Rosemary,
I hope you enjoy this
cast of characters and
the story they tell.
Best,
Cindy Clair

babylonbayou @ comcast.net

BABYLON BAYOU

CONLEY CLARK

Copyright © 2009 by Conley Clark

ISBN 978-0-615-20952-4
Library of Congress Catalog Number 2008905096

Printed in the United States of America

Cover design by Hugh Lambert

Bay Star Press
POB 279
1 Camino Mesteño, Suite B
Placitas, NM 87043

If you wish to reach the author, you may write the publisher and your comments will be forwarded.

Acknowledgments

I would like to thank Louis Ledet, Randy Smith, Greg Border, Marta Burckley, NOPD Officer Tolefson, Detective Winston Harbin, Kermit Bouillon, Sherman McWilliams, Jacob Lee Stuyvesant, Ira Thomas, Randy Loring, Sidney Cates, Mike Fay, PhD and Louis Burkhart.

Thanks to Hugh Lambert for his knowledge and encouragement during the production process. I'm indebted to Abby Broussard, who ran point for me in gaining access to several valuable resources. His generosity made my research especially enjoyable. Special thanks to New Orleans Homicide Detective Erbin "Willy" Bush for his guidance and unvarnished insights into the workings of a homicide unit.

To Peg,

Best friend, steadfast supporter,
and traveling companion on the stony road
to ego disarmament.

ONE

Marty Didian, New Orleans City Councilor, was hunched over his food when I slid into the booth at the café near my office. He was working on a stack of pancakes ringed by a moat of butter and flanked by sides of bacon, hard-fried eggs and biscuits doused with gravy.

I said, "Your financial affairs in order?"

Marty folded a strip of bacon in half, stuffed it in his mouth and said, "Nothing's in order. That's why I eat."

The server brought coffee and a menu. I passed on the food, took a sip of chicory coffee brewed strong as a house jack, then set the mug down.

"Marty, why am I here? Did Jungle Jerry come back and pick your pockets again?"

Marty's a short man. I had to slide the syrup flask over to see his lips move.

"Don't even joke."

After I quit the force and started the agency, Marty came to me to find a guy who had talked him into investing twenty-three thousand in an emu farm, then took off with the cash. I festered for three weeks in the Amazon tracking the guy while being sucked on by leeches and nearly garroted by an adolescent boa constrictor. When I found Gerald, he had gone native and attacked me from a tree with a blow gun. One of the darts caught me in the thigh, but, lucky for me, the guy had picked the wrong plant to poison the tips with. Amateurs.

Gerald was a tad delusional, but when I told him how it was going to be, he pulled the money from a stump and gave it to me, minus what he'd spent on a plane ticket and a burro. I left Jungle Jerry to the trees.

Marty said, "Thanks again, Tag, for keeping that whole sordid mess under wraps."

"My partner and I find that the client confidentiality angle works best for us, Marty. It's that little *lagniappe* we pride ourselves on."

Marty nodded vigorously, the up-and-down motion causing his toupee to dance on the slope of his head.

"Of course, of course. It's just that the press would have crucified me if they found out I had done business with a Certified Public Accountant who was also certifiable."

Marty was working up to something. He'd been a politician too long to get to the point, but it was his rhythm, so I let him run with it.

"Sometimes I wonder why I went into politics."

"Lust for power, bribes, political babes?"

Marty slapped the table and grinned. "I can never take myself too seriously with you, Tag."

"I know I don't."

With all the agreeing motion, Marty's toup had come unglued on one side and pivoted down over one ear. He popped it back on top, and without missing a beat he said, "Your family being part of New Orleans Society, you probably know the name Kanawhite."

"You forget my family cut me loose a long time ago."

"Sure, sure, sure. I just meant—you still gotta have a foot in that circle, right?"

"When I became a cop I got out of the circle and went in the hole, but I know the name Kanawhite. He got plump in real estate, then spent it all trying to find a cure for his wife's one-way disease."

"That's right. When she died, Kanawhite closed himself in the garage, started the Jag, and went out listening to Puccini. Being Irish, I would have chosen the Chieftains." Marty shrugged. "Anyhow, that was a couple of years ago."

"Kids?"

"Adrienne and her younger brother Jackie. Both adults. From what Adrienne tells me, after the parents' death Jackie became a party boy. Ran through his part of the life insurance money pretty quickly."

"Peter Pan bottoms out."

"Bottomed out and disappeared."

"His sister call the police?"

"Adrienne suspects Jackie might be into something illegal. She wants to leave the police out of it."

"Maybe he's missing *because* he's into something illegal. The criminal world tends to be a nasty one."

Conley Clark

Marty lifted an eyebrow. "Tell me about it." By Braille, Marty tried to get his rug lined up with the meager tufts of his real hair. "Jackie and Adrienne haven't been on speaking terms for a year, but Adrienne's worried and I wanted to help in some small way." Marty lifted his noble double chin. "I told her Tag Boudreau was the best private detective in three parishes."

"Modesty prevents me from agreeing." I had never known Marty to play good Samaritan unless there was a hefty campaign contribution or a good looking woman involved. "What's your relationship to Adrienne Kanawhite?"

"She does my publicity photos."

Since the Kanawhite family money was gone and not many photographers could contribute the kind of coin that would make Marty consider himself indebted, I figured she was a looker.

Marty forked a solidified yolk and popped it in his mouth, chewed twice and swallowed, then looked at his watch. "I have to attend a tea."

"Grubbing money for reelection?"

"Two hours with The Matrons of the Sad Poets." Marty looked deflated, then remembered why he was here. "Tag, I told Adrienne you'd drop by and talk to her."

"All right. If she wants me to, I'll look for her brother."

"Great." Marty handed me the address.

"But I have a new policy."

"What's that?"

"No jungles, Marty. I'm through with jungles."

TWO

Marty and I parted at Café Cholesterol, and I walked down Chartres toward my car. Despite the sloppy wet summer heat, the tourists were foraging the shops and taking in the street acts around Jackson Square, sopping up the gumbo-carnival energy of the French Quarter.

During the tourist season parking was a challenge in the *Vieux Carré*. I was lucky to have a permanent spot. Some former clients let me park my car in the carriageway of their townhome on Saint Philip. I had found their sixteen year-old living on the streets in Mobile, and I think this was their way of making right the kid raking my face with the safety pin he wore in his nipple.

I swung the night blue Chrysler Sebring out onto Saint Philip, then turned onto Chartres. It was a short drive from here to Adrienne Kanawhite's studio address. I left the Quarter, crossed Esplanade and Elysian Fields and followed the curve of the river through the Faubourg-Marigny, an old neighborhood of mixed architecture, predominately Creole cottages. I had lived in the neighborhood for a while years ago after I was disowned by my family.

Homes were wedged in tight, and slender ribbons of one-way streets were all that separated one row of houses from another. That close to your neighbors, there were few secrets. We heard the laughter, crying, rage, sex, toilet habits, regrets, revenge, and forgiveness. We knew each other in ways that made it hard to wear the usual masks.

I passed through the residential area and entered the warehouse district. I found the address of Adrienne Kanawhite's studio and pulled into the parking lot of a red brick warehouse that was a relic of the days when "cotton was king." Some of these buildings along the railroad tracks and river were over a hundred and fifty years old.

Clumps of bricks had fallen off Adrienne Kanawhite's building, revealing an even older, chalkier layer of bricks behind. I've been

Conley Clark

told some studio photographers want their buildings to look rundown. The thinking is that thieves won't suspect an outwardly decaying building of housing thousands of dollars worth of photographic equipment.

I parked the car, got out and watched a kid who looked to be about eight skateboard across the lot in my direction. His knee-length baggies and oversized Tulane jersey flapped, flag-like, in the motion-generated breeze. When he reached me he hopped off the board, stepped on the back tip and flipped the skateboard up into his hand.

"Are you the cricket instructor my mom is photographing for the magazine?"

"I don't instruct crickets—just cockroaches and lice. When I'm through with them—any kid picks on you—they'll be all over him."

He cracked a bantam smile, but looked a little puzzled, like he wasn't used to adults cracking wise.

"Actually, I'm here to see your mother about something else. My name's Tag."

The kid looked up at me and squinted into the sun. "That's a funny name."

"They wanted to call me Apgar Snarch, but found that name was already taken."

The kid snickered. "I'm Brent."

He held out his hand and we shook. Firm grip. Brent, no doubt, had been taught the social graces. A handshake was one I liked.

"Are you the detective?"

"That's me."

"Are you going to find Uncle Jackie?"

"I have to impress your mom first—then we'll see."

Brent led me through the door of the studio and into a waiting area the length and width of a single-wide.

"I'll tell my mom you're here."

Brent put the skateboard on the floor and shoved off. He shifted his weight to his back foot, which lifted the front wheels off the floor, then did a three-sixty on the back wheels, shifted his weight forward again. The airborne wheels hit the ground and he was off again. He glanced back to see if I was checking it out. I gave him thumbs up, and he grinned.

The waiting area was hung with several paintings, each done with no more than three or four brush strokes. Very oriental. A little too minimalist for my taste, but they had a certain serenity about them.

The fountain in the corner was a nice touch. A fiberglass oriental monk was pouring water from a bottomless pot into a pool stocked with white and golden-orange carp.

The statue of the monk made me think of the Marathon Monks, a sect of Buddhists that definitely did not adhere to Buddha's philosophy of "the middle way." At some point in their training the monks are required to run a marathon each day for a hundred consecutive days. If they make it they work up to two marathons a day for two hundred consecutive days, and on up to a thousand days. They run in sandals, but that's not the kicker. If they don't go the distance, they're supposed to hang themselves with the ropes that hold up their robes.

Those guys should get together with the religious folks who handle poisonous snakes with their bare hands—swap stories about the ones that didn't make it.

Brent returned and asked me if I wanted to watch the photo shoot, then led me through a metal door as thick as the tax code. Adrienne Kanawhite was photographing a male and female model working out on bungee-type exercise equipment. The models had half-a-bucket-of-protein-powder-a-day bodies. Three other people, who I figured to be the assistant, the stylist and the client suit, stood off camera and watched.

Adrienne Kanawhite looked my way and said, "Mr. Boudreau, we're almost done here."

I could see Marty's interest in Adrienne Kanawhite. Marty told me she had been a figure skater when she was younger. I figured her for about thirty, and judging by her legs, she looked like she could still do a double Salchow and stick the landing.

It looked like she was using a film camera. I guess not everyone is convinced that digital has caught up with film for aesthetic appeal. Adrienne Kanawhite stooped and stood repeatedly while she shot, going after the interesting angles. Four strobe lights "popped" at her flanks, each strobe tethered by cables to a single power pack, like umbilical cords linking newborn quads to their mother. She directed the models with humor and patience, and I enjoyed watching her work.

The models were certainly entertaining. The guy was a demigod with perfect abs, but, strangely, one of his eyes floated involuntarily in random directions. Adrienne had to wait until the floater lined up with the other eye before she could get off a shot.

The woman model flashed big bleached-white smiles when Adrienne was shooting, but between rolls she looked liked she wanted to gouge out the guy's nomadic peeper. I think her face was cramping from having to hold her smile until the male model's drifting eye found top dead center. Adrienne Kanawhite stayed upbeat and handled the models well. Good people skills.

When the shoot was over, Adrienne thanked the models and stylist, then huddled with the client while the assistant broke down the lighting setup. After a few minutes the suit and the stylist left. Adrienne Kanawhite slid the dark slide into the camera and turned toward me.

She said, "Mr. Boudreau, tell me you haven't brought a gun into my studio."

So much for the good people skills.

"I'm not carrying a gun."

"Good."

"But I do carry one in my line of work."

"I don't want one around my son."

"I understand."

"Violence never solved anything."

"It's an ugly part of life. But sometimes it can keep you or someone you want to protect alive."

Adrienne Kanawhite took the roll of film out of her Bronica, licked an adhesive paper band and wrapped it around the film to secure it. I found myself wanting to see her do it again.

She asked, "Have you ever killed anyone?"

"Yes."

The assistant, who had been removing umbrellas from the strobe heads, stopped and stared at me.

Adrienne Kanawhite said, "So, you're comfortable with violence?"

"I was a New Orleans uniformed police officer for four years, a police detective for seven years, and I've been a private investigator for two years, and I've never been comfortable with violence. But there are bad people who are, and they use it to get what they want. Sometimes it's necessary to deal with them on their terms."

Adrienne Kanawhite looked at me for a few seconds, as if she were trying to decide something—like whether I had just recently learned to walk upright.

She said, "Marty told me you pursued someone for three weeks in the Amazon jungle until you found him. That's very impressive."

"Sometimes I obsess—but I've been getting help."

She gave me the arched eyebrow, not sure if I was serious. Maybe I'll nix the humor until she decides about the walking thing.

I said, "Usually, people are easier to find."

Adrienne Kanawhite pulled the light cables out of the strobe power pack, glancing up at me as she worked.

She asked, "Do you always work alone?"

"I have a partner. Koot Loomis was also my partner at the New Orleans Police Department for a number of years. I hold the license, but Mr. Loomis comes in on a case if things go to another level."

"The level that bad people understand."

"Mr. Loomis is very capable at that level."

"I'm sure he is."

"You want to tell me about your brother?"

"Can you find him?"

"Marty told me you and your brother haven't spoken in nearly a year. How do you know he's missing?"

"The manager at Jackie's apartment building called me after a package sat at the door for a couple of days and Jackie didn't answer the manager's phone calls."

"Maybe he just went away for a few days?"

"Jackie never leaves New Orleans. He hates being in unfamiliar surroundings. He's been that way since he was a child."

"Have you spoken to any of his friends or associates?"

"Before we stopped speaking, Jackie spent his time with people you wouldn't normally spend time with. I had no interest in introductions."

"Were his associations the reason you stopped speaking?"

"Jackie was wasting his life with drugs and the party life. He was a bad influence for Brent. I asked him to stop coming around."

"Marty said you were afraid Jackie might be involved in criminal activity and that's why you haven't called the police."

"If he is involved in something illegal, I won't be responsible for Jackie's going to prison by bringing in the police."

"You should know, Ms. Kanawhite, I wouldn't abet any criminal activity I might find your brother involved in. It could cost me my license, or worse."

She disconnected one of the cables from a strobe head and coiled it around her elbow and hand.

"Then maybe I should find another private investigator."

"Most have the same concerns."

"You're telling me I should go to the police."

"I think you should. They have more resources and more feet on the street for this kind of search."

"You could look for Jackie, and if you find that he's involved in anything criminal you could walk away."

"Yes, I could do that. But I would still expect to be paid for the work."

"What is your fee, Mr. Boudreau?"

"Twenty-five hundred dollars, which I get in advance, plus expenses, which I get later."

"And if you don't find whom you're looking for?"

"I charge for my effort, which is considerable. I can't guarantee results."

"My clients don't pay me for photos until I deliver them."

"I don't mean to be indelicate, but if your brother is buried under a cement foundation or was thrown in an incinerator, I could come up empty."

Her body went stiff. She probably hadn't considered the possibility of her brother's death. I had forced it to the surface, and it frightened her.

"Please find my brother, Mr. Boudreau."

It was obvious she cared about her brother. She wanted to protect him, despite their estrangement.

"All right Ms. Kanawhite. I'll take it as far as I can."

"Thank you."

I followed Adrienne Kanawhite into her office. On the walls were more minimalist paintings. No photos. Maybe she was a perfectionist and never satisfied with her own work enough to display it, or maybe she was just humble about it. Adrienne Kanawhite pulled a check book from her desk, then wrote a check and handed it to me.

I said, "Is it too late for introductions?"

She looked embarrassed. "I'm sorry. I guess I pounced. It was just the thought of guns being...made me very..."

"It's all right. When they're pointed at me, I get edgy too."

She nodded and then smiled for the first time. "Please call me Adrienne."

It was a nice smile, warm and without the strain of insincerity.

"Call me Tag."

With clients, I usually preferred the professional distance of last names. With Adrienne, I was starting to feel that distance was not something I wanted.

THREE

On the way to Jackie Kanawhite's place I dialed Koot at his Kenpo studio. Koot learned martial arts after he ran away from home as a teenager, and later dedicated himself to teaching self-defense, inspired by a father with some serious emotional problems.

Koot grew up trying to defend his mother and himself from the routine beatings, and for his effort ended up with cigarettes stubbed out on his skin, or with his face shoved in a tub of live blue crabs—then he was beaten some more. They'd lived in the marsh, so there were no neighbors to report the screaming.

Once, when Koot was twelve, after his father had bloodied his mother for over-blackening the gumbo roux, Koot called the police from school. But when his mother wouldn't press charges, the retribution came swift and savage, and Koot nearly bought it before his mother got him to New Orleans General. Teaching people how to defend themselves became Koot's mission in life.

Koot answered on the second ring.

"Loomis."

"We've been retained."

"What, mama's little Pomeranian on the lam, or has the hubby been coming home with lipstick on his Jockeys?"

"Where's your compassion? Not everyone has their lives together like you and I do."

"You're a riot, Alice."

"It's a real case. Missing person. Name's Jackie Kanawhite. His sister hired us."

"Maybe he flew the coop."

"His sister said he's strictly a homeboy."

I turned onto Esplanade coming out of Marigny and headed toward City Park. It was 9:00 a.m. and a cop was rousting a couple of Lacoste teens who were sitting on the curb drinking sixteen ounce cans of Pabst Blue Ribbon.

10   Conley Clark

Koot asked, "Any lowlife involved?"

"Hard to know where to draw that line. The brother may have been operating in the shade. I'm heading over to his place to look around."

"Anything happens, don't wait till you're in over your head."

"I'll try to give you a jingle *before* any shooting starts."

"That'll be best."

I hung up and turned up Wisner, which hugged City Park heading toward Lake Ponchartrain. I liked passing by the giant oaks at the south end of the park. These titans were survivors of an ancient forest that had canopied the lowland a few centuries before New Orleans rose as a port city.

The grand dame is *McDonogh Oak.* It has the girth of a walk-in cooler and a crown spread that could shade a self-help guru's rally.

Dueling Oak has some interesting history. Under its branches, "gentlemen" would pace off with single shot pistols, then turn and stand very still, providing each other an easy target. It's hard to find gentlemen like that anymore. It's even harder to find these majestic old trees.

From Wisner I turned onto Lakeshore Drive and found the apartment building where Jackie Kanawhite lived. I parked on the street and entered the high rise. The walls of the lobby were papered with a dizzying pink and blue *fleur de lis* pattern. A couple of signing bonus-sized chandeliers, clustered with dozens of tiny pink bulbs on the ends of a tangle of loopy chrome arms, hung from the ceiling. In the corners of the lobby, blue mini-spots lit plants trimmed like poodles. The designer must have been related to or sleeping with the building owner.

I walked to the security guard who was sitting behind a circular desk reading a magazine, *Metal Detector World.* He didn't look up when I approached.

I said, "Lose your car keys?"

Now he looked at me like I was bothering him. I get that look a lot.

"Can I help you?"

"I'm here to take a look at Jackie Kanawhite's apartment."

Suddenly he got friendlier.

"You the PI?"

"That's right."

He grinned. "Sure, no problem." His teeth looked like a slat fence drawn by a two-year old. "I coulda been a private dick."

"What stopped you?"

"I did time in Wyoming for B and E."

"And now you're a security guard."

He smirked. "Background screening's a joke."

"Most people wouldn't be so chatty about a criminal past."

"What, you gonna tell my boss? Be my guest. This job's boring the shit out of me anyway."

The few—the proud—the unscreened.

"The manager said you saw Jackie Kanawhite leave the building Saturday morning."

"That's right."

"Did he mention where he was going?"

"Hey, I don't speak to the tenants, they don't speak to me."

"Friendly's not part of the job."

"Exactly. You think Kanawhite might have been popped?"

"I'm looking for evidence. Conclusions come later."

"You want I should take you up? Wouldn't hurt to have an extra pair of eyes. Be surprised the things I can find in people's places."

"Thanks, but it's probably better if you keep a presence in the lobby. Give the tenants a false sense of security."

He looked disappointed. "Suit yourself." He handed me the key to 1024, then stuck his head back in his magazine.

I punched the elevator button to the tenth floor. Jackie's liking the high life included the location of his apartment, which was at the top. The elevator opened to a hallway lit with wall-mounted electric lanterns. The flickering bulbs were supposed to create the look of gas lanterns from the nineteenth century, but the effect in the confined hallway looked more like some of the strobe-lit drug dens I'd busted. I found Jackie Kanawhite's apartment at the end of the hall and knocked. No answer.

I opened the door with the key and the stench of something rotten made me wince. It was bad, but I knew it wasn't a body. Once you get the smell of rotted human flesh in your skull, it's locked in forever.

The apartment was a wreck. It had been tossed, and by the looks of the place, by more than one person. They wanted what they were looking for pretty badly. The door jamb didn't look like it had been pried. The lock was probably picked, but how did they get past security? Maybe the metal detecting felon downstairs was on duty. Wouldn't take much grease for him to go outside for a Camel.

The couch was gutted, and the tall speakers on each side of the entertainment center were knifed open. The back cover of the TV had been removed. DVDs and CDs were strewn all over the floor. A

12   Conley Clark

DVD with the handwritten label *D and Me* caught my eye. I picked it up and placed it on top of the TV, then went in the kitchen. The refrigerator door was wide open. I closed it on a six pack of Samuel Adams, some moldy bread and the stink of a pan of furry beef Stroganoff.

Pots and cleaning supplies had been raked out of cabinets and onto the floor. Tube-shaped water filters had been removed from the filtering system under the sink and had been tossed, along with the filter casings. These guys were thorough. Maybe IRS agents gone rancid.

I went down the hall and stopped at the bathroom. The clothes in the clothes hamper had been dumped in the floor. The top of the toilet had been removed, then tossed on the floor, where it had cracked.

In the bedroom, the round air mattress had been ripped open and deflated and was draped like a Salvador Dali clock half way off the bed platform. Every drawer in the room was open, and clothes were strewn on the carpet. Next to the night stand lay an aged painting of a voluptuous topless woman with skin the color of cocoa. She wore a red and white Tahitian print skirt and held a large piece of fruit. The painting looked like a Gauguin I'd seen. I picked up the painting and looked at the signature. Gauguin.

I turned the painting over and a tiny patch of canvas in the corner of the frame caught my eye. A closer look showed the pellet-sized patch of canvas to be fairly new. The rip-off artist had carefully and skillfully copied one of Gauguin's paintings, then tried to age the canvas with some kind of varnish. All that effort and he misses a spot. Maybe Jackie thought he was buying an original, or maybe he knew it was forged and tried to pass it off as the real thing to impress women enough to get them into bed. I wondered if that ever worked.

In the nightstand was a bottle of Wellbutrin, a bottle of nasal spray and a pack of condoms. No whips, cuffs or sex toys. Seems Jackie was a fairly conventional party animal.

On a credenza in Jackie's office was a framed photo of Jackie, another man, and a tall attractive woman. Jackie and the man were smiling. The woman made an attempt to.

Jackie's desk had been rifled. On top of the desk an appointment book lay open. I found the last entry, which was on Wednesday. Jackie had written a reminder to himself to get food, water, wine and sunscreen.

I worked my way back through the appointment book. The name "Danika" appeared several times starting in February, around the beginning of Mardi Gras. I'd never heard the name before but was fairly sure it was a woman's name. It looked like Jackie had been seeing her for about four months.

No other names appeared, just entries like "Sailing with Danika" or "Shiner bash" or "Cajun cookout." The entry "Camp" appeared several times throughout the pages of the appointment book. When he wasn't indulging his other appetites maybe Jackie was a Boy Scout leader.

I figured Danika might be the "D" on the disc labeled *D and Me.* I looked around in the desk for a rolodex or something with names, addresses or phone numbers in it, but found nothing. If there was an address book, whoever wrecked the place probably had it, giving them a leg up on me. In the bottom drawer was a loose pile of receipts for gas and docking fees from a marina I was familiar with over in Pass Christian. I stuck one of the receipts in my pocket.

I went back to the living room and turned on the TV. It still worked. I turned on the disc player and slid the video cassette in. Jackie and the woman from the photo were having sex on the carpet. She was on her hands and knees and Jackie was entering from behind. Jackie was nearly as short as Marty, but two large cookbooks and a sofa pillow under his knees brought him up to game level. Resourceful couple.

Adrienne didn't need to see this, so I ejected the disc and stuck it in my jacket pocket in case she came over to straighten up the place.

It looked like Jackie, and maybe the woman too, was on the run from the wrecking crew. Maybe they had what the crew wanted. There was one thing I felt certain of, if the crew caught up with Jackie and Danika, they'd get what they wanted, one way or another. Of course, there was another possibility—that the crew had already caught up with them—and Jackie and Danika were dead.

Conley Clark

FOUR

Traffic was light on the I-10 bridge as I drove across the eastern tip of Lake Ponchartrain. When I entered Mississippi I took Highway 90 along the Gulf Coast toward the marina in Pass Christian. The docking receipt from the marina was all I had to go on, but I'd split the goal posts on flimsier leads before.

When I crossed the bridge at Bay Saint Louis, I thought of the twenty-six foot Jeanneau that Koot, my ex-wife Cile and I used to launch from here. We'd sail out to Chandeleur Islands and the wildlife refuge, or just spend the day tacking our way around the Chandeleur Sound. That was during a time when Koot was out on the ledge after his son was killed. We kept Koot in a pretty tight cocoon of friends then, and being out on the water seemed to put him at ease, if only temporarily.

At Pass Christian I turned off the highway and into the marina parking lot. Koot and I brought the Jeanneau's sails and rigging here once for repair. The marina and docking area was protected by the long concrete and rock jetty that dampened the action of the advancing sea, creating quiet water slips for commercial fishing boats, sailboats and other pleasure crafts.

I parked at the cedar shingled main building. Tackle, bait, beer, ice, food and nautical equipment were all under one roof. I went in and saw that Larry and Oscar were still running the place. Larry was dipping up live shrimp from a holding tank, while Oscar sat behind an antique cash register, blowing cigar smoke up and away from a customer as he took the man's money. Larry emptied the bait shrimp into a plastic bucket and handed the pail to the fisherman, then the man left.

Oscar's eyes were set in shadows cast by a thicket of eyebrows that curled like a hydra in every direction. Years of working in the sun had cured his skin into nut-brown jerky. He looked overripe for AARP.

Larry was younger and was slim almost to bone, and like most redheads with a short supply of melanin, his sunburn would never turn to tan. I remembered him having bad allergies, and noticed his nose still dripped steadily. Fortunately for Larry, his upper lip curled up, which blocked the flow, then channeled it out and around his mouth, where he wiped it with the sleeve of his shirt. The guy was friendly and without guile.

Oscar looked at me and shook his finger as he tried to make me. "I never forget a face. You the fella that caught that shark with the garbage bag of marijuana in its stomach a few years back?"

"I wondered what happened to that bag."

"Hmm." Oscar squinted through another thought. "No, I'm thinkin' you the one that weaseled outta two months' slip fee a while ago."

"Wrong weasel."

"I never forget a face."

"So you said. You're two questions up on me, Oscar."

"All right, buddy. What can I do for you?"

"Does Jackie Kanawhite dock his boat here?"

Oscar squinted again. "Everybody's suddenly interested in Mr. Kanawhite and his lady friend. If you was the law, you'd showed a badge. He owe you money?"

"I'm trying to find him for his sister. You mentioned he had a woman friend. Is her name Danika?"

Larry said, "That's her name. She's a looker. The two of 'em took the *Good Times* out Saturday morning. She's a looker too. Sun Ray thirty-two footer."

I showed them the photo I had taken from Jackie's place. "This her?"

"Yep," said Larry.

"Know her last name?"

Larry said, "Never had the pleasure."

Oscar nodded he didn't know either, then he said, "Unusual, them not coming back. Long's he been docking here, Mr. Kanawhite's been strictly a day tripper."

"Did you notify the Coast Guard?"

Oscar said, "We don't keep up with the comings and goings of boaters unless they ask us to aheada time."

"Then I'll give them a call."

Oscar's face kind of folded in on itself, and you could tell he didn't like that idea. Maybe guilt nudging in.

"It *is* mighty unusual, Mr. Kanawhite being gone this long."

"Yeah." I waited.

"All right, young fella. Maybe I'd better give the Coast Guard a holler."

I took a card from my pocket and dropped it on the counter.

"Will you have them get in touch with me if they find anything? Jackie Kanawhite's sister needs to know."

Oscar picked up the card. "Can do."

I showed them the photo again. "You ever see this man with Jackie and Danika?"

Larry said, "That's Mr. Caveccio. Has a thirty-foot Sundancer diesel with lots of power at the git-go. Mr. Caveccio, Mr. Kanawhite and Mr. Kanawhite's lady friend went out a lot on one boat or the other."

Oscar said, "Mr. Caveccio took his boat out by hisself Saturday, soon after Mr. Kanawhite and his friend went out."

"Back the same day?"

"Yep."

"Alone?"

"I said he went out alone."

"But did he come back alone?"

Oscar looked at me oddly. "Well, there weren't no mermaids with him, far as I could tell."

"What's Mr. Caveccio's first name?"

"Frank."

"You have a phone number?"

Oscar said, "He's got a private number. Hell, you'd think he'd give it to me, seein' I watch his boat for him."

I said, "He might know if Jackie Kanawhite and Danika took an extended trip."

Oscar said, "Might."

"Got an address?"

Larry reached for a card file. "Got it right here."

Oscar grabbed the file from Larry's hand. "We have to protect the privacy of our clients."

Oscar might have been concerned with their privacy, or he might have been fishing for payment for the information.

I said, "If Jackie and Danika are still alive, I'm sure they'll appreciate your concern with your customers' privacy."

He dropped the file card on the counter like it was doused with anthrax. "Whoa, young fella. No one said anything about them not being alive."

"I just did."

"I think you might be jumping the gun there, but of course we wanna help."

"Glad to hear it."

Oscar copied the address on a Post It note, then handed it to me.

"Oscar, you said someone else was interested in finding Jackie Kanawhite and Danika."

"Yeah. Some other fellas was in here yesterday."

"Can you describe them?"

"It's my bladder that's malfunctionin'. My eyes still work fine."

"The best eyes for straight, true stitching I ever saw."

Oscar snapped his callused fingers. "I knew it. Jeanneau, twenty-six footer. I stitched the sails and repaired the rigging a few years back."

"You never forget a face."

"Good boat, sat low and stable. You still got her?"

"Had to sell her when my wife and I split."

"Too bad. Nice boat."

"Yeah."

Oscar said, "You was asking me about..."

"A description of the men..."

"Right. There was two of 'em. The one doin' the talkin' had a nasty scar on his nose," he made a slash across the length of his nose, "and had some kind of a foreign accent. The other one was as hyper as my grandkid on Snickers—and seemed about as mean."

"What were they asking?"

Oscar shrugged. "Same as you. Did they go out? Did they come back?"

"Did these guys leave a name or number for you to reach them?"

Oscar swatted a fly on the tray of bear claws. "No, and they weren't the kind I'd want to be jawing with anyway."

On the way back to New Orleans I was thinking that maybe Jackie and Danika tried to get away in the *Good Times* from the wrecking crew at his apartment. Maybe they planned to sail to Mexico or to one of the Caribbean islands. Didn't seem a likely means of escape unless they wanted to leave the country and were afraid that the airports would be watched. Was it a coincidence that Frank Caveccio took his boat out shortly after Jackie and Danika set sail? Was it Caveccio and someone else that tossed the apartment? Something felt wrong. Maybe Frank Caveccio could tell me something that would feel right.

FIVE

Frank Caveccio's townhouse was just off Metairie Road, across the street from a gym and a dry cleaners. I parked the Sebring in front of the townhouse complex and watched a Hispanic teenage girl with a mesh bag of oranges run flat out alongside a city bus, trying to reach the stop ahead of the bus. She made it about the time the bag split open, spilling oranges in a wide arc on the sidewalk and in the street. The bus driver stopped and helped the girl gather up the oranges. I usually don't like the unexpected in human behavior. This was not one of those times.

Across the street two guys sat in an older model sun-bleached red Mustang Cobra, smoking either hand-rolled cigarettes or joints. I haven't come across anyone who rolled their own cigarettes since the cowboy I tangled with in a Montana roadhouse who mistook me for the guy zooming his wife.

In the front yard of one of the townhouses, an old man gripped his walker with a gnarled hand while he bent and tediously attempted to pull weeds with the other arthritic pincer. I wondered if he'd agree with Plato, who said, "Fear old age—for it does not come alone."

I got out and walked through the black iron gate of the complex. Except for the carved whales swimming through the entablature, the townhouses were Greek Revival, and the landscaping was tropical and well kept.

I found number six and rang the bell. I noticed a woman in her robe sitting in the window of the unit across the courtyard. When she saw me looking, she parted the robe a few inches and smiled. Friendly neighborhood.

I was about to ring the bell again when the door opened and the frame was filled with a van-sized guy with dock pilings for arms. He wore a double-breasted, definitely not off the rack. The big man wore a crew cut, a Vandyke and a scowl, right out of central casting.

Muscle for Frank Caveccio. All we need is for him to say "Whatta you want?"

He said, "Good afternoon. May I help you?"

I love it when they play against type.

"I'm here to see Frank Caveccio. It's about Jackie Kanawhite and a woman named Danika."

I handed him my card.

He looked at the card. "Private detective." Then he looked at me like the card read *Stalker*. Of course he was pretty much looking at me that way before I gave him the card.

He stepped aside, and I entered, then he eased the door shut.

"Please wait." Like it was killing him to be polite.

Big Man lumbered across the foyer and moved through a door to another room, bending his head to clear the frame.

A photograph on the foyer wall showed Frank Caveccio to be a man with unusual interests. Caveccio was holding a plaque and was wearing what looked like a bloodstained apron as he shook a man's hand and smiled for the camera. The photo caption read: Fastest time in the *Kill, Pluck, Fry and Eat* category. In the background was a cage of chickens.

In a couple of minutes Big Man came back and nodded. "Mr. Caveccio will see you."

I walked over and nodded toward his arms. "Nice muscle mass. What do you lift?"

Big Man gave me what could have been interpreted as a grin. "Four by fours."

Seemed plausible to me.

I entered a den, and Big Man entered behind me. Frank Caveccio was standing in front of a bar stocked with some familiar faces: Jack in the black, Johnny Red and the Irishman, Mr. Jameson. He poured himself two fingers of the amber Irishman. Big Man parked himself near the door.

Frank smiled. "You seem to know me, Mr. Boudreau, but I'm at a disadvantage."

"I'm a private investigator hired by Adrienne Kanawhite to find her brother Jackie."

When you tell someone who isn't expecting you that you're a PI, and that someone he knows well is missing, you usually get a reaction: a look of surprise, shock, concern, some body language that's telling. With Frank Caveccio I couldn't get a read.

"Jackie is missing?"

"Since Saturday morning when he left the marina in his boat with a woman named Danika."

Caveccio took a slow pull on the whiskey, then wiped the corner of his mouth with his thumb.

"They probably anchored off one of the islands for a few days."

"That would be a first, according to Oscar."

"First for everything, Mr. Boudreau. Would you like a drink?"

"I don't dance that dance anymore, but thanks."

"Too many feet get stepped on?"

"You could say."

"I respect a man who accepts his limitations."

"Most of my limitations were the result of my drinking."

"I see."

Big Man hadn't taken his eyes off me. Making sure I didn't stick an ashtray in my jacket.

I said, "How well do you know the woman Jackie's been seeing? Her name is Danika."

Frank poured another one. This time it was four-fingered.

"I haven't been in touch with Jackie in quite a while."

"I was asking about the woman."

"I never had the pleasure."

I reached in my jacket for the photo. Big Man flinched. An occupational reflex I could relate to. I pulled the photo out slowly and handed it to Frank Caveccio.

Frank knocked back three of the four fingers, then he looked at the photo. "You say her name is Danika?"

"That's right."

Caveccio handed the photo back and shrugged. "I vaguely remember her. Jackie goes through women like ..."

"Like you go through a bottle of Jameson."

That got some body language. He didn't like the comment, but I didn't like being lied to. Of course, I get lied to all the time in my line. You'd think I'd get used to it.

Big Man had unfolded his arms and glared.

I asked, "Did you take your boat out Saturday morning?"

Caveccio stared at me for several seconds before he answered.

"What does that have to do with Jackie's disappearance?"

"I don't know. But if you'd lie about knowing Danika, I get curious about other things."

Big Man dieseled up and came at me from across the room. I backed up a couple of steps. Frank raised his hand for Big Man to stop, but either Big Man didn't see him or he just wasn't built to stop on a dime, emotionally speaking. I took another step back to the fireplace, then opened my coat on the left side and showed him the Kahr 9mm in my shoulder holster. I wondered if the entire clip would be enough.

He ignored my presentation. I get a little rattled when they call my bluff. I reached behind me for a fire poker and squared up for a swing at the bleacher seats.

Frank, emphatic. "Rocco!"

Big Man's eyes blinked a few times, then he pulled up—a step away. He stood there, glaring down at me, neck veins pumping. I put the poker back, then moved around Rocco. At the bar I stopped in front of Caveccio.

"You can either talk to me or talk to the police."

"I have nothing to say to you, Mr. Boudreau."

"I'm a better listener than the police."

"Rocco, show Mr. Boudreau to the door."

Rocco led me out of the room. When I got to the door, I glanced back at Frank Caveccio. His self-assured expression was gone. He killed the rest of his whiskey. Caveccio was drinking heavily in the middle of the morning. Maybe he was a deep-end lush, but I figured he was washing down a lot of cope because he was nervous about something. Drinking had been my way too.

When we reached the front door Rocco opened it and said, "Maybe we'll have a face-to-face again."

"I'll bring breath mints."

Personal interaction is the best part of being a detective.

SIX

When I came home, my cat Seven ignored me as usual, while my eighty pound mutt Santana leaped up to greet me and knocked over the ficus, sending potting soil into my house shoes. He's a blockhead, but after a hard day of detecting it's good to come home to a wagging tail.

When I got Santana as a pup from the animal shelter, he defied all attempts to piece together breeds. It looked like half the male dogs in the neighborhood had their turn at bat with his mother.

A tan undercoat mottled with dark, odd splotches brings to mind a hairy Rorschach test. Sometimes I lie on the couch and stare at the shapes while Santana snoozes. I've seen Mennonites riding rhinos, gargoyles with pruning shears, my parents at each other's jugular. I've been afraid to ask for interpretations.

I found Seven a couple of years ago in a culvert near the river. Her gray fur was soaked in motor oil, and she had been mangled pretty badly. I call her Seven because I suspect she used up most of her lives before she adopted me. That and because I'm smitten with "Seven of Nine" on *Star Trek Voyager.*

I went to the kitchen and grabbed a bottle of lime iced tea from the fridge and took a long pull. Seven came in and hopped to the counter, then up to the top of the fridge. When Santana loped in, Seven pushed one of Santana's squeaky toys off the top of the refrigerator. They were going into their act.

When Santana went for the toy, clueless as always, Seven dropped down on his back and clawed in. Santana leaped sideways, then spun several times in a circle, Seven hanging on for the ride. Maybe I can bring Brent over some time and we'll watch *Cirque de Dufas* together.

After a while I went in the bathroom and took my kit from the cabinet, then laid everything out on the counter. I picked up the lancet and stuck my finger, then swiped the blood with a glucose strip and popped the strip in the glucometer. Ninety-five. My blood sugar was dandy. I put the kit back in the cabinet and removed bottles of Glucotrol and Metformin and shook out pills from each, then downed the meds with my tea.

I went to the bedroom and put on some sweat shorts, a T-shirt and running shoes, then took Santana for a run. My bungalow is a couple of blocks from the river, so we headed for the levee. At the levee we climbed the slope to the top, then ranged our legs along the ridge. It was the time of day when the sunlight dimmed to a warm glow, and the satiny gleam of things gave me a sense of peace.

From the top of the levee I could see the Mississippi, coursing its way toward the Gulf of Mexico. We ran along the ridge and into Audubon Park, circled the zoo and headed back. The first leg was a couple of miles, and I had worked up a good sweat. Santana wanted me to take the bit out. He would run ahead several yards, then wait for me to catch up, then he'd sprint ahead again. I never ran him more than five or six miles, but I knew he was born for distance.

On the return leg I looked across the road and watched the house lights flicker on in the neighborhood. Low in the darkening sky, the cool light of the first star glittered on. I picked up the pace, then we sprinted the last two hundred yards home.

When we got back to the house I showered, then fed the kids. I put a flounder filet in the broiler and made some cappellini with olive oil and green olive pesto. While the flounder browned on top, I sliced some cukes and radishes. I made a dressing with some chilies, olive oil, coarse mustard, lemon juice and unfermented soy sauce.

When the meal was ready, I took my plate out to the porch and sat in the swing. Santana followed me out and settled on his throw rug against the wall. He pumped his nostrils, sniffing the smells drifting from my plate while his ears swiveled like radar dishes, picking up the sounds of the neighborhood.

The flounder was flaky and tender and delicious. I thought of the times my father and I fished the salt water lagoons when I was a kid. I don't have a lot of good memories of my relationship with my father, but those few years on the water together were among the better ones.

The only time I remember him showing me what he thought was compassion was on one of those trips. I lost the biggest fish I'd ever seen trying to get it into the boat. It was a thyroidal monster to a twelve year-old, and I was miserable. My father (calling my father Dad was not acceptable) reached into the ice chest and handed me my first beer, ever. After two beers I forgot about the fish, and

Conley Clark

temporarily forgot about trying to clear the high bar of my father's expectations.

I had taken my second bite of flounder when the phone rang. I stepped over Santana and went in to answer it. Probably a telemarketer. Despite the commercial solicitation law, I still get calls from time to time. They hire psychics to tell them when you're sitting down to dinner.

It wasn't a telemarketer, and I wished it had been. A lieutenant with the Coast Guard told me a trawler had spotted Jackie's boat, the *Good Times*, that afternoon about twelve miles out in the Gulf. The mast had crashed. A Coast Guard cutter sent a crew aboard and a chopper searched a wide perimeter three times, but no one was found.

I wanted to think they had staged an accident and had escaped to the sunny Caribbean somewhere with the insurance money, but some harrowing experiences I've had on high choppy water didn't support the optimism. The storm could have claimed them. If they were swept overboard by a violently swinging boom, it wouldn't take long for the big swells to suck them under.

There were a couple more reasons I wasn't feeling optimistic—the sacking of Jackie's apartment and Caveccio's lies.

I didn't want to tell Adrienne about the boat. I've had to deliver bad news too many times before. I wanted to swim the twenty-six miles across Lake Ponchartrain. I wanted to crawl into a shark cage with a bag of bloody chum. I wanted to have a drink. Instead, I made a call, then drove over to Adrienne's studio.

When I arrived, Brent was sitting cross-legged on the couch in the reception area, reading a book. You could hear the crisp "pop" of strobes in the studio.

I said, "Catching up on your astrophysics?"

"Nooo. I'm reading the Hardy Boys."

"Which one?"

"*The Twisted Claw.*"

"Scary."

"You read the Hardy Boys?"

"When I was a kid."

"I didn't know the books were *that* old."

"Some of the best things are old—like turtles or Frankenstein. Frankie's been around a while." I did my impersonation. "Frrriend. Goood."

Brent laughed, and I was glad. It might be the last time he laughed for a while. I was hoping he wouldn't ask me about his uncle. He had to deal with his mom and dad splitting, and now he would have to try to comprehend Jackie's death. It was a lot for a boy to face. The early end of an innocence.

"Have you found my Uncle Jackie?"

I didn't want to lie to Brent, but his mother would have to be the one to tell him.

"Not yet."

It was true that the *body* hadn't been found. *You can sidestep with the best of them, Boudreau.* Before Brent could ask another question, I got up abruptly and told him I was going to talk to his mom, then walked into the studio. I was relieved he didn't follow.

Adrienne was photographing a woman who looked to be in the waning side of her forties. The model was holding a small box and displaying it toward the camera. She looked familiar. Adrienne was directing the model to give her "confident." It seemed to me the model nailed that look. Tag Boudreau, talent aficionado.

I was waffling on whether to interrupt Adrienne with the news or wait until she finished the shoot. Finally I decided that, since the dead had no pressing engagements, it could wait.

I went over and stood by Adrienne's assistant, the stylist and the client. The stylist nodded and smiled and I nodded back. The client looked at me as if I might be one of his model's spurned lovers, here to throw things around the set. When he decided that I was probably a harmless spurned lover, he ignored me.

I asked the stylist, "Who's the model?"

"Jill Cherry."

Right. I had seen her in movies maybe twenty years ago. I remembered she was in a couple of films that were huge hits and then she did two or three films in a row that went over the cliff. Then I read somewhere that the phone stopped ringing.

I thought she was exceptional, even in the two bad films I saw her in. It wouldn't be the first time a talented actor or actress who couldn't carry a rotten film was rapped for losing their juice and sacrificed to the box office gods.

I wondered if she had accepted not achieving the recognition she deserved, and I wondered if she was okay with selling diarrhea medicine. She certainly added a lot of class not usually associated with the product.

Adrienne finished shooting the roll and called it a session. The client and stylist went over and hovered around Jill Cherry. I walked over to Adrienne.

Adrienne asked, "Have you heard anything?"

"Yes." Adrienne recognized grimness when she saw it. "We should talk alone."

Without speaking to Jill Cherry or the client or her assistant, she walked toward her office. I followed and closed the door behind me. Adrienne went to her desk and picked up a large stack of papers from one end of her desk and put them down at the other end. She walked to an award plaque on the wall and straightened it, though it had already looked straight to me. Then she walked to a small refrigerator, opened the door and peered in.

I said, "Jackie's boat was found in the Gulf this afternoon. There was no one on board."

Adrienne continued to stare inside the refrigerator. Maybe looking for a portal to a parallel and pain-free universe. Finally she turned toward me. Something like hope flickered on her face.

"Maybe someone borrowed Jackie's boat," she said.

"Jackie was seen heading out Saturday morning with a woman named Danika. They didn't make it back. The boat's mast had crashed."

She struggled with whether to place the information in the *real* or *unreal* bin. Adrienne turned and stared out the casement window into the studio. Besides Brent, Jackie had been the only family she had left. I knew how it felt to lose family. Despite their estrangement, everything I had seen told me Adrienne cared about her brother. I wanted to walk over and hold her, but people usually don't take comfort where trust hasn't been built.

I said, "I'm here if you need anything." Then I went to the couch by the wall and sat quietly.

For a long time she didn't speak, the silence as thick as summer air, the only sound the cadenced hum of the air conditioner. After a while I couldn't sit any longer.

I got up, walked over and stopped just behind Adrienne. I put my hand on her shoulder. She stared at my hand for a few seconds, then she broke. She sobbed quietly for several minutes, then she took a deep, phlegmy breath—and she was done.

Without turning, she asked, "Has anyone called the woman's family?"

"No one knows her last name. The Coast Guard said the only inquiry that's been made was an anonymous call."

"Anonymous?"

"Some people have reason to stay in the shadows."

Adrienne looked tired. She said, "Thank you for helping."

I said, "I'm going to continue looking into this."

Adrienne turned. She looked surprised, then angry. "They're dead. What's to look into? Do you want more money?"

"I've torn up your check."

Again she looked surprised. "I don't understand."

"It was presumed an accident. If that turns out be true, there's no reason to charge you."

She wiped tears from her cheek with the heel of her hand.

"I'm sorry I said that."

"No problem."

Adrienne said, "But I still don't understand."

"There are some questions."

"You don't think it was an accident?"

"I'm a detective. I need for things to make sense. Right now, they don't."

Adrienne looked at me for several seconds, then nodded. "Maybe you should know...two men came by today looking for Jackie. I told them I had hired a private investigator to find him. When I didn't want to tell them your name, they got nasty. I hope it's all right that I told them."

"That's fine. Did one of them have a scar on his nose?"

"Yes, and the deadest eyes I've ever seen. Who were they?"

"I intend to find out."

Adrienne asked me if I would bring Brent into the office. When we came in, Adrienne sat on the edge of the couch and patted the seat beside her. Brent went over and sat. He cut his eyes over to me and back to Adrienne. He knew something was wrong.

Adrienne put her hand on Brent's arm and said, "Sweetheart, your Uncle Jackie..." her throat caught, but she got it out, "... has drowned."

She told him straight.

Brent looked down at his lap, then he jerked away from his mother's grasp and shouted, "It was *you* who didn't want Uncle Jackie around."

Adrienne stammered, and before she could get anything out, Brent bolted from the office. Adrienne sagged against the back of the couch. She told me she wanted to be alone.

I left the office and told her assistant that Adrienne had received bad news and asked if he knew any of Adrienne's friends or family that could be with her. The assistant said he'd make a call.

Outside, Brent was sitting on his skateboard in the parking lot. I walked over and squatted in front of him.

"I can see you loved your Uncle Jackie, Brent. Your mom didn't like what your Uncle Jackie was doing with his life, but she loved him too. I think you know that." Brent stared down at the painted flames on his tennis shoes. "Your mom's going to need your help to get through this. Maybe you don't feel it now, but you might need her help too."

He stared some more at the flames, then he stood.

"Are you going to be around to help my mom?"

"I'll be around for a while. That okay with you?"

Brent wiped his nose on his jersey. "Uh huh." Then he picked up his skateboard and headed into the studio.

SEVEN

I reached down and patted around the foot of the bed for the comforter, but couldn't find it. I opened one eye. Santana was sitting on the floor by the bed with the comforter draped over his back and down around his paws. Royalty with flood-prone saliva glands. When I opened the other eye he gave me the gotta-get-a-move-on look.

I rolled out, pulled on a pair of sweat pants, a pair of Water Buffaloes, and a crew neck my niece gave me that says: *The Voices Told Me To Do It.* Sleep had been fitful and left me feeling like I needed to try again. I wondered if Adrienne and Brent had gotten any sleep.

I took Santana up to the grassy slope of the levee. Owners brought their dogs to this area to do their business and enjoy some social sniffing. Santana followed his nose around, picking up scents lost to humans. In a manhunt, a good tracking dog can bring a dead trail to life.

A border collie left a land mine and the owner started walking away without picking it up. We had some words, he told me to mind my own business, then he left. Stellar citizen.

When we got back to the house, I fed the kids and downed a glass of water, then showered and upgraded to jeans and a Tahitian print shirt. I ate a piece of toast spread with peach butter, then grabbed a handful of roasted pecans and left for the marina in Pass Christian. The Coast Guard had towed Jackie's boat in, and I wanted to have a look. Oscar told me Jackie left his car at the marina, and I wanted to have a look at it too.

I took Carrolton up to Earhart and then did the Claiborne maneuver to make it onto I-10. Crossing the I-10 bridge I watched the sun sparkle off the gently surging water and thought of Adrienne and Jackie. Now that Jackie was gone, I wondered if Adrienne was feeling guilty about turning Jackie out of their lives. I wondered if

Conley Clark

Brent could get past the resentment and be there for his mom. I wondered if she'd let me be there for her too.

When I got to the marina Oscar was sitting on his bar stool, Bogarting a cigarette and looking miserable. On the counter was a can of Jamaican ginger ale, a cup of coffee and a bottle of aspirin. Spidery red veins ran through Oscar's rheumy eyes, and he was sweating like Shaq running both ends of the floor for a half.

I said, "You gonna make it?"

He wheezed, "Some kind of damned bug's crawled inside me."

"Why don't you take it to the house—get some rest?"

"Then I'd have to listen to the wife tell me a hundred times I should take better care of myself."

"Hmmm. What's she thinking?"

Oscar took a drag off his cig. "She's thinking that if I check out, she won't be able to afford any more trips to Cancun."

It made me think of the dying man who rallied, sat up in bed and asked his wife if he could have some of the ham he smelled cooking. The wife responded, "Certainly not. That's for the wake."

Oscar took a swig of ginger ale. "I feel real bad about Mr. Kanawhite and his lady friend. Mr. Kanawhite would be three sheets to the wind some days he came in off the water, but he always paid me on time."

"Yeah."

"You heard anything else from the shore jockeys?"

"They called off the search," I said.

"I told Mr. Kanawhite and the woman a storm was brewing. They was probably washed over or swept over by the boom."

"That would make sense."

Oscar took a drag on his cigarette and eyed me. "Somethin' tells me you're not looking for the logical though?"

I shrugged. "Life often veers away from it."

Oscar moved his head to the side of a plume of smoke at his eyes. He said, "Marriage'll teach you that."

I left the shack and walked to the lot and found Jackie's carmine red Porsche Carrera. Koot and I would come back later for the car and take it to Adrienne. She was planning a memorial service for Jackie and had enough to deal with.

The Carrera was a few years old but was in good shape. It looked like Jackie had it detailed regularly. A bumper sticker in the back read: *Jesus loves you. Everyone else thinks you're an asshole.* So Jackie had a sense of humor.

I took my Slide Jim from the kit I kept for getting in places where I'm uninvited. I slid the flexible metal strip down beside the driver's window and into the door. When I felt the locking mechanism, I worked it until the latch clicked. Then I opened the door and lifted the trunk latch.

In the trunk were some emergency flares, a large embroidered sombrero and the spare tire, which was flat. I got in the car on the driver's side and looked under the seats. I pulled out an empty Corona bottle and a portable cassette recorder. I rewound the tape, then punched the play button. Jackie left himself reminders: pick up laundry and champagne; shipment Tuesday; call about hair weave. I wondered what the shipment was. Had Adrienne's suspicions been right about Jackie being into something illegal?

In the glove compartment was the car registration, a box of Altoids, a combination bottle opener and corkscrew, some crushed peanut butter crackers and a half dozen unpaid parking tickets. Nothing I could call a clue.

I walked over to the pier where the *Good Times* was slipped and went aboard. The mast was down and lay across the deck. The boom was bent, which meant it had likely crashed on deck or across the gunwales.

Two shrouds that secured the mast on the starboard side were dangling free. The cotter rings and the clevis pins, which anchored the shrouds to the gunwales, were missing at each chainplate. Two loose shrouds would have caused the mast to come down.

A crashing mast could have knocked Danika and Jackie over the side. If they ended up in rough water, they could have been pounded by the chop, then pulled under. Only I didn't think that's what had happened.

It was the cotter rings. Two were missing. It was unusual for a cotter ring to shear, even in heavy winds. The fact that *two* rings were missing was more than unusual. I'd been sailing for a lot of years and had never heard of it happening. The cotter rings had been removed to crash the mast and make it look like an accident.

When I came back on deck after looking around below, something caught my eye near the bow, at the base of the railing. I went over and bent to get a closer look. The sun reflected off a piece of chrome and crosslit the area. Dried blood. Time for another visit to Frank Cavaccio's place.

Conley Clark

EIGHT

I drove to a deli on Carrollton and picked up a provolone and jack cheese hoagie with jalapeños and tomatoes, a bag of hazelnuts, some chocolate haystacks, a large bottle of water, and some raw liver. I was going to stake out Frank's place and needed provisions. I put the water and the liver in a small cooler with a chemical icepack and drove toward Metairie.

As I approached the townhouse complex, I spotted the same two guys sitting in the Cobra that had been parked on the street yesterday. I pulled by slowly enough to get a better look. They glanced my way as I passed. The driver wore a flat top and was sucking on a lollipop ,while the other guy drummed the dash to a heavy metal screed. Neither had a bad scar along his nose.

The flat top gave me one of those you-wanna-piece-of-me looks you get sometimes when you make eye contact with the emotionally stunted. My hunch was that these guys were sitting on Frank Caveccio's place.

I circled the block and came around again, then parked on the street, several cars back from the Cobra. Were these the guys that had tossed Jackie's place? Were they from the same crew as the guy with the scar? What was the connection to Frank Caveccio? Did they have something to do with the death of Jackie and Danika? As usual, I had more questions than answers.

I was still asking myself questions as the sun dropped into the frame of two bent apricot trees. I glanced at the clock in the dash— 6:10. I took another bite of my hoagie, and a slice of mustard-coated tomato slid out of the sandwich and onto my lap. I was picking the tomato off my pants when a car pulled out of the townhouse complex and turned onto the street, headed in my direction. I slumped down as they passed.

Big Man loomed over the steering wheel, and Frank Caveccio was beside him. A few seconds later the Cobra pulled out, did a U-turn in the street and followed Caveccio's car.

I watched in the rearview mirror until both cars rounded the corner at the end of the block, then I grabbed the bag of liver from the cooler and got out. A pink Cadillac driven by a woman with an inflated hairdo passed in front of me. Another Mary Kay soldier making the rounds.

When the Caddie passed, I crossed the street and went into the complex. Curtains were open in several living rooms around the courtyard, and people were moving about inside. Standing at the railing at the unit next to Caveccio's, an overweight woman and a gaunt man argued the merits of gastro-bypass surgery. I kept walking.

Frank's townhouse was an end unit, so I went around the corner of his place and to the back. A tall, treated-pine fence enclosed the back yard. I made sure I wasn't being watched, then pulled myself up to the top of the fence to see if Frank had any vicious dogs.

Uh oh. Vicious dogs would have been better. Standing under a mimosa tree was a Komodo dragon. The prehistoric looking lizard stood as high as a mastiff, was as long as a small adult alligator, and had thighs like Mary Lou Retton.

I remembered a show on The Discovery Channel saying it was the largest lizard in the world. Unpredictable and aggressive. Teeth like a paper shredder and strictly a carnivore. Another one of Caveccio's unusual interests.

The lizard was standing next to a crash-test dummy which had its head and most of both legs ripped off. The dragon would think he'd won the carnivore lottery when he saw me drop into the backyard. Godzilla looked my way.

I lowered myself back down to the ground and took the bag of liver out of one coat pocket and a small bottle of chloral hydrate out of the other pocket. I had enough to put a large dog out for about two hours, but I wasn't sure how much it would take to put Godzilla down. I remembered that reptiles had a more delicate system than warm-bloodied animals. I didn't want to kill the lizard; I just wanted to make sure he didn't have me for lunch. I decided on half the normal dose.

I poured some on the liver and let it soak in for a few seconds, then tossed the meat over the fence. Soon I heard gnawing. In a few minutes I heard nothing. I pulled myself up the fence again and saw

Godzilla lying on the ground with his legs splayed, breaths shallow, unconscious.

I glanced around again, saw no one, then scaled the fence and dropped into the back yard. The dragon didn't stir. I went to the back door and looked in through the glass panes, then slid the credit card in the latch. The latch clicked. I turned the handle and the door opened. The deadbolt had not been locked. With Godzilla in the back yard, Caveccio probably figured a burglar wouldn't make it this far anyway.

I went through the kitchen and dining area and into the living room. From there I crossed the hallway and went in an office I had seen when I was here before. There was a large teak desk in the middle of the room. I rifled the top drawer and found nothing but the usual office supplies and a couple of opera tickets, *La Bohème*. The next drawer down was locked. I took my lock pick set out of my coat pocket, chose a tool and picked the lock.

I removed a black ledger and paged through it. There were regular entries about shipments of electronics: CD and DVD players, video game players, laptops, cameras, you name it. Payments were all from *Belissimo Distributors*, a company I knew to be a front for the Cosa Nostra. All the checks were signed by Anthony Liano's accountant. Anthony "Nads" Liano was the head of the Sicilian crime family in New Orleans. Nads was a remorseless killer and as vicious as the Komodo dragon when it came to his business interests, or when someone crossed him personally.

The ledger showed the payments had been made to Frank Caveccio and Jackie Kanawhite. It looked like Frank and Jackie were supplying knockoff electronics to Nads, stuff that Nads could move on the street. Caveccio and Jackie had climbed into a snake pit.

I put the ledger back and closed the drawer. In the bottom drawer was a cheroot box full of sales receipts. I placed the box on the desk and went through the receipts. One of them jumped to the front—a Colt Commander .45 handgun. The receipt was dated ten days ago.

I stuck the gun sales slip in my pocket, then put the box of receipts back and closed the drawer. Caveccio had lied about knowing Danika, stonewalled me about taking his boat out Saturday, and had bought a handgun just ten days ago. Enough information that I was going to have to take it to the police.

When I went back into the kitchen I looked out in the yard. Godzilla was standing about twenty feet away, his primitive eyes locked on me. Wrong dose.

I couldn't risk going out the front door and being identified by one of Frank's neighbors, and I couldn't remember if Komodo dragons were slow or had short burst speed. I needed more food and drug administration.

I took an egg out of the refrigerator, then rifled through drawers until I found an ice pick and some Scotch tape. Over the sink I punched a hole in the egg, reamed the hole a little wider, then carefully poured some chloral hydrate in the hole. Some of the drug spilled onto my hand and the fumes shot up my nose, which made my feel woozy. I quickly cut a piece of tape and sealed the hole with it, stuck the ice pick back in the drawer, then rinsed the chloral hydrate off my hands.

When I got back to the door, the dragon had moved a few feet closer. I opened the door, then quickly stepped outside and placed the egg on the ground. Godzilla moved forward. I leaped back inside the door and closed it. The lizard moved to the egg and inhaled it, then looked my way again. I waited. I had already been in the house a half hour. Too long.

Godzilla and I had been eyeing each other for maybe three minutes when the lock clicked at the front door. I was about to find out if Godzilla had the short burst speed.

I stepped out the door and closed it quickly, then sprinted for the fence, the Komodo at my heels. Just as I hit the fence Godzilla caught my pant leg in his teeth, but my momentum pinwheeled me over the top and my pants ripped out of the lizard's jaw. I came down hard on my back on the other side.

I lay there for a few seconds to make sure nothing was broken, then got up slowly and limped away, grateful this crash-test dummy still had his arms and legs.

Conley Clark

NINE

When I got over to St. Charles, I called Koot. He answered, "Loomis."

A Ray Charles ballad played in the background. Koot likes the classics.

"It looks like murder," I said.

"You tearing up checks from clients—that's murder." The volume on Koot's CD player faded. "What happened?"

"It looks like someone killed them on Jackie's boat, then dumped the bodies over. They tried to make it look like an accident."

"You got a front runner?"

I stopped at a traffic light.

"We've a few contenders. My pick is Jackie's business partner, Frank Caveccio. I invited myself in when Caveccio and his giant were out. The castle was guarded by a dragon, but I slipped it a mickey."

"Uh huh."

That's the problem when you see humor everywhere. When you're telling them straight, they don't take you seriously.

The light turned green. As I was about to pull away, a sclerotic old lady with a canvas shopping bag stepped off the curb and began crossing the intersection. Each step was glacial, as if she carried the weight of a lifetime's worth of memories in her bag.

I told Koot, "A ledger showed Jackie and his partner Frank Caveccio were doing business with Nads Liano, supplying Nads with knockoff electronics."

Koot whistled low. "Of course they didn't know they were in a *permanent* arrangement with Liano."

"Featherweights get involved with the mob and think they can make some cash and pull the plug any time they want."

Koot said, "So maybe Nads pulled *their* plug."

"Yeah. Or maybe Caveccio got greedy and took Kanawhite out of the picture. Maybe the woman was killed because she knew too much."

The traffic light turned red again, and the old lady had barely progressed past the hood emblem on my car. The bag looked heavy for a frail old lady. I leaned out the window, "Would you like some help?" She ignored me.

Koot said, "Help? What, you're gonna give me hints?"

"I was talking to...well...you in about forty years."

"Taggert, you going down the rabbit hole on me?"

"Not yet."

"Sometimes I need convincing."

"I'm still trying to put this all together. This is what I've got so far: Frank launched his Sea Ray Saturday, a short time after Jackie and Danika went out, then lied about it. He also lied about knowing Danika. And Jackie's boat was found with two shrouds missing the cotter rings."

"*Two* shrouds...coming loose accidentally?"

"Exactly. The kicker is that Caveccio bought a Colt Commander a few days before the 'accident'. Then I found blood on deck."

Koot said, "So Caveccio might've followed them out, shot them and tossed the bodies over, then brought the mast down to look like an accident."

"Darkness on the face of the deep."

The light turned green again just as the old woman reached the neutral ground and paused before the next leg of her journey. I started through the intersection and watched in the sideview mirror as she stepped off the curb and shuffled toward her next port of call.

Koot said, "What about a love triangle? You think the woman was the kind that could inspire jealous rage?"

"Definitely. I've seen a photo."

"If Caveccio couldn't have her, no one could."

"Yeah, maybe it was jealousy. Maybe it was greed. Maybe I should spend more time with my inner child."

"So far it's all circumstantial," Koot said.

"Should be enough to get some interest downtown. And we've got some more players in all this."

"Yeah?"

"Some guys have been sitting on Caveccio and his headbanger, and some other guys were at the marina asking about Jackie and Danika."

"Same crew?"

Conley Clark

"I'm not there yet."

"Have you told Adrienne Kanawhite?"

"I'm on my way to her place now."

"You're going to let Homicide handle this, aren't you, Tag?

"I'm out of it."

"I've heard that before."

"I've heard the same from you."

"Yeah, well, you don't need trouble with the department."

"Didn't need it when I was *in* the department."

"Same enemies are still there, Tag."

"Yeah, but it's like testing for diabetes. After a while, the pricks don't bother you so much."

I cut over to Magazine and headed for Adrienne's place. Magazine Street was not your typical milquetoast commercial strip. Along this street was The Buddha Belly—a three-in-one eatery, gaming arcade and Laundromat. A head shop called Rock's Off was not far from a Creole soul food kitchen, which was close to an Indian restaurant called Nirvana, which was across the street from the Second District Precinct.

When I passed the precinct, a couple of cops that looked like they were fresh out of the academy were standing out front. I trained rookies for a while. My favorite recruit had been Munny, a Cambodian whose parents had escaped the wholesale slaughter by the Khmer Rouge and made their way to the United States. Because of what his parents told him of their former life, Munny had a heightened tolerance for obstacles on and off the job. His motto was "No problem."

On Halloween night, Munny and I answered a call about a gunshot fired inside a home. We found the victim in his La-Z-Boy with a shotgun barrel inside his mouth and his finger on the trigger. A lot of people kill themselves on days of observance or holidays. Knowing that others are celebrating together sets in relief the victims' loneliness and sends them over the edge.

When this guy pulled the trigger, the shotgun misfired. Instead of blasting the back of his head off, the bird shot lodged in his skull and the gasses from the blast followed the shot inside and expanded the guy's head to the size of a pumpkin.

I think the irony of it being Halloween escaped Munny. So did his dinner. Between heaves he wiped his mouth and rolled his head up toward me.

"No problem."

The power of positive thinking.

I turned toward the river onto Soniat. Adrienne's house was in the middle of the second block. It was a small Spanish Revival framed by bougainvillea and angel trumpet.

Adrienne answered the door in a blue chenille housecoat. She wasn't expecting any more surprises, so she didn't look surprised. She looked like someone who had just had heart surgery. I guess, in a way, she had.

"Tag, come in."

I stepped inside the living room. A woman who looked to be in her mid-sixties, dressed to blow the circuit on pacemakers, arranged herself on the couch.

"Tag, this is Blanche, an old family friend."

"Hello, Blanche."

Blanche gave me the once over, like she was scanning for tumors, then she smiled. She looked like a vital woman, and it would have come through even without the face lift. Like Adrienne, she looked you in the eyes.

Blanche said, "Adrienne said you were a bit of a hunk. You remind me of Harrison Ford in his younger days, only with a few more imperfections."

Adrienne said, "Blanche, do you even *know* the word 'inappropriate'?"

Blanche looked at me slyly. "He's more interested in what *you* said about him than in my two cents worth."

Blanche had quickly picked up on my attraction to Adrienne.

I said, "I'm thinking I would always know where I stood with you Blanche."

Blanche said, "That's right. Too bad my last husband didn't appreciate that about me. But that hasn't discouraged me."

Adrienne said, "She's trying for number four."

Blanche held her chin up, stretching the lifted skin even tighter.

She said, "It's no fun living alone. And if you choke on a chicken breast, there's no one around to give you the Heimlich maneuver."

I stifled a laugh. This was a strange conversation considering the circumstances. Adrienne asked me to sit, and I eased into an overstuffed chair while she joined Blanche on the couch.

Blanche said, "You think this is outrageous behavior under the circumstances." I looked at Adrienne. She forced a smile through a transparent sadness. Blanche continued. "Outrageous is who I am, but it's also the way I deal with losing our darling boy."

"I understand, Blanche."

As if I didn't understand, she said, "If you think that Jackie was nothing but trouble, then you don't know much."

"I'm sure Jackie had some fine qualities."

"Jackie was very sensitive. Wouldn't hurt a soul. When his mother and father died, Jackie never got over it. He just didn't care anymore. That's why he got involved in all that craziness."

Adrienne gazed down at her huraches. "I turned my back on my brother."

Blanche said, "Stop it. Jackie didn't give you much choice."

Adrienne sighed. "Tag, is there something you came to tell us?" I looked at Blanche and back to Adrienne. "It's all right. I keep very few secrets from Blanche."

Blanche deadpanned, "I know a few you *think* you've kept from me."

I sat up and moved to the edge of my chair. "I don't think it was an accident. I have evidence that Jackie and the woman he was seeing may have been murdered."

Adrienne and Blanche looked at each other, then Adrienne gazed out the window. The rain-laden clouds had the hue of gangrene.

I said, "Right now, nothing's conclusive. Normally, I wouldn't have told you this until I was certain, but you wanted me to keep the police out of it, and I can't do that now. I wanted to let you know before I give the police what I have."

"Do you know who killed Jackie?"

"It may have been a business partner. Or it may have been someone else."

"The men who came to my house?"

I nodded.

"Has the woman's family been told?"

"We still don't know who she was."

Adrienne stared out the window. "Why?"

"We don't know her last..."

"No. *Why?*"

She needed to make sense of a senseless act.

"Maybe the police can find that answer."

Blanche moved over and put her arms around Adrienne. We sat there for a while, no one saying anything. In a few minutes the front door opened and Brent came in, followed by a man dressed in a salmon-colored Polo shirt, slacks creased to a machete edge, and buffed tasseled loafers. I made the guy to be Adrienne's ex, Brent's father, bringing Brent home after spending some time together. Brent didn't look too happy in the man's company, but then happiness was on furlough from the Kanawhite home.

Adrienne's expression shifted from vulnerability to something like the game face you put on when facing opposing counsel.

Brent came over to me, and I stood. He seemed to be glad to see me, which felt good.

"Mom said you might be back."

"And here I am."

He mimicked me mimicking Frankenstein. "Frriend. Goood."

I spread my hands. "Frankie."

Our little exchange seemed to annoy the man. He turned toward Adrienne. "Is this the private investigator you hired?"

"Yes. This is Taggert Boudreau. Tag, this is Brent's father, Clayton Weems." I held out my hand. He ignored it.

Weems. So Adrienne either kept her maiden name when they married or changed back to it when they divorced. I remembered the name Clayton Weems. Trial lawyer. Represented a prominent surgeon in New Orleans who'd killed his wife a few years ago. The DA had uncovered the motive, the wife's blood was in the trunk of the doctor's car, and the weapon was found in the woods nearby, a bloody surgeon's scalpel blanketed with prints. A slam dunk.

But as Yogi said, "It ain't over till it's over." The surgeon had deep pockets. Weems had connections downtown. Palms were larded, and the case never came to trial.

Weems said, "So why is he still around?" Like I was a bulletin board without any notices, Weems continued to ignore me. "Your brother drowned. Does he want more money?"

I noticed Brent looked anxious. I was beginning to see why Brent was surprised at humor from adults.

Adrienne said, "He hasn't taken any money, Clayton."

Weems gave me the up and down, then gave Adrienne a noxious look. "Then I can guess what he wants."

Adrienne said, "Clayton, you're a complete..." She glanced at Brent and bit if off.

"A complete horse's ass." Blanche finished the appraisal. "Have been as long as I've known you."

The remark didn't seem to register with Weems, like he was used to it.

"So, why *is* he here?"

Brent was getting more upset. I stepped over to Weems and stood to his side, so he wouldn't feel physically threatened, then leaned in close and spoke low.

"I came to tell Adrienne something about her brother's death. Brent hearing it would only upset him more than he already is. I'm sure, as a father, you wouldn't want that to happen. Can we drop this so you don't keep rolling gutter balls in front of your son?"

We eyed each other. When I was sure he'd gotten *all* the message I stepped away. Weems looked around the room. I think he was getting basically the same message from everyone, so he left—without saying goodbye to Brent.

Brent looked like he was on the verge of tears. Adrienne stepped over to him and kneeled down.

"Your father disappointed you again, Brent. I'm sorry."

Brent glanced over at me, but quickly looked away, as if he were ashamed for his father. It seemed like both a bad time and the right time to try to lighten things.

I said, "Frankie, how'd you like to take in a Tulane baseball game sometime?"

Brent didn't exactly brighten, but he looked at his mother for permission. Adrienne's look said it probably hadn't been the right time.

She said, "We'll see."

Blanche walked over and stood in front of Brent. She said, "I think there's some mint chocolate chip in the freezer. Could you go for a bowl?"

Brent looked at me. "You want some ice cream?"

"Let me talk to your mom first."

When Blanche and Brent left the room, Adrienne said, "I'm so sorry about Clayton."

"No problem. He was courteous compared to a lot of the mopes I've dealt with. How long were you married?"

"Nine years."

"You must have had some good years too."

She shrugged. "I thought so in the early years, until I redefined *good*. Clayton had all the time in the world for his clients, rarely any time for his family. And then when he spent time with the family, after a while you wished he was with his clients."

"How long divorced?"

"Eight months. I wanted to leave him for years, but I felt guilty. A boy needs a father."

"He still has one."

"But it's not the same."

"Keeping a family under one roof is better if there's harmony and respect. Absent that, putting on a happy face for the kid's sake doesn't work. Kids can see through it. I'm sure Brent did."

"He was always tense when Clayton and I were together."

"Brent will adjust to the new arrangement."

"I think he already has."

"He's a great kid."

"Brent really likes you." Adrienne seemed to be studying my face. "Are all private detectives so wise?"

"You have to know the meaning of life before they'll give you a license."

I think she smiled, but it could have just been me wanting to see it.

Adrienne rubbed her temple. "Do you really think it was murder?"

"Things are pointing to it. If Frank Caveccio killed Jackie and Jackie's friend Danika, proving it could be difficult. But there are some good detectives at Homicide."

She nodded. "I know you didn't know Jackie, but I would like it if you came to the memorial service."

"You can count on me."

"Yes, I believe I can."

TEN

In the backyard the rose-colored dawn light burnished the leaves of the Chinaberry tree, and the air was thick as sorghum with the smell of rain. I stretched my calf and thigh muscles for a run with Santana. Being in the yard made me think of the Komodo dragon and how close I came to becoming unidentifiable remains.

We were running on Carrolton, a block from the house on our return leg, when Grady Herns pulled alongside me in the unmarked Crown Victoria. When Grady found a place to pull over I jogged up to the window and stooped down.

Grady said, "Gotta cut the run short, Sport Model."

In my years at NOPD I'd had only three partners, other than a few short-term trainees. Koot and I partnered my first six years. When Koot was forced out of the department, I partnered with Charlie Gutierrez until he was killed. Then Grady made detective and we hooked up.

Grady hadn't put on more than ten or twelve pounds since we played football together in high school when he carried two-forty on a six-three frame. He was All-State at tackle and made it easy for me to do some good at QB. When he was out in front of me on a sweep it went badly for anyone who got in his path.

By the time Grady and I partnered at NOPD the fun was gone. After half the department turned against me, Grady spent less time out in front and more time watching my back. Besides the grief he got from both sides of the aisle after we crossed racial lines and partnered up, Grady was vilified and isolated further when he stood by me after the hearing. On top of that, Grady, and Koot too, were there to pick me up when I became a fall-down drunk.

Grady's friendship never wavered, but after a year and a half it was a burden I could no longer expect Grady to carry. Eleven years on the force and I hung it up.

I hadn't seen Grady, Rosie or the kids since Koot and I were over for a cookout about a month ago. When Santana recognized Grady he nudged in beside me and stuck his snout in the window. When Grady ignored Santana I knew there was trouble.

I said, "I was coming to the station this morning."

It had been three years since I was inside a police station, so Grady looked surprised.

"That so?"

"I found evidence of a possible multiple."

"Who are the victims?"

"Jackie Kanawhite and a woman named Danika."

"That homicide can wait."

"*That* homicide. Is there an outbreak?" Grady didn't say anything. "So you're not here because Rosie wants to fix me up again?"

"Afraid not, Hossfly. This is bullshit, but Mowery and Fortenberry have the lead on this. They're probably at your place about now. The lieutenant wanted me to come over to see Mowery doesn't go Hannibal on you. We'll get all this straightened out."

When we reached the house they were already there. Detective Hal Fortenberry was standing at the front door. Grady, Santana and I got out of the car and Fortenberry met us on the walkway. Until my last eighteen months at NOPD, Hal had been the lone drunk of our district. Then I made my covenant with the bottle and joined him at the bottom.

Grady asked, "Where's Mowery?"

Forttenberry said, "No one answered. He went around back."

I said, "Long time, Hal."

"Tag."

Hal's face and neck had the wattles of a blood hound and his sweat glands were open spigots. Rivulets ran down through the big folds of skin and were sponged up by his Van Heusen, marinating him in his own juices.

I said, "I heard you haven't had a drink for a year."

"Yeah."

"That's great, Hal."

"It was like saying 'no' to Kim Bassinger every night for three hundred sixty-five nights. Piece of cake. How about you?"

"Sober for two years."

Hal asked, "You able to leave the baggage?"

"Everything but the diabetes. The cost of staying drunk for so long'll have to be paid on the lifetime installment plan."

"Sorry to hear that."

"Don't be. Every time I stick my finger to draw a drop of blood it reminds me I can feel something again."

Hal nodded, then said, "Just so you'll know, I didn't want this assignment."

"I'm thinking I'm not crazy about it either, and no one's told me what it *is* yet."

Detective John Mowery, whom I hadn't seen since I left NOPD, came around the corner of the house dragging his knuckles. Mowery was a hard case who loved to work out on perps. He brought in a lot of offenders with bloodless injuries: contused kidneys and livers, broken ribs, concussions. Some of the perps filed complaints of brutality, but there were never any witnesses. Things had only happened when Mowery's partner wasn't around. And none of his partners stayed around for long.

Because most of the perps had long rap sheets, it was hard for them to get a sympathetic ear downtown. Mowery had collared a lot of bad guys as a uniform and in Vice and Narcotics, so he was tolerated at the department, like a vicious guard dog that craps all over the yard might be. Mowery got away with being Mowery.

Mowery hulked over to us. Santana sensed the stench of malice. He lowered his head, riveted his eyes on Mowery and growled. Mowery froze, his hand went to the weapon on his hip. He popped the snap on his holster strap.

I spoke up. "Santana—no."

Santana put it in park, but his motor was still running. Mowery slowly removed his hand from his weapon while he continued to watch Santana. When Mowery saw Santana wasn't going to attack, he stepped over and stood in front of me.

"I've been waiting for this time to come, Boudreau."

"I've missed you too, Mowery. We can do some bonding after you tell me what this is about."

Mowery bared his pat rictal grin.

"You're going down for the murder of Frank Caveccio and Rocco Givens."

Grady looked at me and sighed, the weight of a lot of bad blood at NOPD behind it.

So Caveccio and Big Man had their okra fried. So much for the evidence I was bringing in. Maybe Caveccio didn't kill Jackie and Danika. Maybe Nads killed them all. Or maybe it was the hoods in the Cobra that staked out Caveccio's place, or the guy with the scar.

Of course, Mowery didn't want to look at anybody else but me on this one. He'd try to pound a square peg of circumstantial evidence into a round hole of the facts.

I asked, "Were Caveccio and Givens killed at Caveccio's place?"

"You'd know," Mowery said.

"Shot?"

Grady said, "Nine millimeter. One each to the chest, one to the head."

"And you found my prints at the scene."

Fortenberry said, "Like politicians before elections. They're showing up everywhere, Tag."

Mowery said, "Caveccio's back door, his desk, his bedroom. Those two fags were ruttin' around in bed when they got it. Maybe you got jealous and doused their flames."

Fortenberry squinted hard, like Mowery's comments had given him gas pains. Grady stared at Mowery.

Mowery pulled his handcuffs out and grabbed my right arm and cuffed it.

"You're under arrest, Boudreau."

He reached around me for my other arm, then Grady stepped over to him. "Take off the cuffs, Mowery."

"I'm lead on this, Herns, and I say we cuff him."

Grady took a step closer. "Mowery, the lieutenant said you were to bring Boudreau in for *questioning*. You don't take the cuffs off, you're gonna be 'ruttin'' around on your face."

Mowery was vicious, but he wouldn't even fantasize about going up against Grady. He unlocked the cuffs.

"You make me sick, Herns. Standing up for a cop killer." Mowery sneered at me. "Any friends you got at the department ain't gonna help if we make this stick, Assassin."

Mowery wanted to pin this murder on me like a drowning man wanted air. This was all about one of my former partners, Charlie Guiterrez, who was killed on the job. Charlie and I were staking out a shotgun duplex on Gentilly across from the horse track. We had gotten a tip that drugs were being dealt out of the house. About one in the morning we heard a woman's scream in the house, so we bailed and approached on the run, weapons drawn. No time to wait for backup.

Charlie went to the front door and gave me a few seconds to make my way to the back door, then we were going in. When I got around back, a guy bolted from the house and I went after him. I was chasing the perp down an alley when I heard two shots back at the house.

I pulled up on the perp and sprinted back to the house. I found a woman on the living room floor with her head bashed in, and slumped over her was Charlie, two bullets to the head. A second perp had gotten the drop on Charlie, then executed him.

I made a judgment call. It was the wrong call. I wasn't there to cover my partner, and it cost Charlie his life.

Before the hearing, I think most of the cops in the department were sympathetic. At the hearing I was cleared by Public Integrity (our internal affairs office), but certain testimony was given that cast doubt. Though I had a few cops in my corner, I became the most hated cop on the force.

Mowery said, "Been waiting a long time, Boudreau."

These guys don't forget. And rarely do twenty-four hours pass without the tape of that night queuing up in *my* mind. It's taken a lot of years and a lot of self-destructive behavior before I could finally forgive myself—but forgetting is not an option.

ELEVEN

Grady saw to it that I got to feed Santana and Seven and change clothes, then we left. Grady took his car, and I got in the car with Hal and Mowery. I was glad Hal was in the car. Hal distanced himself from me after the hearing, but I felt like he hadn't passed judgment. I didn't blame him for keeping me at arm's length. I became a pariah at the department, and Hal had to work with those guys. He didn't want to be shut out.

I had assumed we were going to the district station, but when we turned north onto Carrolton I realized we were headed to the crime scene, Caveccio's townhouse. When we arrived, a couple of uniformed cops I had seen around when I was on the job were at the front door. When they saw us approach they stopped their conversation and stared. As we walked up the sidewalk, Mowery gripped my arm like look-who-I-collared. When we got to the door, Mowery nodded at the uniforms. The uniforms nodded back. Next we'd be square dancing.

Inside the townhouse Mowery, Fortenberry and Grady walked me through the living room toward the kitchen. One of the guys from FLU, the Forensic Light Unit, was examining sheets of paper on the coffee table with a magnifier. The bodies would still be in bed pending the Medical Examiner's call of the deaths. Killed while having sex. The ultimate *coitus interruptus*.

Detective Marie Trammel was on her knees and gloved hands, looking under the L-shaped couch for evidence. As we passed she looked up.

"Hello, Marie."

"Tag."

I never knew whether Marie thought I had set up my partner Charlie to be killed. She always kept her feelings close to the vest. Marie was a good cop, and I wished I had known how she felt.

Conley Clark

When we entered the kitchen, I recognized from behind the hip-heavy body and wafer-thin ears of Detective Ernie Stubbs. He was standing at the back door with an animal control officer, looking out at the Komodo dragon. The dragon stood under his little tree and stared back.

Stubbs said to the animal control guy, "That's one mother of a lizard. Think it'll hold still for you slippin' that noose over its head?"

The animal control guy had a cable stick in his hand. He didn't say anything. I stepped over to the guy, then reached in my jacket pocket and pulled out the chloral hydrate.

I said, "Pour the rest of this on something yummy and toss it to Godzilla. You'll have just about enough time to get him in the cage."

Stubbs turned. "Boudreau." He looked at the bottle in my hand. "Why would anyone want advice from a chronicle liar?"

Stubbs liked words. The fact that he was always misusing them didn't seem to bother him.

I said, "Suit yourself." I started to put the bottle back in my pocket.

The animal control guy asked, "Chloral hydrate?"

"Uh huh."

He held out his hand, and I gave him the bottle; then he went out of the room, probably to his truck for bait.

Mowery said, "Sit down, Assassin."

I sat at the dining table. Mowery stood behind me. Fortenberry stood over by the stove and propped himself against the counter, while Stubbs stayed near the back door, keeping an eye on Godzilla.

Grady said, "Mowery, Lieutenant Tolleson wants to sit in on this. Don't start the interview until I get him."

Passing Grady in the doorway, Payton Doucette sidled into the kitchen. Another cop firmly in the "disembowel Boudreau" camp. Doucette was strung tight as piano wire, and he'd learned a long time ago that he had to drop down a couple of octaves in order to fit in at the department. One of the ways he thought made him fit in was the good-ol'-boy patois.

Doucette said, "Well, well, well. If this ain't better than hittin' the Powerball. They let you off last time, Assassin. Maybe this time you gon' do the time. Ya think?" Doucette sat down at the table to my left.

Doucette and I have history before and after Charlie's death. Ancient history had to do with being handed a high profile homicide case Doucette hadn't been able to solve. I solved the case by getting a key witness to come forward after the witness had stonewalled Doucette.

I gave Doucette the biggest share of the credit, but when the media tried to make me the hero, Doucette's memory got as short as a hit man's eulogy, and I made an enemy for life.

That animosity found an opportunity to express itself at the internal Public Integrity hearing after Charlie was murdered. Doucette offered testimony that Charlie told him that Charlie was having an affair with my wife. My wife was called to testify and corroborated the affair with Charlie.

I had suspected Cile was seeing someone, but had no idea it was Charlie. According to Doucette, Charlie told him that I knew about the affair and confronted Charlie about it. Doucette had played his trump card. He knew no one could disprove the lie. And he knew what would happen next.

Even though Public Integrity had no evidence that I set Charlie up and cleared me of any wrongdoing regarding the shooting, a lot of cops believed Doucette's testimony. They figured I had reason to want Charlie dead and figured I took advantage of an opportunity to make it happen. Just stay outside the house and let Charlie enter without cover, hoping he'd be blown away.

Neither the guy I chased nor the killer were ever caught and there were no witnesses, so it came down to my word against Doucette's. Most of the cops couldn't see what Doucette had to gain by lying, and it seemed clear to them why I would. Doucette wanted my career. After a while, he got it.

Doucette said, "You gon' do time at Angola, Boudreau. When they find out they got an ex-cop among 'em, they gon' draw straws to see who gets to shank ya."

I said, "You turned the department against me and ended my career. That's not enough for you, Doucette?"

"You dug your own hole, Boudreau. Now we gon' bury you in it."

"You lying sonofa..."

Suddenly my chair pitched forward and my chin cracked against the table, then my head bounced off the table and followed my body to the floor.

When I looked up, everybody's face was out of focus. I felt blood course from the gash in my chin. It ran down my neck and pooled up in the notch above my sternum.

I heard Fortenberry say, "Cut the shit, Mowery."

Fortenberry came over and helped me back in the chair, then handed me his handkerchief. Then he went back and leaned against the counter and said nothing else.

Doucette said, "Fall out of your chair, Boudreau?" With all the sincerity of a repeat offender before a parole board, "That's a cryin' shame."

I held the handkerchief to my chin to stem the blood flow. Some blood was also running from my mouth, and I realized I had bitten my tongue. After several seconds the gauzy faces and objects in the room began to take on defined edges again.

I saw Grady and Lieutenant Boyce Tolleson's face come into the picture. Mowery moved from his position behind my chair to the other end of the table. When Lieutenant Tolleson saw me holding the bloody handkerchief to my mouth and chin, he glared at Mowery and Doucette.

"What the hell happened here?"

Doucette and Mowery glanced at each other. Stubbs looked out at the Komodo dragon while Fortenberry looked conflicted.

I got to my feet slowly.

Doucette said, "Boudreau had an accident."

Grady knew who did it. He walked over and stood toe to toe with Mowery. After three years, it was starting all over again. Too many scenes similar to this one, too many times before.

I said, "He's right. I fell out of my chair."

The lieutenant continued to stare at Doucette and Mowery, and Grady was locked and loaded.

"Really, I fell. If I don't get my fiber in the morning, I can't put one foot in front of the other."

Grady glared at Mowery.

I said to Grady, "Not worth it, Papa."

Grady knew that he'd either have to let it go or take it all the way. Finally, he took a step back. Mowery tried to smirk, but with Grady looking at him, it came out looking sheepish.

"You all right, Boudreau?" asked the lieutenant.

I wiped blood from my chin. "It'll feel a lot better when it quits hurting."

"You might need some stitches."

"Let's just get on with it, Lieutenant."

"You sure?"

"Yeah."

Lieutenant Tolleson turned again to Mowery. "I told you to bring Boudreau in for questioning, Mowery. You told him he was under arrest, then this crap. I'm putting Herns in charge of the interview."

Mowery looked incredulous. "Herns and Boudreau are friends, Lieutenant."

The lieutenant said, "And you're totally objective here, right, Mowery?"

The veins in Mowery's neck popped out, but he kept his mouth shut.

The lieutenant moved to the opposite end of the dining table and sat down. Grady walked around the table and sat to my right. He gave me a brief look that said he was sorry, then he was all business.

"Were you here at Frank Caveccio's last night?"

"I was here around 6:15 and left at about 6:45."

"You came to see Frank Caveccio and Rocco Givens?"

"No. I had seen them earlier. This time they were gone and I let myself in."

Doucette sat up in his seat. "That's breakin' and enterin'."

Grady looked at Doucette. "Caveccio's not gonna be pressing any charges—is he, Doucette?"

Lieutenant Tolleson gave me a disappointed look. Doucette looked like he needed something to gnaw on.

Grady continued. "Why were you here?"

"I was looking for evidence that would tie Frank Caveccio to the murder of Jackie Kanawhite and a woman named Danika."

Mowery flared. "He was spouting off that story on the way over here, Lieutenant. I checked with the Coast Guard. That was a boating accident." Mowery looked at me again. "You're not gonna divert our attention, Boudreau."

Lieutenant Tolleson ignored Mowery. "If Caveccio killed these people you're talking about, it'd be a moot point now, Boudreau."

I said, "Yeah. Maybe Caveccio didn't kill Kanawhite and the woman. Maybe all four of them were killed by someone else."

Mowery pleaded, "Lieutenant."

Lieutenant Tolleson looked at Grady and then at me. "Nads Liano?"

I dabbed warm blood from my lips. "You guys have the ledger. Caveccio and Kanawhite did business with Liano. If either of them did something stupid, like try to cheat Liano, Nads would kill them and the woman too if he thought she knew anything about their business dealings."

Doucette said, "Why didn't you bring the information about the ledger in when you found it?"

Lieutenant Tolleson said, "You're not conducting this interview, Doucette."

I said, "I was going to bring it in this morning, but your posse caught up with me before I could get in the saddle. Also, some guys definitely not in Nads' crew were interested in Kanawhite and Caveccio and the woman."

I told them about Caveccio and Givens being followed and about the guy with the scar asking about Jackie and Danika.

Doucette said, "This is a crock, Lieutenant. Boudreau's prints are all over the house. We need to run his gun for a ballistics match."

Grady said, "You at all interested in establishing motive, Doucette?"

"I'll find the motive."

I said, "Doucette, I know you and Mowery are disappointed you didn't get to give me a cavity search—but you wouldn't find a motive there either."

One side of Mowery's lip curled up, but it was a lousy Elvis imitation.

Lieutenant Tolleson groused, "Boudreau, you're not here to tweak my detectives. You're here to answer questions."

"Sorry, Lieutenant." Doucette looked like he was having an aneurysm.

Grady asked, "How'd you get involved in all this?"

"I was hired by Jackie Kanawhite's sister to find Jackie. When I found out that Caveccio and Kanawhite knew each other, I went calling. When Caveccio lied to me about a couple of things, I came back here to see what I could find. There were no dead bodies when I got here." I looked at Doucette. "Nor when I left."

Grady said, "Let us have the Kanawhite woman's number."

I pulled my notebook out, turned to the page with Adrienne's number, then slid the notebook over to Grady. He copied the number down.

The lieutenant said, "Herns will call. If it checks out, you can go, Boudreau."

Mowery's expression went tight as a botched eye tuck. He squeezed out, "Are we going to let him walk without running his gun through?"

The lieutenant sat back in his chair and shook his head back and forth as he looked at Mowery, then Doucette. Then he said, "You guys are never gonna let it go, are you?"

Doucette said, "We're tryin' to catch a murderer, Lieutenant."

Lieutenant Tolleson said, "You're trying to *pin* a murder. You and Boudreau have history, Doucette. And Mowery's rabid about Boudreau because he and a lot of other cops believed your testimony at the hearing."

"Due respect, Lieutenant, but are you implyin' I might've lied at the hearing?"

"I'm saying some of us know you're the kind to hold a grudge."

Doucette and Lieutenant Tolleson eyed each other, the tension in the room as palpable as torch heat in a Mini Cooper.

Finally I said, "Well, I know you guys have a murderer to catch so..." I stood.

Grady said, "Let's go make that call to your client."

Mowery said, "Looks like you get a pass, Boudreau."

I said, "Looks like you got one too, Mowery. That won't happen again."

TWELVE

On the way back to my house Grady said, "I should have seen that coming."

"It was my fault, Grady. They ran their mouths, and I bit."

My tongue still bled, and I wiped it with the handkerchief Fortenberry had given me.

Grady watched me and said, "You bit the wrong guy."

I chuckled, and it hurt.

I said, "Sorry I won't get to see Nads when you bring him in for questioning."

"Maybe we'll keep him and his lawyer waiting for a while in the interrogation room. Another dirt-bag puked up his burger and fries there yesterday and it still stinks."

We both laughed. The image of Nads cooling his heels in the stench made it worth the pain.

Grady said, "Tell that sorry partner of yours we want to see both your faces at the house soon. We'll play some ball."

"You'll have to spot me a couple of baskets." I stuck my chin out. "Injured."

"Won't do you any good."

We tapped knuckles, and I got out and went in the house.

I had called Koot before we left the station, and a few minutes after Grady left, Koot pulled up in his Subaru Outback wagon. I wasn't looking forward to telling him what happened. Dealing with Koot's anger was like trying to put out an oil fire. When he walked in and saw me holding the bloody handkerchief to my chin, his eyes narrowed.

"Mowery or Doucette do this?"

Koot carried a double tank of rage. One tank was because of his father, but the rage that makes Koot a truly dangerous man comes from the death of his son.

It happened eight years ago when Koot was in Narcotics. He was dogging a Honduran drug gang and brought in a couple of the middle managers just to let them know the narc wasn't going away. The Hondurans caught Koot one night outside a Wal-Mart and took him to some place out of the city. They put Koot's head in a cattle lock and stuck a furnace-fired branding iron to the side of his head, just above his right ear.

But having Vasquez's "V" in the side of Koot's head wasn't the deterrent the Hondurans figured on. The next time, Vasquez's men took Koot's and Sondra's five year-old son Toby while the boy was with a neighbor and her kids at a playground. They branded the boy, same as they had done to Koot, but Toby had an arrhythmic heart and apparently the pain caused it to stop. The Hondurans dumped Toby's body at the family's door. Koot became a different man.

Koot sent Sondra and their daughter Fran to Sondra's family in Oregon, then Koot and the rest of Narcotics spent the next seven months busting or breaking down every known dealer in New Orleans until they ate their way up the food chain and put Vasquez and his gang away.

Koot's obsession with bad guys didn't stop with Vasquez. He turned maverick and repeatedly disobeyed orders if they got in the way of a lead or a collar. Everyone in the department was sympathetic, and the Commander gave Koot a lot of slack. The department psychologist made house calls. Every weekend for months Cile and I dragged Koot out of his house to go sailing or to Grady's and Rosie's for a cookout. We all thought that in time Koot would work through the grief and come back into the fold at the department.

It didn't happen. Eventually NOPD had to let Koot go. Sondra had had enough too. Soon after Koot was fired, she filed for divorce. Later she left Louisiana with their daughter.

I knew what I was getting into when Koot and I hung out our sign for the agency. Koot's rage has gotten us jammed up more than once, but when the heat was turned up, Koot was the one you wanted on your side. He'd walk into an inferno of hostiles to bring you out.

Koot is a tortured man. And he's my friend.

"Koot, we're not going to war again."

"I can take care of it myself."

"Take deep breaths. This doesn't mean I'm gonna let 'em keep working out on me. But I get to make that call. Okay?"

Koot pulled in a lung full of air and let it out, trying to get a handle on his anger. He did that a few more times, then looked at me. Finally he said, "You need stitches."

"Could probably use a few."

Since his father had never considered taking himself or Koot to the hospital for any of the various injuries that come from leading a self-sufficient life in the marsh and swamp, Koot learned at an early age how to stitch up wounds. He sat me down in the kitchen and looked at my chin.

He said, "You've got a flap of skin hanging down."

I mumbled, "That's one of the things I like about you—your delicate way with words."

"You want delicate—partner with a Geisha."

Koot walked to the sink and washed his hands. Then he went to the cabinet and took out my sewing kit, some cotton balls and a bottle of alcohol. He pulled a sewing needle out of the kit, walked to the stove, turned on the burner and passed the needle through the flame a few times.

Santana sauntered in and flopped on the floor and looked at me, then at Koot. When Koot looked at him, Santana flapped his tail on the linoleum.

Koot pulled up a chair opposite me. He threaded the needle with some heavy black nylon thread I had used to make minor sail repairs.

I said, "You're not too out of practice with this, are you?"

"Nah. And I've got a drawer full of socks to prove it."

"Dandy."

"You got anything for pain?"

"Percocet."

Koot got up and went to the medicine cabinet and came back with a couple of pills and a glass of water.

After I'd washed the pills down Koot said, "That's gonna take a while to kick in."

"Let's get it over with."

"You sure you don't want to go to the ER?"

"And pay a hundred bucks co-pay?"

"Okay, tough guy."

Koot put a cotton ball against the opening of the bottle of alcohol and tilted the bottle down, then he swabbed the gash in my chin. I flinched.

Koot said, "This is the easy part."

"You liking this?"

Koot grinned. I stuck my chin out farther.

Koot brought the needle close and said, "The first stitch—you'll wanna launch. Don't do it."

"Arrrr."

When he stuck the needle in it felt like a jolt of 110. I broke into a sweat, then went into the room behind my eyes that I used to enter when I couldn't walk into any New Orleans police precinct without getting cussed or called out.

When Koot was finished he tied off the stitch and cut the end with the scissors. Then he went and got a couple of cold orange teas from the fridge, handed me one and sat down again.

The inside of my mouth felt like a sea urchin was lodged in it, my jaw still throbbed from being sapped, and the Percocet was stalling entry into my blood stream.

Seven came in the kitchen and two-hopped to the counter and to the top of the fridge. I took a swig of the tea, which soothed my bitten tongue a little.

I told Koot about Caveccio and Big Man, about Mowery and Doucette wanting to nail me for the hit, about Grady and the lieutenant sticking up for me, and about the cops bringing Nads in for questioning.

I told him I was still thinking Caveccio might have killed Jackie and Danika. The lieutenant was right though—if Caveccio did it, it didn't matter now, except maybe to Adrienne. I was hoping she'd want to know for certain who killed her brother. It would give me a reason to keep looking, reason to keep seeing her. Of course, with everything Adrienne was going through, the timing was bad to try to get beyond a client relationship.

Koot said, "So the investigation is over?"

"Depends on the client."

"You'd go after dead men so she can have closure?"

"If that's what she wants." Koot gave me a look, like he was amused I would try to hide it. "All right, I'm attracted to Adrienne Kanawhite."

"She's grieving for her brother, Tag."

"Grieving comes to an end *sometime*."

"Is she interested?"

"Don't know."

"You find out she is—try not to run this one off."

"That has to come to an end sometime too."

THIRTEEN

After Koot left I got tired of sitting around the house thinking about a bad situation, so I decided to go out and think about it. The Percocet had kicked in, giving me the illusion that I was a well man, so I walked my illusion over to Carrolton and down to a beer joint across from the levee called The Fatted Rat.

"The Rat" was a bouquet of sour beer and fruit, grease and pine-scented disinfectant. The place was a galaxy away from the finer clubs and bars downtown. Not the kind of crowd that comes to "impress 'em and undress 'em." Here people aren't easily impressed, and there's rarely anyone you'd want to undress.

The lunch crowd was in, which meant the first happy hour of the day was underway. A group of power company employees were at the bar drinking Busch in cans and eating parched peanuts, tossing the peanut shells on the floor, a tradition at "The Rat." A couple danced by the jukebox to a reggae tune.

I took a booth in the back and ordered a diet Dr. Pepper. I detest diet drinks. A diabetic with a Jones for sugar is a sad thing. The TV, which was bolted to a platform up near the ceiling, and which looked like it hadn't been dusted since Deep Throat served up Nixon, was tuned to CNN. They were reporting that Israel and the Palestinians had finally agreed on the borders of a Palestinian state. To mark the occasion, a suicide bomber blew up himself and seven Israelis at a celebration rally.

I was listening to leaders from both sides spit accusations at each other when a couple of fashionably dressed pugs walked in the bar. The Sicilians. Actually, only one was a pug—the one with the side of his face partially caved in. I heard he had leaned on some guy for protection money and the guy leaned back—with a claw hammer. Of course, anybody that resists the mob usually ends up worse. The pug walked with his legs wide like he had prostitis—or genitals the size of mangoes.

The other guy was Nads' lieutenant, Giancarlo. Giancarlo was six-four and anorexic as tough guys go. He had long, delicate fingers and a neck that bent forward and bobbed like a pigeon's.

Giancarlo had a reputation as the Ginzu chef of mobsters. He was very effective with a blade in extorting protection money from some hard-working store owner, or getting information from those disinclined to talk.

Giancarlo scanned the room a few times, an occupational habit we shared as a result of making enemies on a semi-regular basis. I hadn't run into Giancarlo since I was on the force. He'd been Nads' main man for about eight years. Unusual that, after all this time, he hadn't gotten on Nads' bad side and been demoted or taken out, or hadn't gotten ambitious and tried to take Nads out in a power play. The loyalty was touching.

These guys stood out in a place like this. The regulars watched them like you'd watch the Komodo Dragon from behind a wobbly fence. When they got to the table, Giancarlo stood directly over me. I looked up into a copse of nose hair thick as an air filter.

"Boudreau."

"Giancarlo. If you're collecting for the Victims of Violence, put me down for fifty."

"Always the funny man."

"I used to think so, before the operation."

"Must have been a lobotomy."

"Who said cold-blooded killers don't have a sense of humor?"

He gave me dead eyes. "Mr. Liano would like to discuss something with you."

I took a sip of Dr. Pepper, then said, "I thought you'd be the boss by now, Giancarlo, instead of still number two. Did you ever wish you'd made another career choice—been your own man?"

Giancarlo looked at me like I was somebody's spoiled kid he wanted to slap, but couldn't because I wasn't his kid.

"Be glad I'm *not* in charge, Boudreau."

"All right, number two. Let's go see your boss."

I left a couple of bucks for the soda. I never know what to tip on something that cost a buck. Seems chintzy to leave less than a dollar, but over the top to leave a hundred percent tip. I should write Miss Manners.

Nads was waiting outside in the backseat of his Lincoln Town Car. One of Nads' sumo-sized soldiers opened the back door, then Nads got out and buttoned his suit coat. These guys decked out when it was ninety degrees with eighty-five percent humidity. The Sicilians were nothing if not image conscious.

That was especially true with Nads. Looks and grooming were part of an image of respectability—a respectability he craved. Nads came up from the streets where homage was earned through violence. Of course, what he got from others was not respect, but fear. I guess if you squinted hard enough the delusion might look real.

Nads had grayed a couple of patches over the ears in the last few years, and had traded his double-breasted designer suits for something like a Brooks Brothers, tailored navy pin stripe, three button single-breasted. Must be bribing a higher class of politicians now.

I said, "You almost look respectable, Nads."

Nads said, "You almost look like you're not pissing your pants."

Nads told the sumo to pat me down. The guy ran his hams over me so thoroughly I was wondering if he enjoyed it. He lifted the Kahr out of the holster under my shirt in the back. When I'm on the job I usually shoulder holster the Kahr under a sport coat or a baseball jacket, a better conceal. It's important not to make the clients and interviewees jumpy.

The sumo took the clip out of the Kahr and stuck the gun and the clip in his coat pocket and kept working his way down. I had to lean against his pawing to keep my balance. When he was done, he nodded once to Nads.

"If I wanted to shoot you, Nads, I could have done it long ago."

"People change their minds. Let's walk, Boudreau."

We crossed the road that parallels the river and climbed the embankment of the levee. When we reached the top we walked along the same section of the ridge where Santana and I run. Giancarlo and the pug walked behind us while the sumo walked along the bottom of the levee.

Nads said, "The cops had me come in a couple hours ago. They hassled me. I hate being hassled. You made some accusations of a hit that you can't back up, Shithead."

Doucette or Mowery, no doubt, had dropped my name when they questioned Nads. Never mind the violation of every departmental confidentiality policy. They figured maybe they'd get lucky and Nads would break some bones for pointing a finger.

"They didn't need anything from me to make you a suspect. They found the ledger that links you to Frank Caveccio and Jackie Kanawhite."

"Some ledger saying I did business with a couple of humps don't prove shit."

"Gives the cops possible motive. Maybe the business deal went sour and you took out Caveccio and his muscle. Maybe Kanawhite and the woman too. Something goes wrong, you're not known to seek arbitration."

"You've been trying to bring me down for a long time, Boudreau, but you're not a cop anymore."

"I'll bet you're glad." I shrugged. "Of course, so are a lot of cops."

"You were a pain in the ass. You were never a *threat* to me; you nor your barking psychotic of a partner, Loomis."

"You didn't have a dozen pols running interference, it might have been a different story."

"But it's not a different story. You gonna hold on to 'if-only' till your dick shrivels up like your career as a cop did?"

"Now you've hurt my feelings."

"Personally, I think you'd like me to put you out of your misery."

"Was that what it was for Caveccio and Rocco, Jackie and the woman—mercy killings?"

Nads looked at me like I'd downed a snifter of squid ink. Then he turned and walked down the hill and I followed. When he got to his car, Nads turned.

"Say hello to your buddy Kiki."

"Kiki?"

"You think I don't know Kiki snitches for you and the cops."

I spread my hands like I didn't know what he was talking about.

Nads said, "I know Kiki's never given you or the cops anything on me. That's why he's still alive and pimping for me."

It made sense that Nads would let Kiki sell information to the cops if he knew most of what Kiki gave them was about street criminals. These small timers were no competition to Nads, but he probably figured an occasional sewer flush was a good thing.

Also, most of the small timers were drug dealers, and Nads hated drugs. He had his own take on morality. Prostitution, loan sharking, extortion and stolen goods were fine, but drugs were a destruction of our youth. Nads actually saw himself as a good Catholic. He gave bags of money to the church. In return for his generosity, the church turned a blind eye to Nads' "business." *Our Lady of Denial.*

Of course the church wasn't the only one turning a blind eye. Nads had to know Kiki was an addict, but Kiki made money for him, so Nads overlooked Kiki's habit. The cops knew Kiki was an addict and looked the other way to get the information they wanted. I had been one of those cops.

"I'd better not get pulled into the station again because of you. Understand?

I did my best marbles-in-the-mouth Brando imitation. "An offer I can't refuse."

Nads nodded to the sumo. The sumo pulled my gun and the clip from his pocket and handed it to me. The clip had been emptied. Nads got in the back seat of the Lincoln, then his soldiers got in and they left.

So, maybe Caveccio killed Jackie and the woman, then Nads found out Caveccio had gotten greedy and had him and his man taken out on principle; nobody gets to kill Liano's business partners except Liano. Or maybe Nads murdered the four of them. And I think to myself—what a wonderful world.

FOURTEEN

Kiki Lebrec had been pimping for Nads and snitching for the cops for several years. I got a lot of useful information from him when I was on the force and still pay him for information from time to time. I knew Kiki wouldn't give me anything about Jackie's and Frank's business dealings with Nads—if he knew anything—but he might know something about Jackie and Frank that would help, and maybe something about Jackie's friend Danika.

Kiki lived off Basin Street, just outside the French Quarter. I parked on Rampart, got out and walked up to Basin, then crossed the street in front of a community theatre. *The Vagina Monologues* was double billed with *The Magic Flute*.

Basin Street has seen both fame and infamy. At one time it was a Mecca for the blues, and before that it was part of Storyville, a brothel district at the turn of the 20th Century. Basin today near the Quarter is just part of another neighborhood in decay.

As I made my way up the street toward Kiki's apartment, black men and women stared at me from porches, their faces seeming to hold neither malice nor goodwill. Maybe people living at the margins could afford neither.

Kiki lived on the second floor of an old Creole townhouse that had been subdivided into four units. The door to the building looked like the entrance to a cage—ten-gauge wire mesh welded to wrought iron bars. Heavy enough to discourage any burglar without a Howitzer. I buzzed Kiki on the intercom. No answer, so I sat on the buzzer.

Finally Kiki answered. He was irritated and his voice sounded shaky. "Who is it?"

"Your favorite employer."

"Boudreau?"

"Uh huh."

"I'm sick. Come back later."

Kiki was a cokie. When he was jacked up he was a dependable snitch, if somewhat testy. When he couldn't score he was a mess. He'd been in treatment programs several times, but the wiring on Kiki's coping mechanism was crossed, so when his world tilted he always went back to using. It didn't help that the streets he worked for Nads were infested with dealers. I knew that at this moment Kiki was doing sweat-soaked combat with a nest of demons, but I needed some answers.

"Kiki, you think because I don't tune you up from time to time like Nads does you can waste my time?"

"You don't understand, Boudreau."

"I understand you'd give your left nut to kick your drug habit, and you'd give your right nut for a nose full about now. I'm sorry you can't turn the corner, Kiki—I really am—but this can't wait."

"You're a heartless S.O.B, Boudreau."

"I've heard it before, Kiki."

Kiki's breath rattled and then the door buzzed open. I walked up the dark stairway and entered the apartment. Kiki was standing at the window in his boxers, holding his Chihuahua out the window.

I said, "Cookie's not a cat, in case you're about to see if she'd land on her feet."

Then I saw that Kiki was gently squeezing the Chihuahua. In a few seconds Cookie peed from two stories up and I heard it splatter on the sidewalk below.

"I would have taken her outside for you, Kiki."

Kiki looked at me from hollow sockets. "She's used to it."

Kiki was a cretin and the lowest on the food chain to Nads, to the cops, and to society, even though Nads and the cops knew Kiki had done something very few people would have done—something truly heroic. About four years ago Kiki barbecued an arm and leg when he entered a blazing and collapsing house and came out with a young boy and his baby sister. Kiki was offered a sizable reward by some private citizens, but wouldn't take the money. No one understood how a pimp could be an unselfish hero, or how an unselfish hero could be a pimp. After a while they stopped trying to understand and Kiki became just another lowlife again.

Kiki pulled Cookie back inside and sat on the couch.

"Can we make this fast, Boudreau?"

"Absolutely. You know Jackie Kanawhite and Frank Caveccio?"

"Should I?"

"I know they supply electronic knockoffs for Nads."

"Don't know anything about any of Mr. Liano's business."

"I'm not asking about that. You know anything else about them."

"Yeah, okay. I've seen them at some parties."

"Parties your girls attended?"

"No street girls. This was strictly high class."

"So what were you doing there?"

"That's *my* business, Boudreau."

"You dealing now?"

"You come here to shake me down? You're not a cop anymore, Boudreau."

"My apologies."

"Not that I give a shit what you think, but I'm not dealing."

"I'm glad to hear that, Kiki."

"I got invited to Dumont Castille's parties. He wanted me to work for him. After I said 'no' a few times the party invitations stopped."

"Should I know the name Castille?"

"You been out of touch, Boudreau. Castille's come on strong the last year or so. Flesh and designer drugs."

Suddenly Kiki's face blanched, and he flopped backwards against the couch. The sudden move scared Cookie, and she sprang to the other end of the sofa. Kiki bent his head to his knees.

I went to Kiki's medicine cabinet and got some Ibuprofen, then went to the kitchen for a glass of water. I took the water and Ibuprofen into the living room and shook three caps out of the bottle and held the water and the pills out for Kiki.

"Take these."

Kiki looked up at the pills. "Not what I need, Boudreau."

"If you can't be with the one you love, love the one you're with."

Kiki looked at the pills some more, then took the water and the Ibuprophen and washed the caps down.

I waited until Kiki's contraction had passed and he was sitting back up. "What can you tell me about Kanawhite's and Caveccio's relationship?"

"You mean do they have a thing for each other?"

"I mean did you ever see any bad blood between them?"

"Like I said. I saw 'em at a couple of Castille's parties. Someone mentioned their names. Some lawyer was with them. They brought some fine women. They all looked like they had a good time. That's all I know."

"Who was the lawyer?"

"I generally don't get introduced."

"How'd you know he was a lawyer?"

"Saw him in court once."

Kiki hugged himself tight and his body began to twist around. He looked like he was trying to shed his skin.

"We're almost done, Kiki."

"I gotta get outta here, Boudreau."

"You ever see Kanawhite with a woman named Danika? She's the kind of woman you'd remember."

"Maybe she was the one with Kanawhite."

"You didn't get her name?"

"Like I said, I don't get introduced."

"Know a guy about six two with a bad scar that spirals down over the entire nose—foreign accent—might have had a connection to Frank and Jackie?"

"I know a lot of guys with bad scars, Boudreau." Kiki twitched from a contraction. "Is that it?"

"You've been no help, Kiki, but I appreciate your not trying to sell me a bill of goods."

"I have a reputation, Boudreau."

"Goes without saying." Irony keeps life interesting.

"If we're done, Boudreau..."

I put a twenty on the dinette table and left. Kiki would be out the door soon after me. He needed to get hooked up so he could keep the demons at bay a while longer.

FIFTEEN

I walked back to my car in a steady drizzle. The sun's heat captured in the street and sidewalks turned the rain to rising steam. The men and women were still on their porches, but the persistent rain and steam prevented us from seeing each other clearly. I wondered if there would ever be a time when we could.

When I reached the car, I took a beach towel with a picture of the U.S. women's soccer team out of the trunk and spread it on the seat, then got in and headed home to get out of my wet clothes. I drove through the Central Business District and onto St. Charles.

St. Charles was two sets of one-way streets heading in opposite directions, divided by a wide grass neutral ground. Running through the neutral zone were the two tracks of the streetcar line. For a couple of blocks my pace on the street matched that of one of the streetcars.

Every few seconds the streetcar's electric contact arm would hit a spot on the wet overhead cable and arc a brilliant burst of fire that cascaded over the car like sparks from a metal grinder.

By the time I reached the house, the rain had stopped. When I walked in, Seven shot from the kitchen and down the hall. Santana tried to chase her but couldn't get traction on the wood floor, his legs moving flat out amounting to no more than a slow drift.

My jaw and mouth were starting to hurt again, and I was feeling out of sorts. I went to the bathroom and grabbed my kit from the cabinet and drew blood, then swiped it on the test strip and stuck it in the glucometer. One-sixty, a little high. I had just downed a couple of my meds when the front door bell rang. As always, Santana headed for the front door, and as always, Seven hid.

I unsnapped the strap on the Kahr holstered in the back of my jeans and went to the door. I put away my share of bad guys when I was a cop, and I've made a few enemies as a PI as well. When I'm not expecting anyone, I'm a cautious man.

Conley Clark

I opened the door and there they were—the guys who had been asking around about Jackie and Danika. I figured I'd run into them at some point, but I thought I'd be the one doing the calling.

One of them was about my height, but had a few pounds on me. His dyed carrot hair was cut to the scalp on the sides, while a waterfall of rope-thick curls fell down the back of his head to his shoulders. The pocks in his face trapped shadows. He wore a New Orleans Saints T-shirt under an unbuttoned denim overshirt.

The other guy had the scar, as Adrienne had described. It looked like someone stuck a knife up his nose and ripped it open. It made me think of the scene in *Chinatown* where Jake Gittes got his nose fileted by the "midget." Where the two halves of meat had been sewn back together, it had collapsed in on itself along the jagged seam. It was an ugly scar.

The guy's eyes looked strangely sleepy and predatory at the same time. Probably hadn't been breast fed. But then neither had I.

These guys were not part of Nads' crew, unless they were subcontractors. Maybe Nads decided to have me tuned up after all. Maybe his regular guys had to be breaking bones in another part of town today and they went to the bench for little ol' me.

The guy with the eyes said, "Mr. Dumont Castille wants to speak with you about your investigation. You'll come with us."

No "hello," no introductions. At least some of the Sicilians said "howyadoin'" before they drug you off or split your skull open. Santana stood just behind me, tensed, his eyes fixed on the two men.

I said, "Tell Mr. Castille he can see me at my office. It's always open—except when I'm not there—or on Thursdays. My cleaning lady won't let me see clients on Thursdays."

The guy with the eyes sighed, then looked up and down the sidewalk. No one in sight. Where were the neck-craning neighbors when you wanted them around? The curly-headed guy shifted from leg to leg and moved his head in quick jerks, popping his neck bones. His whole body seemed to be one fast-twitch muscle hung on a skeleton badly in need of adjustment.

Eyes said, "It can be easy—or not. You've got about ten seconds to decide."

The accent was Slavic, maybe Croatian or Serbian, somewhere in that part of Eastern Europe where the wells of so many hearts and minds were poisoned with ethnic hatred. We stood there sizing each other up for a few seconds.

Then I shrugged, opened the door, and stepped aside for them to enter. Curly moved to the door first. I reached behind me for the prickly pear cactus on the table by the door.

As Curly stepped into the threshold I jammed the cactus in his face. He screamed, and I crashed my weight against the door. He screamed again and dropped to the floor. I drew my gun with my right hand as I yanked the door open again with the other hand and crouched for a shot at Eyes.

Eyes just stood there. No gun drawn. No fight-or-flight. Not even a blink. He looked almost bored. That gave me a chill. He noticed my surprise.

He said, "If I killed you, you couldn't answer any questions."

Can't argue with the logic. This guy's fearlessness reminded me of Koot—except Koot was on my side. I was thinking these guys must have parked up the street, waiting for Koot to leave the house. Lucky for me, otherwise their blood would be all over my newly painted porch about now.

Santana had locked onto Curly's leg and was shaking his head as he chewed in. Curly was writhing, trying to get away. He reached inside his jacket for his gun. I stepped on his hand, pinning it against his stomach.

Eyes looked down at Curly, indifferent. "Call off your dog." We looked at each other some more, him giving me the sleepy look. "If we have to come back – it won't turn out like this."

I didn't like being forced, but I figured he had a sizable crew and was just stating the reality. Mostly I don't like reality—but what are you gonna do?

I called Santana off, but he wouldn't let go of Curly's gnawed leg. Reality is simple in Santana's world: good guys, bad guys. When reality shifts it confuses him. He rolled his eyes up at me to see if I had lost my senses, then, finally, he let go of Curly's leg.

Eyes held out his hand. I gave him my gun.

He said, "Get him up."

I reached down and pulled Curly to his feet. Eyes nodded toward the GMC Yukon parked on the street. I locked the house behind us and helped Curly to the Yukon, Eyes following behind.

Eyes opened the back door of the Yukon, and I poured Curly into the seat. Eyes told me to get in the front, then he got behind the wheel and we pulled away.

Curly made hurt animal sounds. We'd both had enough of needles for the day.

I said, "He'd better get to the ER. He's going to need the cactus needles taken out, and his leg is pretty mangled."

Eyes said, "It's nothing."

Nothing. Maybe Eyes thought the needles had found the acupuncture points in Curly's face —do him some good.

SIXTEEN

We crossed the decaying Huey P. Long bridge and headed west through Jefferson Parish. Curly was slumped back against the seat, his face colorless. His eyes were closed, and he was taking deep breaths, then hissing air out between clenched teeth. He tried to pull a cactus needle out of his face, but the skin stretched with the needle and wouldn't give it up and Curly hissed some more.

We had just passed a ribs shack—pork ribs, barbecue sandwiches and boiled peanuts—when Curly suddenly fumbled for the power window switch, then hit it. He leaned toward the window and threw up. Problem was, he thought he had rolled the window *down*.

Eyes jerked the car off the road and parked by a drainage ditch filled with stagnant water the color of cola. He got out and yanked open the back door, grabbed Curly by the hair and dragged him out of the car.

Curly followed his hair out of the car, yelling, "The fuck you doin'?"

When Eyes let go of his hair, Curly stared at him, challenging. But after a couple of seconds of staring into those eyes, the challenge was gone.

Eyes closed the back door and told Curly someone would be back for him. Eyes got back in the Yukon, powered all the windows down and brought the vehicle back onto the highway. I turned and saw Curly bend over the ditch and heave up a feast for the crawfish. The scene with Eyes and Curly made me think of the kids who joined gangs for a sense of belonging, then ended up dead by the side of the road.

We rode in silence for about fifteen miles, the hot wind in the car circulating the smell of vomit. We passed open fields salted with rocker-armed oil wells, pumping crude millions of years in the

Conley Clark

making. After a while Eyes took a black cloth bag from under the seat and gave it to me.

"Put this on."

I slipped the bag over my head. As usual, I was in the dark. After another three miles or so, Eyes made a turn. The crunch under the tires told me the road was paved with broken oyster shells. We tracked along for what seemed like a couple more miles before Eyes made another turn. Over the odor of vomit, I could smell pine and sweet gum trees. We were pretty far into the woods.

After another mile or so Eyes slowed, then pulled the bag off my head at the gate of a barbed wire compound. A doughboy with a flat nose and a neck boil waved us through.

Just inside the compound was a large Quonset hut. Probably the meditation hall. Farther back, between some white oaks, was a cement block building two stories high, circular, with arched entryways about every eight feet. If you ignored the cheap look of the concrete blocks, it looked like a Roman coliseum shrunk to the size of a Denny's. Eyes pulled up to the cement building and stopped.

"Get out."

I got out and followed Eyes through one of the open entryways. Inside we walked up a ramp that came out into the stands of a circular arena. In the center of the miniature arena, two women armored as Roman gladiators were locked in combat. One woman had a shield and wielded a club with a metal head. The other woman had a steel trident and a net. It looked like the tips of the trident had been blunted, maybe just enough to prevent puncture wounds.

I counted eight couples seated in the stands watching the fight. The usual expressionless cadre of muscle stood nearby. None of the women, who were all beautiful, looked like they were enjoying the spectacle, but they were attentive to the men, in a detached way. These pairings were about business, one way or another.

Blood flowed from open wounds in both combatants. I guess the trident wasn't blunt enough. The women took heavy blows and thrusts from each other, yet continued to attack. It was obvious they were amped on some pretty high-powered drugs.

The smaller of the two women thrust with her trident, but the large woman deflected it, then crashed her club into her opponent's arm. I heard bones snap. The smaller woman crumpled to the dirt, but there was no scream. The big woman stepped in and raised her club for another blow.

The downed fighter quickly shoved the trident hard into the large woman's chest. The big woman grunted, dropped her club and went to her knees. She made a choking sound, then spit up blood. Probably a ruptured lung or heart.

The men stood and cheered at the sickening spectacle, while most of the women turned away. I saw a deep sadness in some of the women's eyes, a sadness and, it seemed to me, a kind of hopelessness.

Six women entered the arena and carried the combatants away. One of the men in the stands looked our way. He stood and slapped the man next to him on the shoulder, said something to the others, laughed, then walked over. Castille, my gracious host.

Castille's wide shoulders and narrow waist shaped his black silk shirt into a wedge pointing to copper-colored slacks and flat green snake-skin boots. His jaw jutted out like a threat. When he stopped in front of us, I noticed the ring. It was clustered with diamonds the size of passable kidney stones.

Castille gave me a big lounge singer grin. "Thank you for coming, cher."

Just another friendly Cajun.

I nodded toward the center of the arena. "I had about as much choice as these women."

"They have choices. They can either serve my business associates' needs or fight in the arena."

"Right."

"Since you were a policeman, you may know who I am."

"Other than a snappy dresser and a bloodlusting headcase—I haven't an inkling."

Something like a pipe hit me hard across the back of my legs. I went into limbo position as the pain shot through my body and out my mouth as a favored expletive. The Percocet euphoria went AWOL.

The people in the stands shifted their attention our way.

Still grinning, Castille said, "I'll tell you all you need to know about me, Mr. Boudreau. I get what I want. I'll ask you questions, and you'll give me answers—kind of like a game show."

I thought about snatching my belt off and wrapping it around Castille's neck, threaten to strangle him unless his goons back off. Take him to the car and get away.

Psychologists say fantasizing can be a healthy thing.

Castille said, "I know you were hired by the Kanawhite woman to find her brother. Why have you continued to look for him after his boat was found at sea and he and the woman were presumed dead?"

"I'm not looking for Kanawhite now. I'm looking for evidence that he and the woman with him were murdered."

"What makes you think they were murdered?"

"Clues." I braced for the hit that didn't come. Maybe Eyes thought I said "shoes" and was waiting for the rest.

Castille said, "What clues?" They were waiting for the rest.

"I was looking at his partner, Frank Caveccio. He followed Kanawhite and the woman out into the Gulf. A gun had been purchased. The sailboat appeared to have been tampered with. None of it matters now. Caveccio is dead. You wouldn't know anything about that would you?"

"I ask the questions, cher. Was the Kanawhite woman paying you to look for a murderer?"

"No."

"So why are you doing it?"

"I have a thing about murder. I don't think people should be committing it."

"I think you're lying. I think you know Kanawhite and the woman are alive, and you're looking for them."

"You already know the answers. What am I here for?"

Eyes drove the pipe into my shoulder, just at the neck, and I went to my knees. I flushed hot with the pain. Forget the healthy fantasies—I should see a shrink about my mouth.

"You will die before he gets tired of hitting you, cher."

Cher. This calling me "friend" while having me sapped was becoming annoying.

"The woman who was with Kanawhite is my property. Her name is Danika. She stole some special drugs at a party at my house —worth eighty-five thousand dollars."

I slowly got to my feet. I moved my arm and felt my shoulder. The trapezius had caught most of the impact, and nothing seemed to be broken.

Castille continued. "I think Danika and Kanawhite faked an accident, hoping that I'd believe they're dead. I think Kanawhite's partner helped them."

I gritted my teeth against the throbbing. "If they were going to fake an accident, it'd be a pretty big red flag to steal from you first."

"Being a detective, you know money makes people do stupid things. I think they stole my drugs and will try to sell them."

"I have nothing pointing to their being alive."

I stepped quickly out of Eyes' range and faced him.

Castille stared at me for about an hour, then made a flicking gesture with his hand, and Eyes lowered the pipe.

Castille said, "Anything you find out, you'll tell me. If I find you're keeping anything from me, we'll get the information from you, then you'll be gutted and fed to my boars."

Boars. At least an undertaker couldn't get his hands on me — rearrange my face so it looked like I was happy to go.

"You put up a good front, Mr. Boudreau, but when you leave here you're going to be thinking about what I said."

I glanced at Eyes and the pipe in his hand. "And you say it so well."

Castille gave me that smug grin, then turned and rejoined his cronies and the women.

As Eyes and I were leaving the arena two more women gladiators entered the ring and squared off. When we reached the car, Eyes opened the front door, then gave me back the Kahr and empty clip. People keep taking my bullets without asking.

Eyes said, "Pyro will take you back." As I got in, Eyes gave me his lizard look. "I'll be coming around soon."

"Call first so I can tidy up."

Eyes put the bag over my head, and the car pulled away. Great. A guy named Pyro knowing where my house is and a reptile promising to pay me another visit.

When we had been on the main highway for several miles, Pyro told me I could remove the bag. When we approached the barbecue shack, Curly was slumped against a tree near the drainage ditch where we had left him. Pyro stopped and told Curly he'd be back to get him. I wondered if I'd be seeing Curly again too.

SEVENTEEN

I called Koot and told him about the cordial invitation to Castille's place. I told him about Castille's sex and combat slaves and about the stolen drugs. I wanted to tell him the rest over a glass of Irish whiskey, so I told Koot to bring over a bottle of Jameson.

I hung up and went to the kitchen. I set a towel on the counter, took a tray of ice cubes out of the fridge and popped the cubes onto the towel. I folded the towel over the ice to make a pack, then molded the pack to my neck and shoulder.

I went to the living room, turned on the radio and stretched out on the couch. Norah Jones was putting a silken finish on a Hoagy Carmichael tune. It eased my spirit, if not the pain in my leg and shoulder. Santana and Seven parked themselves on the rug next to me and kept quiet. I think they sensed I needed down time. I knew I wouldn't get much of that when Koot walked in.

He said, "We going after these maggots?"

Letting Mowery get away with sapping me didn't sit well with Koot. This episode with Castille and Eyes was over the top. Koot was ready to go in, guns blazing. I preferred the bide-your-time and find-the-chink-in-their-armor approach. Gave you a better shot at old age.

"'A time for every purpose', Bayou Boy," I said.

"What's wrong with now?"

"Because I feel like I've been chop blocked by King Kong." Koot's face twitched. "Did you bring my old compadre, the Irishman?"

Koot didn't answer right away. Finally he said, "You don't drink anymore."

"Right now I'm thinking that was a bad idea."

"You need sewing up?"

"No."

"You want some eggs?"

"No."

Give Koot a task, he's in there. With nothing to do, he was looking hangdog.

Koot squeezed out, "So what's the play?"

"Emmy Lou doing *Too Far Gone*. In case you haven't noticed, she's singing it to me." I slowly raised myself to a sitting position. "We've got some new information to chew on. I may have been wrong about Jackie and Danika being murdered."

Koot grabbed a chair, pulled it near the couch, and sat.

"Tell me."

"Jackie's companion was a call girl for Castille. Judging by her looks, strictly upper end clientele. Castille suspects Jackie and Danika faked the boating accident as a way for Danika to escape him."

"I can see how she'd be motivated. Of course, if Kanawhite helped her, he'd have to disappear too. I thought he never left New Orleans."

"Yeah. Danika would have to be more than just a good time to Jackie. He could never come back to New Orleans as long as Castille was around."

"You think they've already skipped?"

"Maybe, but if they were going to use public transportation, they might hold up in the area until the heat on the airport, train and bus station lets up."

"So, maybe Caveccio didn't kill them."

"Castille might have thought Caveccio helped them fake the accident."

Koot said, "Caveccio could have followed them out into the Gulf, helped them scuttle the sailboat, then brought them in and put them ashore somewhere; then returned to the marina alone, like the dock squids said."

"It makes sense. Castille already knew Jackie and Caveccio hung out together. Castille's men found out from Oscar at the marina that Caveccio took his boat out shortly after Jackie and Danika set sail. Maybe Castille got suspicious."

Koot said, "And at that point Castille knew something we didn't know, which was that there was a reason to fake an accident."

"Eyes and some of the goons went to Caveccio's place, and when Caveccio wouldn't give up Jackie and Danika, they killed him and Big Man."

"You think Caveccio would have died for Kanawhite and the woman?"

"Who knows. Maybe he didn't know where Jackie and Danika would hold up. They might've thought it safer that way."

"Not for Caveccio."

"It turned out bad."

"So maybe Jackie the party boy has some backbone after all."

"It could still turn out that Nads had them all hit, or maybe just Caveccio and Big Man. We don't know. But if Jackie and Danika are alive and haven't skipped the country, we have to get to them before Castille or Nads does."

"Ideas?"

"Yeah. Grady misses us. Let's pay the man a visit."

If I had called the Second District Station I might not have gotten the time of day, so Koot called and was told Grady went for lunch at Jaffe's café. Koot helped me to his Outback wagon, and I flopped in on the passenger side, lifted in my crunched leg, then we headed to Jaffe's. As we pulled away from the house, we passed the Cobra with the same lackeys in it. Now they were following *me*.

I wasn't on their to-do list when we checked each other out on the street at Caveccio's, so they might not have remembered my face from there. If they didn't, then they wouldn't know I was on to them. If they had known I'd made them, Castille wouldn't have sent the same two to tail me. It was nice having the advantage for a change.

I looked in the sideview mirror and saw the Cobra swing out and fall in behind us at a distance.

I said, "The Cobra, three cars behind—Castille's men."

Koot looked in the rear view and said, "You haven't had this much attention since that year you busted the Mayor's wife and her boyfriend for the Ponzi scheme."

"Another bad career move."

"Pretty bad for the mayor too."

Koot kept glancing in the rearview until he couldn't stand it anymore. "You want me to lose them?"

"No. I want Castille to think he's in control."

We parked on Magazine near Jaffe's café, just down from the Second District Station. The Cobra parked a half block behind us. We got out, crossed the street and went in the café.

Over the arched entry to the dining room, big purple bunches of artificial grapes hung on plastic vines. On the wall behind was a painting of a vineyard on a hillside overlooking the sea. The scene always made me think of retirement. More healthy fantasy.

Jaffe liked cops and gave them a discount on food, and coffee was always free. Naturally, cops bivouacked at the place. Jaffe served Greek and American food: baklava and burgers, spanakopita and sirloin.

We spotted Grady in a booth in the back. A man and woman leaving the restaurant stared at the large "V" branded in Koot's head as they walked by. Koot had gotten used to it. Vanity wasn't part of his makeup anyway.

At a table off to the side were Doucette, Fortenberry and Mowery. They were debating something intensely—maybe the shrinking rainforest, or the origins of life—something along those lines. When they saw us, or more precisely, when they saw me, Mowery and Doucette went stony.

I said in a low voice, "Rein it in, Koot."

I let Koot lead toward Grady, and I limped behind.

When we got even with them, Mowery leaned back in his chair and said, "Whatsa matter with your leg, Boudreau, somebody pull a chair out from under you?"

I had an urge to shove Mowery's breaded pork chops down his throat, but revenge comes at a personal price. It comes from hatred, and hatred poisons the mind and spirit. I've been trying to detox.

Now revenge is different from *discouragement*. Next time Mowery tries to work out on me, I plan on discouraging him. Maybe a broken nose or arm will do the trick.

Mowery said, "Loomis, you don't give a damn who you keep company with, do you?"

Koot stopped in front of Mowery. He said, "I heard what happened to you, Mowery."

Wary. "What?"

"Someone said you had a near-life experience."

Mowery stood up and stepped over. He gave his best Mohammed Ali glare. Wasted effort.

Doucette said, "Not the time nor place, Mowery."

Mowery stood toe to toe with Koot for a few more seconds, then he dialed it down to a scowl. He finally made the right decision and sat down. It saved him a lot of pain.

Mowery said, "What about Boudreau's former partner— Guiterrez? He had a *short* life experience." Cutting his eyes my way.

These guys are nothing if not persistent.

Doucette said, "You're going to screw up again sometime, Boudreau. We'll be there when you do."

I said, "That's the problem with you guys—always looking to the future. You've got to stop and smell the roses."

I nodded to Koot and we walked on back to Grady's table and sat down. Thea Helena came to the table; Koot ordered a gyro and some baklava, and I ordered a falafel platter.

Grady had watched Mowery's chest thumping. He said, "They give badges to dickheads and call 'em cops." He nodded toward my gimp leg. "You tangle with another of your admirers, or you just gotten clumsy?"

"I had an interview with a Cajun named Dumont Castille. Wrong answers drew penalties. You have anything on him?"

"Model citizen. He came on the scene about a year and a half ago. Into high-class prostitution and makes and sells some powerful designer drugs. Narcotics hasn't been able to get anything on him ,and Vice can't get any of Castille's women to testify."

"No surprise."

"Most of the women are Eastern European, Balkan region."

I said, "Castille's main man is Eastern European. He'd be point for recruiting the women."

"We could bring Castille and his man in for assault."

"Harrassment's a waste of time. Does Castille have any juice downtown?"

"Higher. We think he's connected in Baton Rouge. We need something solid on him, something that can't be covered up."

I asked, "You have any fun with Nads? I told Koot about the bouquet in the interrogation room."

"We kept them waiting for an hour. By the time we got to them, Nads and his lawyer were both ranting."

"That's a shame. Pillars of the community having to waste their valuable time," Koot said.

Grady and I grinned.

I said, "Nads caught up with me after you guys hauled him in. He had his tail in a knot for pointing you guys to him."

Grady looked pissed. "Doucette and Mowery..."

"Yeah, they told Nads it was me, but it worked out. Nads hates Castille. Maybe we can use Nads to get to Castille."

I told Grady about Danika being one of Castille's call girls, and that Castille thinks Caveccio helped Jackie and Danika stage the accident so she'd have a way out. I told him I thought Castille might have gone to Caveccio to find out where Jackie and Danika were, and that Caveccio either wouldn't give them up or didn't know where they were.

Grady said, "You're thinking Castille wouldn't give Caveccio the benefit of the doubt and popped him and his man Rocco?"

"And when they found out I was still on the job after Kanawhite and the woman were supposed to be dead, they thought I might know something they didn't, so they reached out to me—with a pipe."

"You give them anything?"

"Mostly batting practice."

Grady said, "So, Castille and Liano both may have had reasons to kill these people."

Koot said, "If Jackie and Danika are still alive..."

Grady said, "We need to find them before Castille or Liano does. We can protect them. What about Kanawhite's sister?"

"They know Adrienne hired us because she didn't know Jackie's whereabouts. She's safe for now."

"We'll be working this from our end. You bring me something we don't have, the lieutenant will move on it."

"Already have an idea, but I need Caveccio's cell phone from the evidence room."

"Hold on, Tag. You trying to get my ass in a sling?"

I said, "Grady, you were born with your ass in a sling. But you still turned out to be a good cop."

Grady took a macaroon from a bag in his coat and popped it in his mouth, chewed a few times, then swallowed. "All right, Hot Rod. This better catch us a bad guy."

We left the café with Grady, climbed in his Crown Vic and rode over to headquarters. The right front fender of the car was crunched and barely cleared the tire. It had been like that for a year. Given the department's budget, it wasn't likely to be fixed. Battles were waged almost daily over the allocation of funds.

Grady told me he'd gone head-to-head with the assistant DA that morning over money. She wanted the department to pay to send a tow truck to North Dakota for a car she wanted as evidence in a homicide case, even though the car had already been printed and combed by the North Dakota forensics team. Grady argued that she had more than enough evidence and that the expense was unwarranted. And on it went.

When we got on Napoleon, heading toward Broad Street, I glanced behind us to see if the tail was with us. They weren't. They must have been watching the Outback instead of the café and didn't see us leave in Grady's car. The Darwin Award contenders would figure it out eventually.

When we got to Headquarters, we parked underneath the building. The evidence room was down under, just off the parking lot. When we entered the receiving area, the woman officer behind the horizontal steel bars at the counter greeted Grady with the affection of an old friend.

Grady had helped the woman out a few years ago when she was being harassed by her ex-husband. The uniforms had paid the guy a few visits, but the schmuck kept giving the woman a hard time. Then Grady went to have a talk with the guy. The gift of gab coming from a two hundred fifty-pounder is particularly effective. The woman had no more problems with her ex.

Koot and I took seats by the door while Grady chatted with the officer. There was no one else in the receiving area. She pushed the log across the counter for Grady to sign, then went through the door where evidence was inventoried. In a minute she reappeared with a plastic bag with a cell phone and power cord in it. She slipped the phone and cord through the bars to Grady, then Grady said something to the woman and we left.

Grady giving me the phone was a serious violation of departmental policy. If it was discovered, the department could come down hard.

It could also jeopardize any case against Castille that any of the divisions might be building if Castille's lawyers found out. Even though the phone had already been dusted for prints, if the lawyers claimed that evidence was tampered with, the judge could dismiss any charges brought.

I had put a friend at risk, and down the road could be responsible for a murderer and a dealer in human slavery walking. But two lives could depend on whether Koot and I found them before Castille did. I couldn't see any other option.

Grady gave me the phone and didn't say a word about getting it back. He put his trust in me, and it weighed on me.

EIGHTEEN

If Jackie and Danika were alive and Frank Caveccio had helped them, Frank and Jackie would stay in touch, probably by phone. Since he was supposed to be dead, Jackie wouldn't be answering the phone. He'd be the one to call. Koot and I would monitor Frank's phone for a couple of days and see if we got lucky. Of course, if Jackie already knew Frank was dead, there was no place for luck to go.

We left headquarters, and Grady dropped us off at the Outback in front of Jaffe's. The Cobra was still parked in the same place. These guys were going to have to tell Castille there was a blank space in the sequence of their pursuits today. If they had any sense they wouldn't mention anything about blank spaces. When I was drinking heavily, I never did.

We decided to do our first stint at Jackson Square. We got in the wagon and took Magazine Street through the CBD and then into the French Quarter. The Cobra slithered in behind us. We knew we'd have to do something about these guys soon, but for now we'd let them waste their time.

I plugged the charging cord into the cell phone and plugged the other end into the dash outlet to top off the charge. In the French Quarter the streets choke down into narrow one-way lanes. On Chartres, a car pulled out of a parking slot ahead of us and Koot pulled in. Sometimes you get lucky. I glanced in the side-view mirror and saw Heckle and Jeckle in the Cobra, turkey-necking to find a parking spot.

I unplugged the cell phone and put it in my pocket, then Koot and I got out and walked toward Jackson Square. One of the mopes would get out and stay with us on foot while the driver circled the block.

As I limped along, Koot said, "Walking will help the circulation in that leg."

"It's not helping the pain."

"Yeah, but the pain'll help you remember to watch your mouth next time someone with a pipe stands behind you."

"I'll keep that in mind."

Jackson Square is a nice little park with flower lined sidewalks and ornate cast iron benches. We strolled by the large stone pedestal in the middle of the park where a life-sized bronze of Andrew Jackson sits on a rearing horse. Jackson was a talented and courageous general, a contentious president, an evictor of Indians, a duelist, and a widely popular figure with the common people.

We found an empty bench, then sat and watched the street entertainers work the crowd. A tuba led band played Dixieland jazz, while a contortionist crammed himself into a box the size of a mini-bar. Teenaged boys with bottle caps stuck in the soles of their tennis shoes tap danced in front of Saint Louis Cathedral. Tarot card readers set up around the perimeter of the square, flipping cards and telling people whether their lives would be a fest of fulfillment or mostly a challenging mess.

Then there were the guys who painted themselves gold or silver and stood still for long stretches of time. Mimes without motion. I guess if you put a hat on the ground in front of you, someone'll take you for talented.

After a while, we got tired of sitting. When we stood, Koot nodded toward our tail who was trying to hide behind a Girl Scout troop being led on a tour of the square.

Koot said, "Somewhere a ditch is not getting dug because these mopes took a wrong career turn."

We left the park and crossed Decatur, the tail keeping his distance behind us. When we climbed the steps to the riverwalk, he hung back near the streetcar track.

The slow stroll along the river loosened my muscles and made my leg feel a little better. We watched a cargo ship nearly ten stories high from waterline to the top of the pilothouse head up river. Traveling in the opposite direction, a push boat pushed four linked barges loaded with crated goods. Strung together, the barges were the length of two football fields. So wide is the Mississippi these Leviathans have room to pass each other and still leave plenty of river for other craft to travel.

New Orleans is the first deep water port for cargo ships heading up river from the Gulf of Mexico. Steel from Brazil, Mexico and Japan. Natural rubber from Indonesia and Malaysia. Grain, coffee, plywood, copper and manufactured goods—all find their way into

New Orleans before being trucked or railed to the coasts and into the heartland.

Shipping pumps a couple of billion dollars into Louisiana's economy and produces tens of thousands of jobs. The river is economic plasma for New Orleans and for towns along its banks all the way to St. Louis and beyond.

My father's business serviced the shipping industry, and my family enjoyed the financial success that business created. I was supposed to inherit the reins, but when I became a cop instead, I was disinherited by a father lousy at handling disappointment.

The cell phone rang, but it was a guy Caveccio had met at a club in the Quarter. He wanted me to tell Frank that he had a fabulous time the other night and for Frank to please give him a buzz. I could have told him Frank was dead, but the guy might have had a need to eulogize and I didn't want to tie up the phone. I told him I'd pass on the message and hung up. He'd get the truth from the papers.

We walked until it was time for Koot to go teach a class. When we padded back across Decatur, lackey number one was watching from behind one of the horse-drawn sightseeing rigs parked in front of the square. He was on his cell phone, likely to number two, who was probably still circling the block in a holding pattern.

We weren't giving these guys anything to report, and I knew how they felt. Surveillance is mostly boring. As cops and as PIs, we've spent days, sometimes weeks on a job waiting for some guy to do something incriminating, either in the eyes of the law or in the eyes of our client.

Mostly, the person we'd tail just went about his day—picking up his dry cleaning, seeing his therapist, taking in a porno flick, having late night milk and cookies before the sheep traipsed through his troubled psyche. Castille's guys were bored now. Later on we'd make it interesting for them.

We got in the Outback and lackey one scrambled for the Cobra, which was rounding the corner of the block. Then Heckle and Jeckle fell in a few cars behind and we formed a little parade up Canal to Koot's studio.

The studio was a Victorian that had been gutted by a fire a few years back. The fire started when the mother of a teenaged girl made an unauthorized entrance into the girl's room. The lit Virginia Slim the teen tried to hide behind her back ignited the flounced curtains, and soon after, the entire house.

Koot picked the house up cheap. Our first year as PIs we had a lot of time on our hands between cases, so we spent it repairing the structural damage and doing the build-out. For several years before he bought the house, Koot rented studio space in crumbling buildings in shabby neighborhoods. The Victorian was a dream finally fulfilled, and Koot was proud of it.

By the time Koot had changed into his *Gi,* his students had arrived. It was a diverse group of women: professionals, soccer moms, a couple of teenagers and the grandmother of one of the teens who had been Koot's student for seven years.

Koot is an excellent teacher. Precise and patient. Like Arjuna in the epic Bhagavad-Gita, Koot is a warrior in the noblest sense. He's a born protector and never uncoils his fierceness without just cause or provocation, despite the rage and pain he carries around like twin anvils.

I watched Koot take his students through their warm-up exercises: left neutral bow into a scissoring arm break, a sword hand to the throat, then a leopard fist to the ribs. I particularly liked watching one of the women with the grace and balance of a puma. I think she enjoyed me watching. She kept glancing over and smiling in between crushing snap kicks to the imaginary groin.

After the session, she came out of the dressing room in neoprene pants and a neoprene florescent yellow halter top and sauntered over. She filled out neoprene nicely.

She asked, "Want to spar sometime?"

Maybe she hadn't noticed my limp. Or maybe she had and liked the advantage. Maybe she had full contact in mind.

I was unequivocal. "Maybe."

"Not sure your male ego could handle being beaten by a woman?"

"I got used to that when I was married."

She gave me a smile that said unfinished business. "It's a standing invitation." Then she left. I had a feeling if we got together we wouldn't be standing for long.

After his class Koot dropped me off at the house, then went back to the studio. I glanced up the street before I went inside. Like I was a snake charmer with a flute, the Cobra stayed fixed on me.

I went in and checked on Seven and Santana, then put on my white shirt, leaping marlin tie and my navy suit for the memorial service. I hoped we would be memorializing the end of an old *way* of life for Jackie and Danika, not the end of life itself.

I locked the house and eased into the Sebring. When I pushed in the clutch my leg felt like glass had splintered along the sciatic nerve. I barked with the pain and the couple walking past stepped up their pace.

By the time I got to Our Lady of the Assumption Church, my jaw was sore from gritting my teeth when I worked the clutch and I was sweating, despite having the AC on high. I parked in the lot under a diseased sycamore and went in.

The small chapel was sandwiched between the main church and the rectory. Inside, except for two pools of green and gold light that spilled through the stained glass windows and onto the slate floor, the chapel was dark. Dark granite walls and pews as dark as bittersweet chocolate. High in the chapel and presiding over all the darkness was Jesus, spiked to the cross. Another church emphasizing suffering over a message of love.

Adrienne, Brent, Blanche and an elderly couple sat in the front pew. Besides the priest, they were the only ones attending. It looked like Jackie had burned a lot of bridges.

I had been to Our Lady of the Assumption for memorial services a couple of times before. The first time was here in the chapel for an ex-con I had tried to help go straight. A buddy of mine at the docks gave him a good-paying job, and he did fine for a while, until some of his old drug-using chums found him and sucked him back into the streets. He eventually got popped by one of his "friends" for seven hundred dollars worth of crack. He had vowed he'd not end up in prison again, and he was right.

The other memorial service I had attended was in the main church. It was for Charlie Gutierrez, my partner who was killed when we were on the job. The church had been full of cops, and except for a handful of supporters and friends, the entire department made it a point not to sit near me.

When I reached the front of the church, I sat down by Adrienne. Blanche looked at me and nodded. All the brashness was gone. She was letting the pain wash over her. Brent gave me a little wave, and I winked at him. Adrienne had been crying. She placed her hand on the top of my forearm, and a charge shot through me. It's funny how passion can be aroused by a simple touch from the right person; and neither dark churches nor grieving hearts kept it from happening.

Adrienne said, "Thanks for coming, Tag." I put my hand on top of hers and nodded. "Has Danika's family or anyone else come forward?"

"Not yet."

Her asking about someone she didn't know, under the present circumstances, showed an uncommon compassion. Or maybe it wasn't that uncommon. Maybe it was just that I rarely saw it in my world.

The priest continued the memorial mass. "O Lord, do not bring your servant John Coats Kanawhite to trial, for no one becomes holy in your sight unless you grant him forgiveness of all his sins."

The priest said something about mercy, then my mind went to Adrienne, Brent and Blanche. I felt a strong urge to take them out of this darkness and tell them Jackie might still be alive. Instead, I sat quietly.

In a few minutes the quiet was broken by the chiming of a tango —Caveccio's cell phone. I got up immediately and headed to the back of the chapel. On the way up the aisle, I punched the answer button and tried to imitate Caveccio's granular voice.

"Yeah."

"What the hell is going on, Frank? I've been calling since yesterday."

"Jackie, listen to me. Frank's dead. Castille didn't buy the boating accident."

Silence. Then, like he didn't really want to know the answer, "Who's this?"

"I'm a private investigator hired by your sister. You and Danika are not safe."

Just getting it. "Frank's dead?"

"I'm sorry, Jackie. It looks like Castille killed him trying to get to you."

"That...couldn't...Frank doesn't know where... It's safer that way." He spoke as if Frank were still alive. Acceptance would take a while.

"It turned out bad, Jackie. Castille will be coming for you both. We've got to get you into police protection. Where are you?"

There were several seconds of silence, then Jackie hung up.

The priest had stopped speaking, and Adrienne and the rest were twisted in the pew, staring at me. The anger at me taking a call during the service was obvious. If I told them Jackie was alive they'd quickly get over the anger, but if I told them now, and Castille killed Jackie and Danika before Koot and I could get to them, Adrienne might not get over the heartbreak of hearing for a second time that Jackie was murdered.

I walked back down the aisle, feeling bad that I had to tell Jackie about Frank's murder. If Frank was willing to stick his neck out to help Jackie and Danika, they must have been good friends.

When I got to Adrienne I said, "I have to go."

The look of betrayal from Adrienne and Blanche knotted my stomach.

Adrienne said, "I wanted you to be here. Brent wanted you to be here. I guess I was wrong about you."

"I hope soon you'll see it differently. It's important to me that you do."

I turned and walked quickly out of the chapel, trying to turn my mind from the ones I hurt to the ones we could save.

NINETEEN

On the way to the studio, I punched in Vickie Cohen's number on the cell. Vickie works as a technician in the womb of one of the wireless phone companies. She and Cile had been long-time friends until Cile and I divorced. When we split, Vickie refused to choose sides, then Cile turned her back on Vickie, and Vickie and I remained friends. Vickie's a wild woman, a "stem-winder" as Koot calls her, and I liked her right away.

Vickie answered, "Cohen."

Clicking sounds were in the background.

I said, "Did you get it?"

"I'm betting I get it more than you."

"I refuse to compare notes."

"Could be embarrassing, huh?" Vickie laughed sharply. "Of course I got a lock."

I had given her Caveccio's phone number to monitor. When I answered Jackie's call, Vickie put a trace on it. Illegal, of course. I had asked another friend to put themselves at risk, and again, another friend came through.

"I appreciate you doing this, Vick."

"You tell me it's life or death, I'm going to say *no*?"

"Where'd the call come from?"

"The middle of nowhere as far as I can tell. You want me to fax a map of the area to your office?"

"Fax it to Koot's studio. I'm on my way there."

"I guess it pays to have friends in low places." Vickie cackled.

"I owe you a dinner at Antoine's," I said.

"I have a big appetite."

"I'll bring a big friend."

Vickie roared and then hung up.

When I got to the studio, Koot was in the middle of a session. I went in the office and grabbed the map Vickie had faxed. She was right about the call coming from the middle of nowhere. It came from a vast marsh and swamp south of New Orleans.

I remembered the entries in Jackie's daily calendar—"camp." He and Danika were probably holding up at a fishing or hunting camp until they were ready to make their move. They'd know Castille had his men watching the airport and bus and train depots.

Vickie vectored the call to within a mile radius, but if the camp was deep in the swamp, hidden by the trees, it might still be hard to find. Koot has a family friend who's fished and trapped in that marsh and swamp all his life and I was hoping he would know the camps in the area.

I walked into the back of Koot's class. When Koot looked my way, I pointed a finger up and moved my hands in a circular motion a few times. Time to mount up.

Koot let his most advanced student, Iris, the grandmother, finish taking the class through their routine, while Koot and I went in the office. I showed him the map, and Koot confirmed that his Cajun friend Hadley knew the area well.

Koot said, "Hadley's losing the sun, so he'll be bringing in today's catch before long. We can be there about the time he comes in."

"Good. First we need to see Grady."

I called and caught Grady at the station. I told him we needed to see him and the lieutenant and that we were on our way. We left the studio and got in the Outback.

I said, "It's time to lose Heckle and Jeckle."

Koot smiled. "At the bayou?"

I nodded.

Koot swung out of the driveway and headed up Canal toward City Park. Castille's men did a U turn and came up behind, keeping the prescribed three cars distance between us.

We headed up Canal for several blocks, then turned right on Carrolton. We took a right on Esplanade and another right over the bridge crossing Bayou St. John. Koot immediately took another right on Moss, which curved along beside the winding bayou.

Koot drove a short distance, then stopped across the street from Cabrini High School. The lackeys pulled to the curb, keeping their distance. I got out, then Koot pulled away and continued down Moss along the bayou.

As expected, Heckle and Jeckle stayed with me. I turned and strolled along the banks of the water, the throaty sound of the muscle car idling along behind—as stealthy as the Tin Man on linoleum.

Walking along the bayou made me think of the times Koot, Grady and I camped in the marsh. On moonless nights we'd fire up gas lanterns with cloth mantles and curved metal reflectors and walk the shallows next to shore, looking for flounders to gig. Magic time. The warm night breeze, the stars flared in a raven sky, the sound of water lapping the reeds, the hissing of the butane-fueled mantles burning, even the high-pitched drone of mosquitoes trying to penetrate a barrier of Deet. The sights and sounds a gift from a sometimes benevolent cosmos.

When I got to the footbridge, the only pedestrian walkway crossing the bayou in that neighborhood, I walked half way across, turned and grinned at Heckle and Jeckle. They pretended they were just here admiring the scenery, trying not to look directly at me.

When Koot pulled up to the curb at the footbridge on the *opposite* side of the bayou, the mopes didn't pretend anymore. When they saw the Outback they knew they had been had.

I finished crossing the footbridge, limped to the Outback and opened the door. In desperation, Heckle and Jeckle bailed out of the car and ran to the footbridge.

I yelled, "That makes twice you lost me, boys." They'd already be thinking about what Castille might do to them. "I hear Belize is a nice place to live."

As I got in the Outback, Heckle, or was it Jeckle, kept insisting loudly that I have sex with myself. I was going to miss all the attention.

Upstairs at Homicide, not much had changed. The coffee maker still sat on the rickety table next to the charger for the radios. Along the baseboards and around doors and windows was the same snake nest of phone and electrical wires. The banner was still stretched above the doorway: HOMICIDE — OUR DAY BEGINS WHEN YOURS ENDS. Cop humor. Homicide detectives see death on a regular basis. The banner was a bad attempt to keep it light so they could keep it together.

Grady was at his desk listening to Mertie, an elderly woman who had been coming in for years with crime "tips." Several years ago one of her tips actually led to an arrest for a domestic homicide. From then on Mertie saw herself as the station informant. It didn't matter to Mertie that we only dealt with homicides. She came in with tips on drug dealers, domestic disturbances, auto theft, you name it. She once tried to turn in one of her best friends because the friend had her deceased husband's body exhumed a couple of days after he was buried.

According to Mertie, her friend had the hots for one of her husband's former business associates, and before the last shovel of dirt had been tossed on the hubby's grave, the woman was ready to give the guy a jingle; only, she couldn't find the phone number. When it occurred to the woman that the number might be in the suit her hubby was buried in, she had him dug up. Mertie railed about it violating all conventions of decency, but I think Mertie was just bent out of shape because she was interested in the same man.

Lieutenant Tolleson and Mowery were at Mowery's desk going over a crime report, and Fortenberry was pouring himself a cup of coffee. Doucette and Stubbs were just coming in the back door.

When he saw us the lieutenant said, "Boudreau, Herns said you had a run-in with Dumont Castille."

"I think I'm on his A-list."

"Herns said Castille was looking for Kanawhite and one of Castille's call girls and thought you might know something."

"That's right."

Grady stopped listening to Mertie and turned his attention our way. Mertie looked back and forth between Grady and us.

When she realized Grady was ignoring her, she said, "Herns, how are you ever going to make lieutenant if you don't pay attention?" Then she left, looking indignant.

Grady rolled his eyes. I eased over to his desk and slipped Grady the cell phone to return to the evidence room.

The lieutenant said, "So you've switched parties as to who killed Caveccio and Givens?"

"It looks more like Castille had Caveccio and his muscle-lover hit because Castille thought Caveccio knew where Kanawhite and the woman were."

Doucette chimed in, "This what diabetes does to your brain, Boudreau? Everybody knows where Kanawhite and the woman were—deep-sixed in the Gulf of Mex...ico. You think Castille kills someone trying to get to someone he knew was already dead?"

Koot's eyes narrowed. He was more sensitive than I was about the diabetes remark. Of course, Koot was touchy about a lot of things.

I said, "Kanawhite and Danika are not dead."

Doucette said, "First ya tell us they didn't drown, they were murdered. Now ya tellin' us they're alive and kickin'. You some detective, Boudreau."

Koot said, "You can work homicide cases till your lolly goes limp, Doucette, and you won't solve as many cases as Tag did."

Doucette went red. "Watch ya mouth, Loomis."

The lieutenant said, "Cut the crap, all of you. All right Boudreau —we're listening."

"I spoke to Jackie Kanawhite an hour ago. The boating accident was staged. Jackie was helping Danika break free from Castille. Frank Caveccio helped them stage the accident. Only Castille figured it out."

Grady said, "That makes Kanawhite and the woman material witnesses to Caveccio's murder."

Koot said, "They'll need protection."

Fortenberry asked, "Where are they?"

"At a fishing camp in the swamp in Jefferson Parish. Koot has a friend that knows that area. We're going down now. We'll launch at the ramp in Lafitte, and from there head into the swamp."

The lieutenant said, "Bring them to the safehouse near the expressway. Herns will set it up."

Doucette said, "Lieutenant, let me go with them."

The lieutenant said, "I know you sometimes forget we have no jurisdiction outside of New Orleans, Doucette, but then I'm here to remind you." Lieutenant Tolleson turned to Koot and me. "They'll have to testify."

I said, "I'm more concerned with keeping them alive."

"You know we'll see to that. That's the thing with you two—it's always personal."

"Doesn't get any more personal than murder."

Doucette said, "You'd know."

Some people say your adversaries make you stronger. Mostly, Mowery and Doucette just make me tired.

TWENTY

Hadley Poteet lived in a clapboard shack at the edge of the marsh and swamp near the small community of Lafitte, about twenty miles south of New Orleans. We parked at the end of the sand driveway between a twenty year-old pickup and a large butane tank painted electric blue. At the side of Hadley's cottage was a statue of the Madonna set in a small grotto. Mother Mary was the saint of choice for most South Louisiana Catholics.

Hadley was under a large oak in the back scooping up iced crawfish from a fifty-gallon plastic garbage can and bagging them. Like his father and grandfather before him, Hadley made his living wading hip-deep in the dark waters of the cypress swamp—pulling his skiff, or sometimes his pirogue, and bringing up meat-baited chicken wire traps full of crawfish. The men and women who make their living from the swamps and marshes have become as rare as courtesy and ethics, and Hadley was the last in his family to choose the life.

When we got out of the Outback, Hadley recognized Koot and broke into a grin. He moved his shoulders up and down in a kind of footless dance.

"Koooot. How you been, cher?"

It was Hadley who had given Koot his nickname. When Koot left home at fifteen, he never again answered to Cyrus, the name his father had given him.

We stepped over to Hadley and the crawfish catch.

Koot said, "Firing on all cylinders, Hadley."

"I can hardly believe dat. You get away from the land and water as long as you have, your spirit gets restless."

"Wouldn't have any spirit left if I'd stayed down here."

"Your daddy was a mean one, him. Dat's a fact."

"I just brought the good memories with me today, Hadley."

"Dat's good, Koot. You and me had some good times when you was a little shaver. Catch a lotta good eats out dere in de swamp."

"That we did, Hadley."

"You was a good kid, Koot. You daddy didn't beat that out of you. And now you done grown into a good man."

"Don't get sentimental on me, Hadley."

"Will if I want to." Suddenly Hadley was light as filo dough again. He turned to me. "I see you done brought Tag wid you. Tag, you was down at Hadley's place just before de bayou flooded."

I nodded toward the statue. "Koot told me the Virgin Mary was doing the breast stroke."

That brought on another little shoulder dance. "Dat's a fact. Found her down the bayou safe in the arms of a Tupelo Gum."

Koot said, "We need your help, Hadley."

"It would be a blessing if ol' Hadley can help."

Koot unfolded the map and pointed to the area we had circled. "We're looking for a camp somewhere in this area."

Hadley studied the map for a few seconds, then pointed to a spot on the map. "Dere's a camp right here. Tres jolie."

I said, "Can you get us there, Hadley?"

"Of course. When you want to go?"

Koot said, "Now."

"Den we better get goin' 'fore de night creep up on us."

Hadley dumped four bags of ice over the crawfish, then we helped him move the plastic garbage cans into the shed. Then Hadley backed his Chevy pickup to a trailer carrying an ancient wooden skiff with a twenty-five horse Evinrude outboard. Hadley had us hook another trailer to the Outback that carried an aluminum skiff and a forty horse Mercury.

We followed Hadley out of his driveway and onto the main road. About a mile down the bayou road we turned onto a deeply rutted dirt road. Soon we were at the clearing in the woods next to the bayou where the ground sloped down to the water. This was the only public boat launch in the area and was used primarily by fishermen.

Hadley backed his trailer to the water, got out and winched the skiff off the trailer and into the bayou. When Hadley pulled his truck out of the way, Koot backed the trailer and aluminum boat to the water's edge, then I cranked the cable until the skiff slid into the bayou. Hadley climbed into the wooden skiff while Koot and I got into the aluminum boat, then Koot and Hadley primed the motors and cranked up.

For me the smell of gas and oil burning in an outboard was usually the prelude to a great day on the water. If we brought Jackie and Danika out of the swamp alive, today would be no exception.

Hadley throttled his flat-nosed thirteen-footer, and we followed him down the broad bayou. After about fifteen minutes Hadley turned off the main bayou onto a narrow ribbon of water that led into the stillness of the marsh.

Before long we were easing through the heart of the marsh. Bull tongue, cat tails and maiden cane grew in patches along the sides of the narrow estuary, and egrets and blue herons rose out of the marsh reeds on big gangly wings. We had traveled maybe two miles when Hadley killed the engine. Koot throttled down and eased up beside him. The cypress swamp lay about a quarter mile ahead.

Hadley nodded toward it. "Dis leads you 'traight into the mouth of the big swamp, boys. When you get inside, stay to de right. The camp is up a ways. You'll have to paddle from here if you wanna go in silent."

Sound carries on the slightest breeze in the quiet of the natural environment. Koot shut off the Evinrude, swung it up and locked it down.

Hadley asked, "You expectin' trouble in dere?"

I said, "Trouble finds you, Hadley, expected or not."

"Ain't dat the truth." Hadley gave us the look of a caring parent.

Koot said, "We'll see your craggy old face in the morning."

Hadley smiled with his eyes, then dug a paddle in at the back of his skiff and pivoted it around in the narrow bayou. He cranked up and slowly motored away.

Koot and I paddled the quarter mile to the edge of the swamp, then entered the dark cypress silence. The gray-brown trees rose all around us from the tannin darkened water, their canopies overlapping so that the sunlight could only penetrate in scattered shafts. Spanish moss hung from cypress limbs, sucking invisible nutrients from the hot wet air. Around the base of the trees, knee-shaped roots jutted out of the water, adding to the primordial feeling of the place. A large alligator with its ridged back slid off a mound of earth and into the water as we swept by, causing a primitive-looking gar fish to break the water in front of the bow.

We threaded our way through the swamp for a few hundred yards—then, through a drape of moss—we saw a cabin sitting on a narrow spit of land. A sixteen-foot Crestliner angler's boat was tied to a small dock.

People are interesting partly because of their contradictions. Jackie liked the high life, but it appeared he also liked the solitude of the swamp. Maybe in the past he came here to fish, or maybe to reflect on the road not taken in his life.

We slowed our paddling to dampen the sound of the skiff cutting the water. Except for the modulated squawking of a heron in the distance, the swamp was as silent as rising smoke. We were now a hammer throw from the cabin.

Suddenly a flash of fire came from the window and two slugs pierced the bow of the boat and passed through the bottom. One shot just missed Koot's foot.

I grabbed the bow line as Koot and I peeled over opposite sides of the skiff and went under. Another shot penetrated the water and hit me in the hip. Fortunately, a couple feet of water absorbed most of the velocity so that it only stung like a rock from a slingshot.

Holding the bow line, I swam underwater until my hand found the large cypress I had aimed for, then I surfaced on the safe side of the tree. Koot surfaced a second later behind a cypress about thirty feet away. I put my feet down and found bottom. The water was nearly chest deep. We both reached into the water and pulled our weapons out of our holsters and held them up to drain, though we didn't intend to get into a firefight with Jackie.

Another shot cracked and splintered a section of the tree just above Koot's head.

I shouted, "Jackie, I'm the guy on the phone with you today." He held his fire. Progress. "If we can find you, so can Castille. We came to bring you in. Then we'll get you and Danika to a safe place."

Two rounds hit the cypress over my head and another round hissed by my ear. Not progress. They were scared.

I shouted, "Call Adrienne."

I hoped he'd make the call. Either way we couldn't stay on the defensive. The skiff had taken on a lot of water. The gunwale was nearly at the water line. I signaled Koot with a crescent movement of my hand that I was going to circle behind the cabin. He waved the dripping Glock to let me know he would get Jackie's attention when I was in position.

I squatted low in the water and backed up slowly, keeping the cypress between me and Jackie's sight line. When I reached a denser grouping of trees, I used the better cover to begin a slow wide arc around the camp. I duckwalked through the algae-covered mire, holding my gun up. Bending my bad leg was difficult, but the water seemed to soothe it some. With all the cypress knees and roots under the water I was glad I had worn my jungle boots. Air Cajuns Koot calls them.

I glanced back in Koot's direction. The skiff had slipped completely under, bubbles the only evidence that a boat had been there. I turned back toward the cabin. Out of the corner of my eye, I saw something move from my left. A cottonmouth moccasin was several yards out and heading straight for me. If I shot it, Jackie would think I was shooting at him. If I tried to move away quickly, Jackie would spot me and maybe get lucky and put one through my head.

The snake came on. Cottonmouths usually aren't aggressive unless they think their territory is threatened. This one was hormonal about it. I kept my eye on the three-footer as I stepped the last few feet to the cover of the next tree, then I switched my gun to my left hand and waited. The moccasin closed in.

Just as the snake opened its mouth to bite I shot my arm out and snatched it up by the tail and held it at arm's length. The snake tried ferociously to bring its head up far enough to nail me. I was concerned that the cottonmouth's wild writhing would catch Jackie's eye.

Still trying to keep out of Jackie's sight line I moved a step away from the tree, then, in a fly-fishing motion, I brought the snake back, then whipped it forward and let go. The cottonmouth sailed off through the swamp in an enraged tangle. I peeked around the tree to make sure Jackie wasn't looking my way, then pushed on, hoping the moccasin wouldn't return for a rematch.

When I made my way even with the side of the cabin and beyond Jackie's view from the window, I moved in toward the cabin. The sun had dropped and twilight came on fast. I beached on my stomach, then got up and slipped over to the side of the cabin. Just as I started toward the back of the shanty, Jackie fired three shots in rapid succession into the fading light of the swamp. I could barely see the slugs splinter the tree Koot was hugging. I guess Adrienne's phone was busy.

I stepped around the cabin and saw that it had a back door. I was counting on it being unlocked. I took a step out from the cabin and waved at Koot. I couldn't tell if he saw me, but then the Glock barked. Koot would put a tight pattern in the wood around the window, distracting Jackie. I quickly moved to the back door.

Jackie returned Koot's fire. I was banking on him emptying his clip. The problem was that I didn't know how many rounds that would be. I counted seven shots, then it went silent. Seven it is. I burst through the door and lunged across the cabin toward Jackie. He spun around, eyes wide, and fumbled to insert his next clip. Just as he got the clip locked in and brought the handgun up, I kicked his arm and the gun skidded across the room.

I felt, more than saw, the frying pan coming from behind. I jerked my head and upper body to the right and the cast iron pan blurred by me and hit the wall close to Jackie's head. I spun around. Danika was standing by the stove. She was more beautiful than the photo, a leggy poetry of form. The impulse to savor the poetry was cut short when she broke for the gun in the corner of the cabin.

I ran, or more precisely, stumbled to the same spot. She arrived a step ahead of me and bent to grab the gun. Before she could pick it up, I hip-checked her against the wall, then bent down and I had it.

The pistol was a Colt Commander .45, the gun I thought Caveccio bought to murder Jackie and Danika was bought for their protection. Some detective.

I heard a noise on the porch, then Koot burst through the front door in a full layout, hit the floor in a roll and sprang to a crouch with his gun leveled, all in a single motion. The Cajun twister touches down. Koot scanned the cabin and saw that I was the only one holding a weapon.

"Clear?"

"Yep."

Jackie had crumpled against the wall beneath the window. Danika moved quickly to him and they huddled together on the floor. Beauty and the dumpling. I'd seen stranger pairings, but it'd been a while. They were pretty scared. The look on Jackie's face made me think of Santana when he gets dragged to the vet for his shots.

Jackie said, "Castille sent you to kill us."

I hobbled over to them. "Have you heard a word I've been saying? Look at us." I glanced at Koot. He still had his warrior face on, which could be unnerving. "Okay, look at *me*. Do I look like a killer."

They didn't look convinced.

"I'm telling you, your sister sent us."

"My sister and I haven't spoken in two years. She wouldn't have hired detectives to find me because she didn't know I was gone —nor would she have cared."

"Your sister found out you were missing because the manager at your apartment building told her that a package sat at your door for a couple of days. He suspected something wasn't right and called Adrienne. I went to your place. Castille's men had already torn it apart looking for the drugs. And if your sister didn't care about you, she wouldn't have sent the dynamic and dashing duo."

Jackie and Danika looked at each other and then back at me, confused.

Danika said, "You're not here to kill us?"

I looked at Koot. "I thought I've been the only one bushwhacking off the trail." I pulled my wallet from my back pocket and took out a soggy copy of my PI license and handed it to Danika, then I handed Jackie the Colt. "What's for dinner?"

Twilight turned to onyx and a glee club of nocturnal swamp life began to croak, click and wail around us. Jackie loaned Koot and me some shorts and T-shirts that were too small while we dried our clothes by the fire. Jackie and Danika were still shaken about Caveccio's murder, so Koot stepped in and cooked a pot of rice and canned red beans. He opened a couple of tins of smoked oysters while the rest of us sat at the rough cut pine picnic table. Danika removed a bottle of Shiraz from a cedar chest and filled coffee mugs for Jackie, Koot and herself. I declined.

Jackie looked disoriented, like he'd been spun and released on shifting ground. I guess the pain of losing a friend and the fear of being stalked relentlessly had taken its toll. Danika seemed to be holding up a little better. After what she had been through in the last few years, she had probably learned to compartmentalize her fears pretty well.

I said, "Were you two going to stay out here and eat alligator until Castille retired?"

Jackie said, "The camp was temporary, until we were sure Castille wasn't on to us."

Danika said, "Then we were going to fly to Spain. I can never return to Crotia."

"Were you going to disappear, Jackie, and leave your family to mourn?"

"I was going to get in touch after things cooled off."

Koot said, "It was damn lucky Castille didn't kill your sister—trying to get to you—like he took out Caveccio and Rocco."

Jackie looked like he had been rabbit punched. Koot got that look he gets, like he knew he was a bull in a china shop, but regretted the damage.

Koot backpeddled. "But she and Brent are safe, so it worked out."

Pure luck that it did—if you believe in luck. If a package hadn't sat at Jackie's door for a few days, the apartment manager wouldn't have suspected anything and wouldn't have called Adrienne. If Adrienne hadn't known Jackie was missing she wouldn't have called us, and if she hadn't hired detectives to find her brother, Castille might have thought she knew where Jackie was and Adrienne might have ended up like Caveccio and Rocco.

Koot was sautéing onions and cumin seeds for the rice and beans and the smell made my stomach butt into the conversation. I think Danika's stomach was griping too.

I said to Danika, "Castille used the aftermath of war in Croatia to lure you here?"

Danika said, "Our country was torn apart, and there was little work. Young women like me were promised good jobs, and when we arrived..."

Koot said, "You were forced into slavery."

"They threatened to have our families back home killed unless we cooperated. We have sex or we fight each other with weapons. These are our choices—choices worse than in Croatia. I am one of the fortunate ones. The women who fight are eventually injured badly. A few have died. The ones who have to work the street corners are with so many different kinds of men. Sometimes they are injured as well."

Danika's beauty assured she wouldn't have to work the streets. Men would call for her by name and pay a premium. Jackie must have spent a lot of the money he made working for Nads to spend time with Danika.

Danika pushed her hair back from her forehead. "Those of us who are too old or too much trouble are taken to make Castille's poison—his drugs." She started to say something else, but the words wouldn't come. Finally Danika spoke. "There are those of my religion who will never forgive what I have become."

"It wasn't your choice."

"It does not matter."

"To them. Does it matter to you that they don't represent the truth of your religion?"

"Tag, you do not understand."

Danika knew she was blameless, but it didn't prevent the anguish she felt from knowing that some, or many, of her own people would reject her. Being rejected by family was something I understood.

Jackie put his arm around Danika's shoulder. It occurred to me for the first time that Jackie might be able to help Danika get past some of her grief. Maybe Danika could help Jackie as well.

No one spoke for a couple of minutes.

Finally Jackie said, "Why did they kill Frank?"

I said, "Castille wanted an answer. Frank didn't have one. That's the only reason Castille needed."

"Even if Frank knew where we were hiding, he wouldn't have told them."

Jackie was acknowledging the loyalty of a friend. I didn't want to tell him that, given time, Eyes would have gotten whatever Frank knew out of him, and would have enjoyed the extraction. Somewhere beyond loyalty, we all have a breaking point.

"We're going to take you both to a police safehouse until we can get to Castille. It's already set up."

Jackie said, "What if Castille finds out?"

Koot said, "He won't."

Jackie and Danika looked at Koot and me and then at each other, then Danika said, "We will go with you."

"Good."

I poured some water from a pitcher on the table and drank.

Then I said, "Danika, do you know where Castille's drug operation is?"

Danika said, "No, but I once overheard two of Castille's men talking. I think it is underground."

"Do either of you have a taste for Castille's product?"

Jackie sat straight. "Danika has never used drugs. I'm sure Adrienne told you all about my appetites."

"Yes, she did."

"I'm done with that life."

"What about dealing?"

"You said something earlier about Castille's men looking for drugs in my apartment. Is that what this is about? You think we stole drugs from Castille?"

"Castille said a large amount of drugs disappeared from his house the night before you staged the accident."

Danika said, "His precious Sojourn."

"That's the name of the drug?"

"Yes."

"You were at the party where the drugs were taken. The next day you two staged an accident. Selling the drugs would give you a good run at a new life."

Danika said, "We were trying to convince Castille that we were dead. We would have to be...how do you say...up in our tree...to steal drugs from him first."

Jackie glanced at Koot and me. "She's working on her expressions."

Koot said, "She makes more sense than most of the amoebas I've collared."

Jackie looked at me directly. "We didn't steal Castille's drugs."

I looked at Koot. He believed them too.

"Okay," I said.

Koot opened a can of asparagus, then dished up the rice and beans and oysters and set the food on the table. I was hungry, and the food was hot and satisfying.

Midway through the meal I suddenly felt bone-tired and my mouth was dry as desert dust. I got up and went to the sink to fill the water pitcher. It felt like I was dragging an Airstream. I poured a glass and drained it, but my thirst wouldn't be quenched.

Being hauled in by Mowery this morning made me forget to take my diabetes meds, and I didn't have to test my blood sugar to know I needed them right away. I reached into the side pocket of my cargo pants for the plastic bottle, but it was gone. The pocket flap was open, which meant my meds were out there somewhere under four feet of water and silt. It was going to be a long night.

It became a struggle to form thoughts as my body and mind began to shut down. I told Koot to call Grady and tell him we were coming in at first light, and to swing by my place for both bottles of my meds.

I collapsed in a stupor on a cot in the corner and spent an eternity waiting for the earth to spin toward the light of dawn.

TWENTY-ONE

Ahead of the sun, Koot rolled off his cot and made coffee, then brought me a steaming mug. I pulled myself to a sitting position and took a sip.

Koot asked, "How you feeling?"

"I'm not."

"We'll get you out of here soon."

Koot woke Danika and Jackie. While they loaded their belongings into the boat, I finished the coffee, then got up and poured another cup. I needed to prop myself up long enough to get Jackie and Danika to the safehouse.

I took my coffee and shuffled out to the front porch and flopped onto a cypress plank bench. Koot waded out to the sunken skiff and retrieved the "Merc" motor and gas tank and loaded them into Jackie's Crestliner. We were going to have to buy Hadley a new skiff. I hoped he hadn't been attached to the old one.

Jackie turned off the generator in the cabin and shuttered the windows, then we left. I sat up front by Koot and laid my head back on the seat while Koot and Jackie paddled us out of the thick of the swamp, then Koot cranked up and headed toward the main bayou.

When we were nearing the boat launch I looked for Grady, but he hadn't arrived. Farther up the bayou, tied off along the bank was a large powerboat. Something didn't feel right about a pleasure boat anchored around here. Koot spotted it too and just as he throttled down, shots cracked and hit the water around us. Castille's men.

Koot throttled full and turned sharply, then pointed the Crestliner back up the bayou. The powerboat lurched away from its mooring and accelerated toward us. The boat had more muscle in the water and came on fast. We'd be overtaken soon unless we could make it to one of the narrow sloughs running into the marsh. If we could do that, we had a chance.

I shouted for Jackie and Danika to lie down in the bottom of the boat. I could see Eyes in front of the powerboat next to Curly, who was steering. Two other men stood behind them.

I pulled my Kahr and fired. The powerboat quickly swerved, then swung back around and came on, but kept a greater distance.

Eyes's and his men fired, and I heard fiberglass splinter. If they hit the Crestliner's gas tank, we'd be flash-fried in the explosion. It looked like Castille wasn't as concerned about getting his drugs as he was about feeding his sense of revenge.

As the hail kept coming, Koot and I scanned the shore for an opening to the marsh and spotted a narrow inlet. Koot turned hard right and headed for it. The powerboat angled in behind us, still keeping a distance. I squeezed off a clip and a couple hit the powerboat, but I didn't get lucky enough to hit the fuel line.

When we reached the vein of water, Koot throttled way back. At higher speeds the engine sits too low in the water for these shallows. A stump or log could take out the prop. The weight of the powerboat behind us meant Curly would have to go even slower. We had counted on that.

We idled through the curves of the slough deeper into the marsh. The throaty engine of the powerboat idled in behind us, maybe eighty yards back. After a couple of hundred yards the bayou began to taper in. If it dead ended, we were trapped. We had to do something.

I spotted a small stand of swamp red maples ahead of us and told Koot to stop there. When he pulled to the small patch of solid ground I got out with the gas tank from the sunken skiff. Koot knew what I was thinking.

Koot said, "You're not in shape for this. I'll do it."

"No time, partner." I turned to Jackie. "Give me your lighter." He pulled it out and handed it to me. At the moment I was glad he smoked. To Koot, "I'll signal."

Koot nodded, then pulled away from the bank and continued up the bayou.

I squatted behind the stand of trees with the gas tank. I ripped one of my sleeves from my shirt, then rolled it to make a fuse. The powerboat was getting close. I unscrewed the gas cap and fed one end of the rolled cloth into the tank, then back-poured to saturate the shirt with fuel.

When Eyes and his men were within thirty feet I flicked the lighter, but got no spark. I kept flicking it. The boat was now even with my position in the maples. On about the tenth try the lighter lit, but the boat had pulled past. I put the fire to the fuse, then stepped out of the trees and heaved the gas tank as hard as I could. The tank slammed the stern of the powerboat and bounced in.

Castille's men tried to dive off the boat as the tank exploded. I saw two of them stagger to the gunwales, hair and clothes in flames, and fall over into the water. I shoved another clip in the Kahr and waited for someone to pop up. I saw Curly sprawled face down in the reeds on the opposite side of the bayou. Eyes had disappeared.

The two guys surfaced next to the bank on my side of the bayou. They were dazed and one had lost his hair, but the water had saved them from severe burns.

The boat was soon in full blaze, giving off an acrid chemical smell of composite resin. Rolling plumes of black smoke billowed into the air, causing two passing egrets to veer off their flight path.

I stepped to the bank where the two were clinging to shore. While looking for Eyes, I bent and grabbed one of the gunmen by what was left of his shirt and drug him halfway onto the bank, then turned him over. No gun. The other guy wriggled onto shore beside him. I rolled him over too, took the weapon from his pants and tossed it in the water.

My whole body was stiffening up. Rigor mortis in the living was not a pretty sight. On top of being tight and exhausted, the chemical smell of burning resin and the heat of the rising flames made me dizzy.

I went to my knees on the spongy ground and continued to scan the reeds, but still no sign of Eyes. If the concussion of the explosion knocked him out, he should have floated to the surface, unless he snagged on a log at the bottom and drowned. I was concerned that he'd crawled into the reeds and was waiting to take me out at close range.

The burning boat had drifted sideways and blocked the narrow waterway. We'd have to find another way out of the marsh. I told the two men on the bank to lie face down, then I fired a shot into the air and five seconds later fired another shot. The signal for Koot.

Koot idled backwards down the tributary. When the boat got to the stand of trees, Koot and Jackie hopped out. Koot checked the two on the ground, then he and Jackie helped me into the Crestliner. As we idled forward up the bayou I stared into the marsh, trying to decide if it was breeze-nudged cattails moving or human limbs.

Koot found another tributary near the end of the vein we were on, and after winding through the marsh for about twenty minutes we came out into the main bayou again.

Koot pointed the boat toward the launch and said, "Now we have another problem."

I nodded. No one was going to like hearing it either.

When we arrived at the boat launch, Grady was waiting. If any of Castille's men had been at the dock while we were chased, they were gone now.

Koot and Grady helped me out of the boat and over to Grady's Crown Vic. Jackie and Danika followed us. Koot opened the front door and poured me into the seat, then Grady handed me the two bottles of meds and a bottle of water.

Koot went to load the Crestliner onto the trailer Jackie had parked at the launch, then he'd take it to Hadley's to store.

"You've looked better, Sport Model," Grady said.

I grunted and poured out two caps of Glucatrol and a couple of caps of Metformin and washed them down.

Grady turned to Jackie and Danika. "I'm Detective Herns. We're going to protect you."

"For how long can you protect us, Detective—a week, a month, a year?" Jackie asked.

"As long as it takes, Mr. Kanawhite."

"That means as long as Dumont Castille is still alive."

Grady glanced at Koot and me and then looked at Jackie. "Or until we can get to him."

I thought of the one in 10,000 people born with the heart on the right side of the chest. That'd be about the odds for Jackie and Danika to be alive in a year if we didn't take Castille down or out.

Grady asked, "Tag, how did Castille find you?"

I straightened myself in the seat and faced Grady, Jackie and Danika. I knew that telling Jackie and Danika might destroy any trust we had gained, but they had placed their lives in our hands and I wasn't going to lie to them.

"A homicide detective."

TWENTY-TWO

On the way back to New Orleans I sat up front with Grady, and Jackie and Danika sat in the back.

Grady said, "You're telling me we've got cancer in our house, Tag?"

The meds were finally beginning to lift the concrete blocks off me.

"Has to be."

"Who else knew about the camp?"

"The man who guided us in."

"How can you be sure about him?"

"Same as I'm sure about you."

Grady looked at me for a few seconds, then nodded once.

Jackie said, "While you two sort out who's working for Castille —as soon as we get to the city, we're out of here."

Grady said, "Mr. Kanawhite, I assure you we'll find out who this is and deal with him." I wondered if Grady had already suspected who it could be. A couple of names jumped to the head of my list. I knew Grady would take this extremely personally.

Jackie said, "It could be you for all we know, Detective."

I turned in the seat and faced Jackie. "Jackie, this is what you know—you know Koot and I got you and Danika out of a dangerous situation. This is what you *need* to know. Grady would have done the same thing."

Jackie said, "That leaves us with what you *don't* know."

I took a deep breath and let it out. "I can understand not having your trust, but I'm asking for it just the same. We made a mistake. It won't happen again."

Danika and Jackie looked at each other. They looked conflicted.

Danika said, "Now that he knows we're alive, Jackie, Castille will never stop looking for us. I think Tag, Koot and Detective Herns are our best hope."

Jackie looked like he wanted to shrink into himself. "This is a nightmare."

Grady said, "Nightmares end."

Jackie said, "So do lives."

Danika put her arm on Jackie's arm. After a few seconds Jackie nodded.

Danika turned to me. "Please protect us."

"We will." I was trying hard to believe we could do it.

Castille knew we were bringing Jackie and Danika to the safehouse, but he wouldn't come for them until well after dark, so we had some time. Grady called Lieutenant Tolleson to set up a meeting with Grady, Koot and me.

We stopped at a grocery store to buy food for Danika and Jackie, then we took them to the safehouse. A couple of uniformed officers were there to take the day watch. When we got Danika and Jackie settled in, Grady took me home so I could get some rest. Later, I'd bring Danika and Jackie some things to make them comfortable.

The meds helped get my legs under me enough to negotiate the porch steps. When I walked in the house, Seven gave me the stare, miffed I hadn't made it home last night. I'd have to atone.

After I fed the kids, Koot came in.

I asked, "Are we in the doghouse with Hadley?"

"He said sinking that old skiff did him a favor."

"Then he should be happy when we get him a new one."

"Yeah."

Koot volunteered to take Santana for a walk in the neighborhood. While they were gone, I gave Marty a call. I told him what had happened and what needed to happen. He okayed the plan, then we hung up.

I grabbed a quart bottle of water from the kitchen, then went back in the living room, turned on the radio, and collapsed on the couch. Diabetics are especially prone to dehydration when the blood sugar spikes and I drank like a lost desert hiker at a found spring.

Seven hopped into my lap, and I stroked her back until she was satisfied that I was contrite, then she hopped down and went to her cushioned basket and curled up. The weatherman talked about a tropical depression building in the Atlantic. That was the last thing I heard before falling asleep.

I stood knee-deep in the surf and shined a light into the darkness toward the voices calling for help. I heard someone call my name, then a swordfish leaped toward the light and speared me in the chest. Then I heard a bell chime and I was lying on a simple pallet in a bare room. My eyes were closed, but somehow I could see the ochre-robed monk who sat on the floor at my side, chanting something I could not understand. I wondered why I couldn't feel the stab wound, then I realized the monk was doing Otsuya, the Japanese Buddhist practice of spending the night with the newly dead.

A bell rang again, and I found myself back in the more familiar world of pleasure and pain. At the moment, mostly pain. I grabbed the portable phone off the coffee table and answered it.

Grady said, "How're you feeling, Swamp Rat?"

"Like a dream."

"You gonna be up to this tonight?"

"If I get to refuel the sleep tank."

"If we can take one of Castille's men alive, maybe he'll give us the pus boil in the department."

"Unless the cop is a mystery man to Castille's crew."

"Yeah, that's possible."

I shifted on the couch.

"It took a long time to clean up the corruption at NOPD. One way or the other we're gonna nail him. Can you and Koot meet us in Audubon Park at the dock in say, forty minutes?"

"Sure, who needs sleep?"

I hung up, then climbed in the shower and got the smell and grime of swamp off me, then put on some clean jeans, a shirt and my running shoes. When Koot and Santana got back, Koot got a shower while I made a couple of turkey melts on onion rolls for the road, then we took off in the Outback.

We hadn't eaten since last night, so by the time we reached the park the sandwiches were a memory. Koot wound past the zoo and over the railroad tracks, then approached the docking area for the John James Audubon, the three-decker tour boat that ran up river to downtown and back. The Audubon disgorged passengers while a new line of sightseers waited to board.

Koot pulled in beside Grady's Crown Vic, then we got in the back seat.

Lieutenant Tolleson said, "Let me have it."

I said, "Besides Koot's friend, your detectives were the only ones who knew where we'd be putting the boat in."

"Loomis, what about your friend near the swamp?"

Koot said, "Not a candidate."

The lieutenant looked at me, and I nodded agreement.

"Maybe Castille had you followed."

I said, "We got rid of the tail before we left New Orleans."

Koot said, "But the cop didn't know we got rid of them. He probably figured that when Castille's guys showed up, we'd assume we were followed."

The lieutenant said, "So he wouldn't think suspicion fell on anyone in the department."

I said, "Yeah. He'd feel secure enough to tell Castille about the safehouse."

Grady said, "We gonna turn this over to Public Integrity, Lieutenant?"

"We do that now, it plays our hand. Let's give our criminal some line, and if he surfaces again, we'll try to set the hook."

Grady said, "The lieutenant likes your idea about tonight, Tag."

Lieutenant Tolleson said, "I cleared this with the commander. I want you and Loomis at the safehouse with Herns tonight. No one else will know you two are there. If any detectives get curious why only Herns was assigned, I'll handle it. I have a dinner with the mayor's office tonight, but I'll have my cell on if you need me."

Koot said, "They'll come tonight."

Grady said, "That'd be good. I hate waiting."

Koot dropped me off at the house, then went to teach his women students how whacking windpipes and punting gonads were sometimes the best negotiating skills when dealing with aggressive males.

I went to the kitchen and downed a glass of water, then tested my blood sugar. Back to normal. Maybe the rest of me would be before long. I ate a barbecued almond Mojo bar then locked the house, got in the Sebring and headed over to Bucktown to see my niece Trish.

I still wanted to find the drugs stolen from Castille. It might give us a bargaining chip for Danika and Jackie, in case we couldn't get to Castille any other way. I was hoping Trish could help. I was also hoping I might be able to help her.

I took Carrolton up to City Park, turned onto Marconi Boulevard and headed up toward the lake. When we had partnered as rookies on the force, Koot and I answered a call in this neighborhood about a domestic disturbance. When we got to the house we found a woman sitting on her deck in the backyard under a mercury vapor light, drinking a can of Old Milwaukee.

Koot noticed the red light flickering on top of the roof about the same time the woman offered to buff our nightsticks.

The plan had been for the boyfriend to videotape a couple of cops having sex with a complainant, sell the tape to the tabloids, then take off to Bimini. Their travel plans got canceled.

When I got to the lake, I turned east on Robert E. Lee then eased over the canal into Bucktown. Trish had a summer job as prep help at a seafood restaurant near the lake, and I wanted to catch her before the lunch crowd arrived. I parked in front of a sign on an easel outside the restaurant. Specials of the day: oyster gumbo and fried softshell crabs.

The smell of gumbo met me at the door. I walked over to a skeletal waiter who was digging something out of his ear with a butter knife. I asked him if he'd tell Trish that her favorite and only uncle wanted to see her.

The waiter went in one side of the swinging doors to the kitchen, and a minute later Trish came out the other side. She was dressed in baggy black jeans and a black halter top with *Raging Babysitters* scrawled in neon pink across the front. A tourmaline stud was stuck in the side of her nostril, and another stud with a small steel ball was fastened under her bottom lip. Except for an ice blue topknot of sorts, her hair was cropped to the skin.

This look was a recent development and was allowed only after fierce infighting with her Mom and Dad. A sixteen year-old trying on identities. A loss of light in her eyes was also a recent development and concerned me.

"Hi, Trish."

Her voice flat and detached. "Hey, U.T."

She had recently stopped calling me Uncle Tag. Too many syllables I guess. She keeps paring down, next time it'd be, "Hey, U." The minimalist approach to relationships.

I said, "Can we talk?"

She led me through the kitchen and asked a guy dressed as a chef if she could take her break. He gave begrudging approval, and we went out the back door.

Outside, a boy about Trish's age was cleaning fish on a concrete table. He wore a maroon rubber apron and heavy gloves, and his pants had as much material gathered around his ankles as above them.

Conley Clark

The odor of fish parts and shrimp heads rotting in the dumpster draped us, so we walked across the alley until we were out of range. We sat on a retaining wall partially shaded by a dogwood tree. Trish took a pack of Camels and a disposable lighter from her apron and lit a cigarette.

I looked at the metal ball below her lip. "This is new."

"Uh huh."

"Looks like a little trailer hitch."

She tried to blow a smoke ring, but it came out shapeless.

"I don't pull any weight but my own."

"Not even that from what I hear."

She gave me disgusted. "God, did Mom and Dad send you to lecture me?"

"Have I ever lectured you? I ran into your mom. She mentioned that you've been calling in sick lately, and that you're not showing up at home—even when you're there. They're concerned."

"They just don't want me to lose my job."

"It's not the job they're worried about being lost."

Her voice took and edge. "They don't trust me."

"You given them any reason not to?" She ignored that. She tried to blow another smoke ring. It looked like a shredded tire.

"Do your mom and dad know you're doing drugs?"

She looked at me, giving me *et tu.* "You don't trust me either."

"Save the theatrics, Sweetness. You're using as we speak."

It caught her by surprise, and her face was a wave of emotions. Shame, anger, confusion. I thought I saw them all. Anger stepped to the mike.

Trish said, "At least I've never been a drunk." Her face twitched. She regretted it as soon as it popped out. Shame took the lead. "I'm...I shouldn't have..."

"It's okay."

"I hate people who are judgmental. I'm really sorry."

"You just stated the fact. I was a menace to sobriety."

Trish stubbed out her cigarette on the wall, then she fidgeted. She wanted to ask me. Finally she did.

"Why did you...you know...become a drunk?"

"To make the pain go away."

"Did it?"

"Only thing that went away was my marriage and career."

"What made you stop drinking?"

"I finally forgave myself."

"For your partner getting killed?"

"That was the big one."

"I know your partner getting killed and all must have been a drag for you, but I don't get high because I'm in some kind of pain."

"There's different kinds of pain. One is the pain of not being understood, not knowing where you belong in the world."

Trish blinked, then looked away. "Getting high makes me feel good. What's wrong with that?"

"Everyone wants to feel good. But after a while it takes more to get you up. Then up starts to feel like down. Things start to come unraveled, then maybe you become another casualty."

"But my life sucks. My parents are on me all the time, I got dumped by a guy I really liked, and nobody gets me at school."

"Using's not going to change those things. Many of the circumstances of life are beyond our ability to change. You can't keep someone from dumping you if they're ready to move on. I couldn't keep cops from hating me."

"That was so unfair—them hating you. You could never do what they said you did."

"I appreciate that, Trish. At the risk of sounding like a daytime talk show shrink, it's the changes we make inside that give us some measure of contentment about our lives."

"How do I do that?"

"We all have to figure that one out for ourselves, Sweetness. But you're one of the lucky ones. You've got family who are here for you while you do. I'm here for you."

Neither one of us spoke for a while.

Then Trish said, "Aunt Cile shouldn't have left you when you were down."

"Everyone has limits."

"Did you hate her for having the affair?"

"Yeah, until I realized I had loved my job more than I had loved her."

"Do you ever miss her?"

"You can miss someone and still not belong together. I didn't figure that one out until I was sober again."

The kid at the table had been looking over at Trish as we talked. Whenever Trish looked vaguely in his direction he pushed up a bent goofy grin. It didn't seem to bother him in the least that he smelled of fish offal or that Trish didn't encourage him in any way. He was confident. Maybe he was even content.

Trish said, "I'd better get back to work."

Conley Clark

"Trish, you know anyone who deals designer drugs—ecstasy or 'G' or a new one called Sojourn? Someone who knows people around town?"

"So is this how you get me to stop using—you bust my supply?"

She was joking, and the light moment between us made me feel good. Then she squinted, turning it over.

"Your name will not come up," I said.

"Why do you want to know?"

"Two people's lives could depend on it."

Trish put her upper lip over the little ball tacked to her bottom lip and rubbed it for a while. Then she said, "There's a guy everyone calls Shaman. He'll probably be at this party tonight."

I took a small notepad and pen out of my pocket and handed it to her. Trish took it and wrote an address, then handed it back.

She said, "You won't cause a scene at the party, will you?"

"Sweetness, when have you ever known me to cause a scene?"

Trish smiled. She had seen me drunk going head-to-head with my ex-wife, sometimes in public places.

She said, "Do me a favor, U.T. Don't call me Sweetness around anyone I'm hanging with."

"No problem. We wouldn't want them to know the real you."

TWENTY-THREE

I called Adrienne's studio, and her assistant told me Adrienne canceled a photo shoot and went home, so I drove to her house. I was about to bring her out of mourning and felt as good about delivering the news that Jackie was alive as I had felt bad about keeping it from them.

When I arrived, the front door was open. Through the screen door and down the hall I saw Adrienne on her knees on the kitchen floor. She was wiping a wall.

I spoke up. "Adrienne."

She turned and looked at me, then turned back and continued wiping.

"You'll want to hear this. I promise you."

Adrienne stopped wiping and turned again. She looked tired.

She said, "You're good at making promises you can't keep."

She turned toward the wall again, but didn't wipe it.

"Adrienne, I'm coming in."

I opened the screen door and walked down the hall and into the kitchen. On the floor at Adrienne's knees, what looked like a chocolate cake with a raspberry colored icing lay in a disfigured heap. Chocolate and raspberry streaks were smeared on the wall above the glob. Jackson Pollock does dessert.

I could think of a few reasons why Adrienne would heave a cake against the wall. Maybe she was feeling guilty—thinking if she hadn't turned Jackie away he'd be alive. Or maybe she felt Jackie had abandoned *her*. It can get pretty irrational when you lose someone—or when you *think* you've lost someone. My abandoning her at the memorial service might have been in the mix. Selfishly, I'd hoped it was. Whatever the reasons, it was time for the grief to end.

I said, "Adrienne, Jackie is alive."

Adrienne's head whipped around and she gave me hot eyes. "Get out of my house—now."

"I mean it Adrienne. The call I took at the chapel was from Jackie."

Adrienne stared at me. I think she was trying to decide if I was capable of demonic cruelty. Experience told me she'd need to be talked through the shock and disbelief.

"Jackie is in love with Danika. He tried to help her escape a very dangerous man. They faked the boating accident, then hid in the swamp. We found them and brought them back. Right now they're someplace safe."

I'd have to tell her Castille would keep coming for them, but I wanted to take it a step at a time.

Adrienne looked up at me with an expression of desperation, like someone who had the wind knocked out of them and was struggling to catch a breath. She said, "I don't know who you are. I don't know..."

I took her shoulders in my hands. "Adrienne, I didn't tell you they were alive sooner because if the man got to them before we did, he would have killed Jackie. Then I'd have to tell you for the *second* time that Jackie was dead. I couldn't do that."

She stared at me some more, then she flared. "Why does he do this to me?" Relief masquerading as anger.

Then Adrienne put her arms around me and sobbed—tears of relief, tears of gladness. In a minute she leaned her head back and looked at me.

Adrienne said, "You let me hate you in order to spare Brent, Blanche and me."

"Don't think I could stand to do that again."

Adrienne's eyes were softer than I'd seen before.

She said, "I don't think you'll have to. Can we see Jackie?"

"Soon."

Adrienne nodded, then pulled me to her. We kissed. I was glad to feel her hunger match mine. Then she took my hand and led me into the bedroom. She didn't close the blinds, and I got to enjoy the beauty of her body under the northern light of a cloud strewn sky.

After, we lay facing each other, glossed with sweat despite the chilled air blowing from the window unit. I felt better than I'd felt in a long time.

Adrienne said, "My first time with a detective."

"My first time with a client. You know I'm not the only one who has a thing for you."

"Marty, I know."

I said, "I'm going to have to tell him how I feel about you."

"How do you feel?"

"Like the more I'm somewhere else, the more I want to be here."

Adrienne smiled and ran her hand over the ridge of an old scar on my back. She asked me about Danika and Castille and whether Jackie and Danika were still in danger. I answered all her questions and told her I'd take her to see Jackie tomorrow.

I had hoped she would let me know how she felt about me. I guess she'd tell me in her own time.

Adrienne said, "Jackie has been lost since our parents died. I'm glad he's found someone to care about again." She forced a smile. "*We* were family once."

"You could be again. Jackie may have made some mistakes, maybe a lot of them, but he showed a lot of courage when he signed on to help Danika break away from Castille. I think Jackie's put his old ways behind him."

She seemed to consider that. She said, "Courage is not that common." Then she caressed my face. "Lately, I've found myself surrounded by it."

My hand followed the curve of her back and came to rest on creviced perfection.

Adrienne asked, "Is it difficult living with diabetes?"

"It beats wearing a colostomy bag."

"I guess there's always something worse. Do you give yourself shots?"

"No. Mine is non-insulin dependent. I take pills. If I eat right and exercise I might never have to inject insulin."

Adrienne put her leg over mine. "Does diabetes run in your family?"

"The gene is there, but I'm the only one who has diabetes. I opened that door when I became a drunk."

"Do you still drink?"

"At times I've wanted to—a couple of times lately—then I remember where I've been."

She nodded, then asked, "Why did you become a private detective?"

"Because I couldn't be a cop anymore."

"Why not?"

I told Adrienne about Charlie, about Doucette's lie at the hearing, about how impossible it was because nearly all of NOPD hated me, or at least had doubts about what happened that night.

"Was it difficult to leave?"

"A cop was all I ever wanted to be."

"Why?"

"It's an unjust world. I have a hard time with that."

"You're intelligent. You could have been a lawyer. Lawyers can help people find justice. I'm not talking about my ex-husband, of course. With him it was more about jackpot than justice."

Adrienne reached and pushed a ringlet of hair away from her eyes. A simple gesture I found sexy.

I said, "Lawyers are too far removed from the hot zone."

"I see." She seemed disappointed. "But the front lines can turn violent. You could end up like your partner, Charlie."

"Cops know the risks."

She raised her head and looked at me. "You and Koot put yourselves in danger for us. I'll never forget that."

"Are you in bed with me because of gratitude?"

"That's right, and Koot is next." Adrienne grinned. I didn't. "I'm in bed with you because you're a good man who can deal with the harder realities and still keep a sense of humor about it all. I find that very attractive. Also, I like looking at you."

It's interesting the connection between intimate conversation and arousal. I said, "So how's it looking for us to spend time together after all this is over with."

Adrienne lifted the sheet and peered down.

"It's looking up."

TWENTY-FOUR

It was 9:00 p.m., and we had been staked out at the safehouse for a couple of hours. Grady was inside, Koot was bivouacked behind some azalea bushes to the side and near the front of the house, and I was nested in an azalea bush on the opposite side of the house, at the back of the lot. The shrubs had been planted long before the city acquired the property and were large enough to give us good cover.

Two other lots abutted the yard, one on Koot's side and one at the back fence. Just outside the fence on my side of the yard was a railroad embankment and at the top of the embankment, the tracks.

The new moon was no more than a sliver, so Koot and I had the additional cover of darkness, but so would an assassin. The street light in front of the house gave us some visibility if anyone approached from that direction.

The bedroom at the back of the house was dark, but the rest of the house was fully lit. Grady, Koot and I had radios to give each other a "heads up" when things started happening.

It was quiet. My thoughts went to Adrienne and her complete lack of inhibition this morning in bed. I thought about how being with Adrienne soothed a restlessness in me, a restlessness I'd had for a long time, a restlessness beyond my understanding.

I was looking forward to bringing Jackie and Adrienne together in the morning. I thought they had a good chance at a new and better relationship. Deep character reveals itself under pressure, and the fact that Jackie risked his life to protect Danika spoke more to the truth of the man than did the lost life he had led in recent years.

But first we had to get to Castille. I was hoping we wouldn't have to go through all his soldiers to do that, but it was hard to see a way around it.

I was thinking about how I might fit in the picture of Adrienne's and Brent's lives when I heard rocks crunch behind me. It sounded

Conley Clark

like a couple of people coming down the railroad embankment. Before I could get on the radio to Grady and Koot, I heard the assassins scramble over the chain-link fence and drop to the ground, just a few feet away. Too close to use the radio, so I turned it off in case Grady or Koot called and gave me away.

An azalea bush rustled, and I heard breathing. The smell of sweat from a bad diet drifted my way.

One of them spoke quietly. "Locate the woman and man and the cops."

The voice. Eyes made it out of the marsh. That was disappointing.

I heard the guy Eyes had instructed come out of the bushes, but I couldn't see him until his silhouette was framed by the lights in the house and the street light. He went low to the front of the house, then looked in the side living room window where Grady would be. From there he worked his way back down the house, peering into the lit dining room, the bathroom, a bedroom. At the back of the house he looked through the window into the darkness of the back bedroom.

Soon he headed back across the yard. He hadn't gone to the other side of the house, which meant he knew the rooms of the shotgun house were all on one side, off a long hallway. Castille's cop would have given them the layout. Since the scout hadn't checked out the other side of the house, Koot didn't know they were here.

Eyes' man came back into the bushes and rasped, "The man and woman are asleep in the back bedroom. There's one cop in the living room."

Eyes said, "You're sure—only one cop?"

"The place is lit like Vegas. There's nobody else."

A cell phone beeped out a number. In a couple of seconds Eyes spoke. "We're set here." Then the muted snap of the phone being folded together.

Eyes said, "Silencer."

I heard the faint sound of silencers being screwed onto gun barrels. After about a minute there was a loud crash on the street in front of the house. I raised up to have a look. Under the street light I saw the front end of an old Dodge embedded in the tail gate of an even older pickup truck. A man got out of the pickup and a woman got out of the Dodge and they surveyed the damage. A dog barked in a yard nearby. The man from the pickup spouted loud obscenities at the woman. The man grabbed the woman by the arm and pointed at his truck.

Grady appeared next to the man and woman. Grady said something to the man, and the man started in on Grady. The phone call. The accident was a setup to get Grady out of the house.

I heard Eyes say, "Let's go." The two men moved quickly out of the bushes and toward the house.

When they were near the house I pulled the Kahr and turned on the radio. Then I felt a gun barrel at the back of my head. A *third* guy.

The guy hadn't so much as grunted "Right, boss" the entire time. It's the quiet ones you have to watch out for. That is, if you can see them. The guy kept the muzzle pressed tight to my head while he took my weapon and the radio.

Against the kitchen light I saw Eyes and the other guy move to the back door. Eyes' thug broke a pane of glass in the door with his weapon, then reached in and turned the lock, and they were inside the house.

Thug Three shoved the gun to my head harder. "How many more?"

I said, "It's just me and the detective you lured to the street."

"If you're lying, you're dead."

"I wouldn't lie. I have a dog and a cat that need me."

"Shut up."

The light in the back bedroom came on. Through the window I saw Eyes aim his weapon, then heard five muted pops. Eyes yanked the cover off the bodies, then the surprised look when Eyes saw the mannequins.

He and the other guy quickly left the room. I heard Koot yell "Freeze," then gunfire roared in the hallway.

Thug three must have raised up to look because the gun came off my head. I quickly pivoted to the side and thrust a sword hand where I thought his windpipe would be. It connected squarely, and he gasped. I placed my leg behind his and threw him over my hip to the ground and followed him down. He tried to bring the gun up, but I pinned the arm with my left hand and slammed my right fist into the side of his head twice and he went limp. I ripped the weapon from his hand, then grabbed my Kahr from the guy's waistband.

I looked up in time to see Eyes bolt from the house and head this way. I dropped to the ground and shouted "Drop your weapon."

Eyes' gun flashed four times, and I heard the shots whizz by my head. I saw Eyes in silhouette wheel and run. I couldn't return fire because the house next door was directly behind Eyes' flight line. He cleared the fence and disappeared in the darkness.

Koot and Grady came to the back door, weapons drawn. Koot yelled, "Tag."

I shouted, "You guys okay?"

Koot said, "Yeah. One down and one out the door."

"Eyes did an Edwin Moses over the fence, heading south. I've got one here, alive."

Grady switched on his flashlight, and they ran over.

I said, "What about the decoys?"

Grady said, "They took off."

"Koot and I are on the sprinter."

Grady bent over to cuff the one on the ground. "I got this one and the one down."

Koot and I ran to the Outback and jumped in. Koot did a hard U and headed south.

I said, "The other one dead?"

"Leg and shoulder. He'll make it."

At the end of the block we turned right, then sped up to Claiborne. We looked right and left, then spotted Eyes under a street light about a block and a half away, near the Ponchartrain Expressway. He was standing at the curb talking on the cell phone.

Koot pulled onto Claiborne, but was hemmed in by a bloated Chevy Caprice in one lane and an Acura in the other. Beyond where Eyes was standing, I saw a pickup truck turn onto Claiborne from a side street. It was the decoy truck.

We were a block away when Eyes spotted us. He turned toward the decoy truck and vigorously waved the driver toward him. Koot swung out into the oncoming lane of traffic and floored it. A minivan came directly at us. The van braked, and Koot swerved back into our lane just ahead of the Caprice.

The pickup squealed to a halt in front of Eyes a second ahead of us, but before Eyes could get in the truck, Koot whipped in broadside and blocked the pickup. Eyes ran. We bailed and drew down on the guy in the truck. He tossed a weapon out, then got out with his hands in the air.

I said, "I'm on Eyes."

I took off down Claiborne after him. By the time he got to Earhart, I'd lost distance on him. With my gimp leg, it was a mistake not to have Koot go after him. I had let it get personal.

When Eyes reached the expressway, he ran up an exit ramp against traffic. Horns blared. When I got on the ramp I ran as close to the railing as I could so I wouldn't get clipped by a big rig coming down the ramp. When I got to the top I saw Eyes about sixty yards down the expressway. He was looking for a break in traffic so he could dart across.

When he saw me, he crouched and fired. I hadn't been a cooperative informant, so Castille must have signed off on Eyes taking me out. There was too much traffic to return fire and I was exposed, so I stuck the Kahr in my holster and scrambled over the expressway barrier for protection. I hung on, feet dangling in air. A freight train was moving on the track directly below me.

I pulled myself up to look for Eyes. He was several yards down the expressway, peering over the concrete barrier at the train. Then he hopped up on the barrier, and leaped.

Eyes landed in the center of a boxcar, the motion of the train sending his feet out from under him. He caught himself just before going over the edge. Eyes got to his knees, took aim at me and squeezed off several rounds.

I dropped onto the top of the train and tumbled headfirst off the end of the freight car. On the way over I grabbed the metal ladder at the end of the car, which whipped me around and crashed me against the ladder. It knocked the wind out of me, and my arms felt like they had been ripped out of their sockets. My mind flashed on the Komodo dragon's crash-test dummy. I glanced down and saw that the impact had jolted the Kahr out of my holster.

When I got my wind back, I stepped up a rung and looked down the line of cars. Eyes was four cars back. He saw me and fired again ,and I ducked. He would soon realize I didn't have my weapon and move on me like a crab moving on a wounded gull. Time to fly.

I leaned out and looked down the tracks. Under the expressway lights, I saw a large pile of railroad ties about seventy yards away. Just behind the pile were straw bales stacked maybe five wide and four high. If I could clear the railroad ties, the straw bales would break my fall. Of course, the ties would break my fall too, but I could end up a lot shorter. Still, short beats dead.

I stuck my head up above the car again. Eyes was two cars closer. I grabbed one side of the ladder with both hands and got back as far as I could toward the center of the car. When I was almost even with the railroad ties, I pulled hard on the ladder and catapulted out. I barely cleared the ties, then hit the straw bales. They collapsed over me.

Eyes fired three times from the train, and I heard the shots "phoomp" into the bales, then I was out of his range.

Eyes didn't get off the train, so I climbed out of the hay bales and took a couple of minutes to brush the straw off before I hobbled back down the tracks to find the Kahr. When I had it, I made my way back down Claiborne to Koot.

Tonight hadn't gone as planned, but it worked out. We had moved Danika and Jackie to Marty's house this afternoon where they were safe, and we took three of Castille's crew off the board. Three less between us and Castille.

TWENTY-FIVE

The lieutenant met us at the Second District station a little before 10:30 p.m. Two of Castille's men were locked up, and the other was under guard at Charity Hospital where he was being treated. Marie Trammel was the detective on duty at the station and had been called to the scene of a stabbing.

The lieutenant was in his office sitting behind his desk. Grady and I sat in the wood slat chairs, and Koot leaned against the wall.

Lieutenant Tolleson said, "You guys did good work tonight. And I like it when my guys come back in one piece." He looked at me. "Or almost in one piece."

I said, "I liked being one of your guys again, Lieutenant."

Koot nodded in agreement. "Like old times."

Lieutenant Tolleson looked at each of us for a few seconds, then nodded and leaned back in his chair. "We've got live bodies locked up. My detectives are gonna want to know why you two were at the safehouse. Any suggestions."

I said, "Koot and I got an anonymous tip that Castille's men were on their way to the safehouse. We got the tip around 8:30 and went directly to the safehouse. Things went down before Grady could call for backup. How's that?"

The lieutenant said, "That's probably why you're a good detective, Boudreau. You think like a criminal."

"Around here I *am* a criminal."

"Feeling sorry for ourselves?"

I shrugged. "Maybe so. Sometimes I pick at the scab of the same old wound. You'd think it would've healed by now."

"My wife's been dead for four years. Some things are hard to get past."

I nodded, appreciative.

The lieutenant said, "Tomorrow you guys come in and make your story official."

Grady said, "Maybe one of these guys we got locked up will give us our renegade."

Koot said, "If they know."

I said, "Koot's going to take the watch at Marty's place for the rest of the night."

The lieutenant said, "What about you?"

"I'm going to a party."

The double gallery mansion was the size of a boutique hotel and stood out among the other large old homes in the neighborhood. Cars lined both sides of the street for a block in each direction, so I pulled past the estate and parked a block over, next to the cemetery.

I got out and walked back past the rows of mausoleums. New Orleans is low land and holds river and rain water like a sated sponge, which is why the dead are entombed above ground. It insures that the only "floaters" are the homicide victims dumped in the Mississippi.

As I approached the house, the synthesized thud of techno music grew louder. I was guessing a teenager was throwing this bash while the parents were out of town. Unless the teen had free run of the house this shindig would be a trust-buster when the parents found out. And they'd find out. Some neighbor would gladly serve the kid up.

I climbed more steps than my leg wanted me to and entered the house without knocking. Just off the hall in the living room a couple of teens were lying on a large Persian rug, pretending there weren't two layers of clothes between them. I continued down the hall toward the music.

The next room off the hall was a trophy room—animal trophies. Lining the walls were the heads of a tiger, two bison, an elephant, a polar bear, and some other exotics. A couple were on the endangered list. They had been stalked and shot, not for food or population control, but for the pleasure of killing.

At the end of the hall, I entered a large den packed with teens dancing. They undulated to the synthesized music like kelp on the tide. Several looked as if they were lost in trance. A few just looked lost.

Most of them were cruising—maybe on GHB—"G"—or maybe crystal meth. The ones sucking baby pacifiers were probably doing ecstasy, which causes a lot of users to grind their teeth. The baby binky keeps them from grinding the enamel down.

I looked around for Trish but didn't see her. A girl wearing a gold mini, a black bra and a long strand of red glass beads stopped dancing and came over. She looked about seventeen and seemed acutely aware of how well her body was maturing into womanhood.

She shouted over the music, "Who are you?"

I pitched my voice. "Tag."

She motioned with her head, and I followed her into the corner of the enormous room, away from the music's epicenter. I could still feel the bass in my temples and chest. We spoke up.

"I'm Charlotte."

"Hi, Charlotte. I'm looking for..."

"You're here to see my mother."

"What makes you think so?"

"They all come to see my mother."

"What about your father?"

"He's away on business, as usual."

"And that's when they come to see your mother?"

She smiled, having fun with this. "Which is often."

"And your mother lets you have these little gatherings while Daddy is away?"

"My mother is upstairs in her room with one of my classmates."

Trying to shock me.

"So much for role models."

She studied me. "You're not like the others."

"I get that a lot. It's usually not meant as a compliment."

"You want to go upstairs?"

"I'm not here to see your mom."

"I meant with me."

"Is this a thing with you, Charlotte, propositioning men you just met?"

She gave me coy. "My first time."

"Uh huh. You're very attractive, but has it occurred to you that having sex with strangers could be dangerous?"

"I was counting on it."

A body maturing ahead of the rest of her. Or maybe with parents like hers, she just didn't care. I looked at her until her eyes quit skittering and she held my gaze.

"You can't change your parents. But you don't have to be like them."

Her eyes blinked rapidly several times, then her expression went blank. Charlotte turned and in exaggerated nonchalance she moved back into the crowd of dancers. My chest felt heavy. *Let it go, Boudreau.*

I couldn't find Trish in the crowd, so I went in the kitchen. Through the copper pots and pans that hung over the butcher block table, I saw her talking to a teenage boy. After the conversation with Charlotte, I felt like taking the guy aside and issuing a warning, but I really liked having a niece who would speak to me.

I moved to the butcher block and pretended I was interested in copperware until I caught Trish's eye. When the guy she was talking to looked away, Trish nodded toward the dining room. I tapped a sauce pan with my knuckles, then eased into the next room.

A guy with a ponytail, late twenties, was sitting at the large dining table surrounded by several teenagers. Holding court. The teens appeared to be mesmerized by the guy's trippy riffs on setting your mind free. Of course, drugs were the short cut to a freed mind, and he was just there to help—for about twenty-five bucks a mind. Had to be Shaman.

A liter of Gatorade and a stack of Dixie cups sat on the dining table at Shaman's elbow. A couple of kids plunked down cash, and Shaman poured them each a cup of designer high.

I recognized a guy leaning against the wall in the corner of the dining room. Darius Lewis played cornerback for the Saints a few seasons back. He blew out his knee and three miniscus operations couldn't give him his speed back, so he was cut from the team. From the bored look on his face I knew he wasn't there to party. He was Shaman's hired head-thumper. Times must be tough after the pros.

When Lewis noticed me he casually straightened himself. A good cornerback has an instinct for where the play is going. I smiled as I strolled past Lewis. He worked his wad of gum as his eyes stayed with me. When I got to the table I placed my hands on it and leaned down, facing Shaman.

I said, "They say a shaman's soul can leave his body and journey to the underworld."

Shaman stared, sizing me up, then glanced toward his man to see if he had a bead on me, then looked back at me.

Shaman said, "The soul and the journey are everything, bro." He glanced at Lewis again, then gave me a smile I wanted to wipe off his face.

I said, "What if he has no soul to begin with?"

"Then he wouldn't be a shaman."

"I guess that's right. He'd be a drug dealer."

The room went quiet. One teen voiced his disapproval. "Who is this dude?"

Shaman said to me, "Look around you, man. You're the only one has a problem with that."

"They haven't seen the casualties you and I've seen, have they, Sham-man?"

"You a cop?"

"No."

Lewis took a step closer, and I swiped up the Gatorade bottle, twisted the top off and tilted the bottle just short of pouring. The dealer held his hand up for Lewis to stop. I was holding about fifteen hundred dollars worth of pleasure cruises and one or two casualties at the ER, and it was all profit for Shaman.

He asked, "You on a crusade, man? Save them from themselves?"

"Naa. I just don't like drug dealers."

"No shit." He looked at the Gatorade bottle. "So what now?"

"You're going to love the irony, Sham-man. I need some information, and you can help."

Shaman studied me for a couple of seconds and then shrugged. "You the one holding the bottle, man."

"So let's you and I and the bottle take a walk out back."

Shaman stood, then glanced at Lewis. Some teens stood and blocked the way.

Shaman said, "It's cool, my flock."

The teens got their hard stare practice in, then they parted.

I turned toward Lewis. "It's a busted play, Darius, but if you stay here no one gets penalized."

Shaman nodded at Lewis. "It's cool."

Lewis cocked his head, then gnawed his gum and watched us go out the door.

Shaman and I went out back into a rose garden. We stopped, and I handed the bottle to Shaman to hold, then patted him down. He was carrying a .22 caliber in an ankle holster. I removed it and put it in my sport coat.

The light above the detached garage sent shafts of light through the thicket of rose bushes that surrounded us. We stood in the glow by a birdbath with a small marble statuette of an angel in the middle.

I said, "I want to know if somebody around town is trying to move a large amount of Sojourn."

"*Sojo*. Only one player has that sweet stuff. He makes it <u>and</u> moves it."

"Well somebody else has a few thousand hits of it. Castille's not a happy scumbag."

Shaman chuckled. "Somebody stole eighty-five thousand worth of product from Castille. That's one stupid fucking corpse. What's your interest here?"

"I want to get the drugs back to Castille."

"So you work for Castille?"

"No."

"Yeah, I see. You want the Sojo for yourself. Think you can move the stuff and live to spend the money."

"It's like I told you, Sham-man."

Shaman looked at me for a few seconds, then he grinned. "You had me goin', man. They know you escaped from the asylum?"

"The deal is, Sham-man, you get a name for me, and I don't have you busted. Sound fair?"

"So you *are* a cop."

"Close enough as far as you're concerned."

Out of the corner of my eye I caught a movement and turned just as Lewis sprang out of the dark. I sidestepped his charge, but the long reach of his arm caught me around the neck and we careened into a stove-sized rose bush.

As we went down I twisted my body so I'd land on top when we hit the ground. I intended to get the first punch in. When we hit, I popped up and straddled him, then drew my arm back. The thorns of the rose bush dug into the sleeve of my sport coat and checked my swing.

From his prone position Lewis backhanded me hard on the side of my head, then shoved me off and kipped up to his feet.

I yanked my arm hard and the sleeve ripped away from the thorns, leaving a broad swath of linen on the bush. I go through sport coats like bookies go through antacids.

Before I could get to my feet, Lewis planted and threw a side-kick aimed at my head. I ducked to the right and the blow caught me in the meat of my arm and sent me to my back. He might not be able to run down pass receivers anymore, but the man still had quick feet.

I rolled away from him so I could get to my feet, but only made it to my knees before Lewis stepped over and planted again for another side-kick. This time I blocked his kick with my forearm, but

I hadn't regained my balance and the force sent me into the birdbath, which toppled over on me.

I grabbed the statuette of the angel. When Lewis went to kick again I rolled toward him and under his kick. With my right leg I swept his planted leg from under him. When he hit the ground I cracked him in the nose with the statuette, and blood in the shape of teardrops sprayed the seraph's wings.

Lewis grabbed his nose and looked at me in disbelief. I got to my feet.

"Man, you hit me with something."

"The angel of mercy, Darius. You should take it as a sign to find a new line of work."

I checked him for weapons and removed the blade from his back pocket. I handed him my handkerchief, and he wiped the blood gushing from his nose. When I turned toward Shaman with the bloody statuette in my hand, he stumbled backward a couple of steps.

I said, "You can keep the bottle Sham-man, as a token of good faith. But tomorrow you'd better have a name for me."

I hated giving the bottle back, just like I hated the idea of giving Castille's Sojo back, but if it could free Danika and Jackie, it would cut the bitter taste.

"Yeah, all right, man. Where do I find you?"

"Meet me at Jackson Square at noon. You don't show, I'll find *you*."

"How 'bout my gun?"

I pulled it out of my jacket pocket. "These things are dangerous, Sham-man." Then I put it back in my pocket. He didn't like it, but kept his mouth shut.

I helped Lewis to his feet and followed the two of them into the house. When we walked in, a group was standing over a teenaged boy who was blacked out on the floor. I told a girl who was bent over the kid to move away, but she ignored me. I lifted the girl by the arm out of the way and bent down to feel the boy's pulse. His breathing was shallow and his pulse was hammering. I turned to Shaman.

"What's he on?"

"GHB. He's just in a 'G' hole, man. He'll be all right."

"You'd better hope so Sham-man, or you're gonna be in a shit hole."

I stood and grabbed the bottle from Shaman, uncapped it and poured the venom into a rubber plant.

Shaman said, "You just cost me..."

I pointed at him, and he shut up. "This doesn't change our deal, Sham-man."

I got a couple of the kid's friends to help me get the kid to my car. The teens went with me to the ER. While the doc and nurses shoved a tube down the kid's throat and pumped, I got the parents' phone number from the friends and gave it to the ER nurse, then I left.

As a uniformed officer I brought these overdoses to the ER on a regular basis. Sometimes I was glad I wasn't a cop anymore.

TWENTY-SIX

Some of Nads Liano's women would still be working the streets in the French Quarter at this hour, which meant Kiki would be around. I needed him to set up a meeting with Nads.

I parked my car in the carriage way on St. Philip and walked toward Bourbon Street. Most of the art galleries and bistros in the Quarter that shared walls with pizza stands, T-shirt and souvenir shops were closed. Now, full bore hedonism was getting traction in the clubs and bars on Bourbon.

Tourists, college kids and the serious Quarter rats strolled and staggered past the stench of vomit and urine that lingered in alcoves and recessed doorways, while barkers stood in the doors of bars, baiting the crowds with the promise of bargain drinks, loud music and bare flesh.

Two teenage girls teetered my way, sucking frozen drinks from salami-sized fake plastic syringes. They were laughing. Bourbon also had its share of angry drunks. When I worked Vice, I arrested a lot of them, then I became one and spent most of my off duty time running the same joints.

I found one of Kiki's hookers negotiating with a couple of frat boy types. The boys got jumpy when I approached, and it took me a minute to convince them I wasn't trouble. The hooker was pissed at me for interrupting the negotiation, but I got out of her that Kiki was at the Pink Pearl.

The Pearl was jammed, and at this hour, few were sober. Kiki, another man and a woman were sitting in chairs on the stripper's stage, biting into hot peppers. The crowd was hooting and cheering them on. It was a contest. Footlights illuminated the contestants' red faces, and aides fanned the pepper eaters furiously with towels.

The Master of Ceremonies roared to the crowd. "Do these contestants know how to suffer or what?" More cheers. "Or do they?" The M.C. waved his hand with a flourish. "I think it's time to open the gates of hell."

A curtain opened in the back of the club and a guy in red with a satin cape, a tail and horns emerged and made his way through the crowd toward the stage. He carried a red satin pillow with three bright orange peppers on it. Habaneros.

The M.C. bellowed, "Satan has brought us his proudest achievement—next to sin, of course. The hottest pepper and the reason for human spontaneous combustion. We call it—Satan's blow torch."

The crowd howled.

The devil walked on stage and, in turn, each of the contestants took a pepper. The M.C. gestured toward a sexy brunette off to the side of the stage who was wearing a firefighter's coat and hat and nothing else that I could see. She was holding a fire extinguisher.

The M.C. said, "We have one of New Orleans' finest here in case someone ignites." Whistles for the brunette. "All right contestants—time to light up."

Kiki and the other two took a bite of their peppers. Immediately the man and woman grabbed their throat. The woman gasped and the man screamed. Their aides handed them slices of bread, which they stuffed in their mouths. Bread was supposed to absorb some of the fire, but, judging by the looks on their faces, it was like trying to smother a garment warehouse blaze with a blanket.

Kiki sat silently and smiled strangely.

The M.C. stared at Kiki for a few seconds, then threw his head back and bellowed. "We have a survivor!"

The crowd boomed.

When the noise subsided, Kiki looked at the M.C. and croaked. "I won?"

"If you say so."

Kiki skipped the victory lap and headed straight to the bar, eyes bulging. Kiki's friend Mae, who hooked part-time, followed him back.

Kiki reached over the bar and grabbed about a dozen packets of sugar while the bartender drew him a beer. Kiki ripped open the packets and poured them into his mouth while Mae wiped sweat from his face with the towel. Kiki downed the entire glass of beer, then motioned for the bartender to draw him another one.

I walked over and sat on a stool next to Kiki and Mae.

I said, "How you doing, Mae?"

Mae smiled wearily. "Too old to be desired, too broke to retire."

"That'll cover most of us, one time or another."

Mae was nudging into her mid-forties. I took a lot of prostitutes through the revolving door when I was in Vice. Mae was one of the few who had worked the streets for more than ten years who wasn't strung out, walled off or in some other way dead inside.

At least Mae had chosen the life. I thought of Danika and the other women Castille had forced into prostitution; young women who, before they were abducted, had dreams of careers, of starting a family, of accomplishing goals. Young women who had hope for the future. I wondered how many of them still held any hope.

Liano would let his women walk away from the streets as long as they didn't try to freelance. Mae stayed because it was all she knew.

Mae asked, "How're *you* doin', honey?"

Kiki grunted and looked back and forth between us. "Best pals."

Mae looked at Kiki and said, "Taggert Boudreau treated me better when he was arresting me than you do when you're lovin' me."

"See what kind of trouble you bring, Boudreau."

"I'm not the one who decided to eat fire. How does it feel to be a winner?"

"Like the last one standing in a knife fight." Kiki took a long pull on his beer, then wiped his mustache. "Weren't you banned from this place, Boudreau?"

"I promised to behave."

"You were more fun when you drank."

"*You* were more fun when I drank, Kiki."

Mae grinned.

Kiki gave me bored. "So whatta you want?"

"I want you to set up a meeting with me and Nads."

"Like I'm going to put you two together."

"Don't worry. He already knows you snitch for me—and for some of the cops."

"Jesus Christ, Boudreau. You told him?"

You'd think the peppers made Kiki sweat as much as he was going to, but new beads popped out on his forehead.

"Kiki, I thought we had a relationship built on trust."

"We got a relationship built on money. I give you information, you give me money."

"I'm hurt."

"Don't shit me, Boudreau. Then how did Mr. Liano find out?"

"You move in a world of scumbags. Take your pick."

"If Mister Liano even suspects I might of...I'm screwed."

"Don't worry. He knows you've never snitched on him. That's why you still have a life— such as it is. He likes that you rat out his competition."

"How do you know all this?"

"I pissed Nads off. He came calling and mentioned it."

Kiki took several deep breaths. "So why would Mr. Liano be interested in meeting again with a dick that pissed him off?"

"Business."

I didn't tell Kiki I wanted to ask Nads for help. I didn't want to risk a thrombo.

Kiki's cell phone rang, and he answered it. "What, I'm in the middle of something here. The john wouldn't pay? I'll be there in a coupla minutes. I find you pocketed the money, Carli, I'll break your hands." Kiki hung up.

Mae looked at me and frowned. Kiki wouldn't hurt any of the women, and the women knew his threats were empty, but Kiki wouldn't try to protect them either if Nads thought someone was skimming the take.

"Why you gotta bring this on me, Boudreau?" Kiki looked like he was being forced to eat another habanero. He squinted hard and bit at his finger tips, then said, "I hear they make diamonds from the carbon of cremated bodies. Anything happens to me, will you see they make me into a diamond and give it to Mae?"

Mae said, "That's the sweetest thing you ever said."

I said, "A romantic. Who would have guessed?"

"Bite me, Boudreau."

TWENTY-SEVEN

I fell in bed with my clothes on around 2:00 a.m. and listened to my heartbeat slow to the rhythm of the throbbing in my neck and leg. Then the phone rang and pulled me out of a dreamless murk. I glanced at the clock. 6:00 a.m. I fumbled for the phone.

"Speak."

"Jackie and Danika are on the run," Koot said. I propped myself up against the headboard. "They crawled out the bedroom window. I heard a car stop on the street. When I looked out, they were pulling away in a cab."

"Why do we do this, Koot?"

"The pressure got to them."

"Maybe I shouldn't have told them about the cop at Homicide."

"They needed to know. We got a break, though. They booked a 7:00 a.m. flight to Cabo San Lucas."

"Notepad?"

"I got a clear impression of the flight number. American Airlines. We'll be at your place in a couple of minutes."

"We?"

"Marty wanted to tag along."

"Great—now he's a crime stopper."

When we got inside the airport terminal, we looked at the monitors to match the flight number to the gate, then Marty went to see if Danika and Jackie were at the American Airlines counter while Koot and I headed for the security check area.

We didn't see them in the security area line, but standing against the wall by a smoothie concession was Curly and another one of Castille's men. So, Curly made it out of the marsh too. I had hoped he parted ways with his soul in the reeds.

We knew Castille would have men here and at the train and bus stations. Danika and Jackie knew it too, but probably figured they had a better chance of slipping by Castille's men than waiting at Marty's for Castille to find them.

Curly and the other guy faced each other and moved in close. Curly held his flight jacket open and the other guy reached in and pulled something out, then put it in his own jacket. Gun. It looked like Jackie and Danika had managed to get through security before the goons could reach them, and now Curly was going to follow. Curly got in the security line and pulled a boarding pass from his jacket.

How'd Curly find out where Jackie and Danika were headed? Maybe money changed hands at the ticket counter. Maybe Curly got in line behind Danika and Jackie and listened for their destination at the counter. Maybe he was psychic. Detectives have "maybe" on the brain.

The guy with the guns in his jacket flipped open a cell phone and dialed. He'd let Castille know that Curly was on Danika and Jackie, but Curly wouldn't be trusted to get the job done. Eyes would be on a later flight to Cabo.

Koot said, "Seven minutes before flight time."

I couldn't get to the gate without a ticket, so I ran over to the American counter and barged my way to the front.

"I have to catch this flight to Cabo San Lucas."

"Sir, we've passed the cutoff."

"You've heard this before, but lives are at stake."

"It's the first time I've heard it *today*. I'm sorry, sir. You'll have to go to the end of the line."

"When's the next flight to Cabo?"

"11:35."

"Can you get me on it?"

Out of patience. "Sir, you'll have to go to the end of the line. Then we'll see."

I needed to break her sense of the order of things. I took a chance that she wouldn't call security and barked sharply, "I'll go to the end of the line. Just tell me if there's a seat."

She gritted her teeth and gave me the hard look, then she looked in the computer.

"There's been a cancellation. One seat available. However, if anyone already in line wants it ..."

I turned to the ten or so people in line. "Anyone without a reservation planning to buy a ticket to Cabo San Lucas?" No one. I turned to the ticket agent. "I'm going to the end of the line now."

Still gritting her teeth. "Thank you for your cooperation."

I circled out to the back of the line while passengers glared at me. Marty and Koot had followed me over.

Marty said, "Politics is definitely not in your future."

Koot said, "I'm going with you."

"Only one seat left, partner. That means Eyes and his stump necks will have to get the late afternoon flight. That gives me some time."

I knew Curly would keep his distance from Jackie and Danika in Cabo until Eyes got there. I was glad I thought to bring my passport and meds. I looked around, then opened my jacket.

"Take care of this."

Marty stood close to screen us, then Koot slipped the Kahr from my holster and quickly stuck it under his shirt.

Koot said, "I'll catch the afternoon flight."

"The same one Eyes is on? Maybe you and he can play gin rummy."

Koot looked frustrated. "You're going to need backup, Boudreau."

"I'll have Carlos meet me in Cabo. You stay and keep Grady and the lieutenant informed."

Koot said, "I don't like it."

"Always the serious one. Me, always the joker. Between us we've got one well-adjusted personality."

Marty hacked a laugh.

Koot said to Marty, "Don't encourage him." Then he turned back to me. "I don't hear from you, I'm coming anyway."

I said to Marty, "This is what you have to put up with when they care."

Marty said, "The two misfit amigos."

After I bought the ticket I called Carlos, a friend in Cabo that Koot and I got to know when we worked an insurance fraud case about a year ago. I gave Carlos a description of Jackie and Danika and the flight number. He agreed to follow them from the airport to wherever they were staying and then come back for me when my flight arrived.

I told Carlos they had a tail and described Curly. I told him we were dealing with bad people and that it'd be fine if he wanted to sit this one out. He asked me if I ever associated with anyone who wasn't "bad people."

Carlos was waiting when I cleared customs at the San Jose del Cabo airport. Below a scrub of premature gray hair was the sanguine face of an optimist and the lacerated hands of a career fisherman.

"Tag, mi amigo. You look like shit."

"Tengo hambre y estoy cansado."

"We can take care of that. I brought you a chimichanga and some sopaipillas, and a bed waits for you anytime you want it."

"Gracias, Carlos."

We walked out of the terminal and got into Carlos' faded red Ford van. Carlos swung out of the parking lot and onto the highway to Cabo San Lucas.

He asked, "This is a bad situation?"

"Si. A man and his thugs want the man and woman."

"Are you in danger?"

I shrugged.

"You and Koot attract trouble, no?"

"You think it's too late to change?"

"Unless they cut off his cojones—a bull remains a bull."

"I'm going to try to get that picture out of my head, Carlos."

Carlos grinned.

Leaving San Jose del Cabo the Transpeninsular Highway curved toward, then paralleled the shoreline of the Sea of Cortez. In the two years since I had been here, several new hotels had gone up on the beach between the quieter mission town of San Jose del Cabo and the tourist Mecca of Cabo San Lucas.

Cabo San Lucas had been a sleepy fishing village until the forties, before wealthy movie honchos started coming to fish the clear waters of the Pacific and the Sea of Cortez around the tip of the Baja. The word got out, development followed and over the years the sleepy seaside village in the desert swelled to a clamorous tourist town of fifty thousand.

People still came for the fishing. The harbor was usually jammed with expensive high-tech private and charter fishing boats. But now the fishermen share the tip of the peninsula with sun devotees, golfers, surfers, shoppers and the party crowd.

When we reached Cabo San Lucas, Carlos took Lázaro Cárdenas, the main drag running through the tourist area, toward the harbor. Along Lázaro the restaurants, watering holes and high-end boutiques nuzzled up against hundreds of small family owned shops: tour packages, T-shirts, beach wear, shoes, jewelry, crafts, and lots of chintz.

When we got to Ignacio Zaragoza we turned north away from the harbor. After a few blocks the shops and restaurants gave way to residences. After a few more blocks Carlos did a U turn at an intersection and came back down the narrow street, then stopped in front of the Hotel Santa Fe. One of the older hotels in Cabo, the milk-white stucco building stood in the middle of a working-class neighborhood.

"The couple checked into room 209. The other man who move like...how you say..." Carlos jerked his head and arms around.

I asked, "Twitched?"

"Si. One big twitch. He checked into a room upstairs, across the courtyard. All the rooms face the courtyard. The man named Jackie came downstairs and bought some things at the store, then returned to the room. The man who twitch bought some things later, then also returned to his room. All still in their room when I came to pick you up at the airport."

"Where are the hotel entrances?"

Carlos pointed as he spoke. "Three: through the Laundromat, through the small store attached to the hotel, and through the walkway off the parking lot."

I caught a break that all the entrances were visible from the street. A dodge pickup pulled up and stopped next to the truck. Carlos nodded at the driver, then turned back to me.

"Maybe I should stay with you."

"No se preocupe."

"I am a father of six. It is my job to worry."

"Go home to your family, Carlos. Will you give Koot a call and tell him to sit tight?"

"Of course."

We both got out of the van. Carlos climbed into the truck with his friend, and they drove away. I got back in the van on the driver's side, then opened the Styrofoam container and ate the still warm chimichanga, and waited.

Since all the rooms faced the courtyard, I couldn't get up to Jackie and Danika's room without being seen by Curly. I was going to have to wait for Jackie and Danika to leave the hotel. When Curly followed, I'd tail him and wait for a chance to take him. Problem was—Eyes' flight arrived in about an hour.

The tropical sun bore down on the truck like a welder's torch to sheet metal, and the few splinters of shade from a coconut palm were no more than a tease. The salsa on the food punched up the Fahrenheit even more and made me think of Kiki eating the peppers. My shirt was soaked with sweat, but I was hungry and finished the food. I turned on the radio, then gulped water from the quart bottle Carlos had left for me. I understood enough Spanish to know that the tropical depression in the Atlantic had upgraded to a storm, then to a hurricane. It now had a name: Katrina.

I wondered how much money Jackie and Danika had brought to live on. Jackie carried a briefcase out of the swamp with him that may have been full of cash made from the knockoff business with Nads, but you can only take ten thousand in or out of the country. That might be enough to last four or five months if they lived modestly. I wondered if Jackie could live modestly. Judging by the hotel they were staying in, he may be learning.

I had waited about forty-five minutes and neither Jackie nor Danika had left the hotel. Soon I'd have to go into the courtyard and deal with Curly out in the open.

I had finished the bottle and was still thirsty. Alone on a stakeout, drinking a lot of liquid is a bad idea unless you have something to urinate in. I now had an empty bottle for that, but it felt like getting more water was a matter of survival. A boy of about twelve in lime green jeans and a white shirt came up the street on an old Schwinn bicycle.

I said, "Amigolito."

The boy stopped. "Si?"

"Puede usted ayudame." I held out five dollars and nodded toward the store across the street. I was sure the store stocked bottled water for the guests. "Tengo cinco dolores por uno galón de agua." I hadn't had time to exchange dollars for pesos, but in a tourist town, the locals were used to dealing with U.S. dollars.

The boy looked at the store and then back at me. He was trying to figure out why I wouldn't walk across the street and get the water myself. Most kids would have gotten the water, taken the five bucks and peddled off. He knew there was a reason that I couldn't or wouldn't go in the store.

In a few seconds he looked toward the sun and squinted. "Hace calor."

"Si."

He figured that as hot as it was I wanted the water pretty badly. The kid was about to ask me for more money.

He said, "Siete dolores."

We were haggling over the cost of twenty steps for a bottle of water. I knew the kid would take the five, but I was impressed that the he sized up a situation so quickly. He didn't know the circumstances of what was going on, but figured he had an advantage.

I said, "Seis."

The kid wiped his forehead and was going through his spiel again about how hot it was when Danika and Jackie walked out of the hotel and headed down Zaragoza in the direction of the harbor. They were dressed for the beach.

I sank down in the seat so that I was looking through the steering wheel. The kid stopped chattering and looked at me, then followed my gaze as I watched Curly exit the hotel and follow Jackie and Danika.

I let Curly get about forty yards ahead, then I got out of the van.

"Hasta luego, amigolito." I turned and trailed Curly, trailing Danika and Jackie. The kid caught up to me and paced alongside.

The kid nodded toward Curly. "Mister, that man does not know you are following, si?"

The kid spoke English. And again he read the situation.

"Go away, kid."

"Okay, mister. Maybe I will go and walk with him."

Hustled by a twelve year-old. The kid created his own opportunities and would probably make something of himself. Hopefully, he'd stay on the sunny side of the law. While we walked, I pulled out my money clip and removed a five and two ones and gave it to the kid.

He tapped his chest twice with his closed fist, like an NBA player after a windmill jam, then he nodded toward Curly and said, "Be careful, mister."

"He's not a problem. It's smart kids I've gotta watch out for."

The kid grinned, then peeled off and headed back up the street.

I couldn't see Danika and Jackie ahead of us. I stayed on Curly and hung back, but wasn't too concerned with him spotting me. He was focused on his quarry and thought he was at the end of this caravan.

As we got closer to the harbor, the streets were strangled with autos and the pedestrian traffic on the narrow sidewalks bulged and slowed to a lava flow. In the crowd it was harder to keep Curly in sight, and I had to close the gap between us so I wouldn't lose him. I veered into the street several times to get around tourists window-shopping or huddles of locals jawing. Once I stepped into the street and a guy in a lowrider sat on the horn and growled, "Gringo loco."

When Curly reached Lázaro Cárdenas, he crossed the street and walked east. By the time I got to the light, it had changed and a steady flow of traffic kept me from crossing. I turned up Lázaro Cárdenas and kept pace with Curly from the opposite side of the street. I glanced ahead and saw Jackie and Danika, just before they turned right on a street leading to the bay.

When Curly made the right behind them I dashed through traffic to the other side of the street, then trailed them all to the water. From the top of the hill I could see Jackie and Danika get in one of the water taxis that run across Bahia San Lucas to El Arco, a natural rock arch jutting up from the sea at the tip of the peninsula, and to Playa del Amour, Lover's Beach.

Curly hung back beside one of the patio bars until Danika and Jackie were a third of the way across the bay, then he boarded one of the water taxis. When he was underway I made my way down to the water and got my own taxi.

The boatman, Miguel, introduced himself. After we shoved off, Miguel pulled a bottle of Cuervo tequila from under his seat and swilled it. When he held the bottle up in offering, I begged off. Miguel's bloodshot eyes were coated with the milky film of a boozer whose liver was not long for the world. And since Miguel wasn't likely to get on any list for a transplant, Miguel wasn't long for the world either.

In the distance, I saw the boat carrying Jackie and Danika run up on the beach at the little cove on the bay side of the peninsula. The water was calm here and Jackie and Danika went ashore.

Curly had his boatman slow to an idle about eighty yards offshore. I had Miguel curl off toward the arch. As we passed to within forty yards of Curly's taxi, I slumped down and turned away in case he glanced in my direction.

When we got close to the arch, I had Miguel nestle in along the rocky granite cliffs within sight of the beach. We were at the southernmost tip of the Baja Peninsula where the muscular waters of the Pacific Ocean met the Sea of Cortez, only slightly less brawny.

I stayed low in the boat and watched Danika and Jackie swim the sapphire water of the protected cove. Curly and his boatman sat tight on the other side of the cove while Miguel and I moored near El Arco. If Miguel was curious about what I was up to, he didn't ask.

After a while Jackie and Danika swam ashore, gathered their things and walked over the dunes toward the Pacific Ocean side of the peninsula. Curly had his boatman move in and put him ashore.

I gave Curly a minute to top the dunes, then had Miguel zip us to the beach. I had to pay him in advance to wait, but I wasn't worried that he'd cut out on me. These water taxi guys were licensed and depended almost entirely on the tourist trade. A few reported rip-offs and they'd be out of business. I felt even more certain he'd stay put when Miguel pulled another bottle of tequila from under the helm.

From the cove I scrambled up the small sand dune that cut a swath through the jagged gray rock outcroppings. From the top of the rise I could see the bay and the Sea of Cortez behind me and the Pacific Ocean ahead. I looked to my right and saw Curly peering from behind a large rock formation, then saw Danika and Jackie strolling down the beach.

It was easy to understand why they called the Pacific side of the peninsula Divorce Beach. Monstrous waves, riptides and undertows, metaphors for the treachery of a marriage beyond redemption. Also, it could divorce your body from your soul.

Jackie and Danika strolled toward the cliffs that jut out over the ocean. I watched Curly move with them, hugging the many rock outcroppings for cover, then I moved in behind. Since the ocean on this side was too dangerous to swim, few people were on the beach. A teenage couple examined some sea creature that had washed ashore, and a family of four picnicked.

When Jackie and Danika got to the cliffs, they climbed up through the crevices of the sharp, angular rocks. When they had disappeared among the boulders, Curly jogged to the base of the cliff and made his way up into the rocks. I ran to the cliffs and climbed a different route to avoid Curly spotting me.

The crevices were wide enough to get through, but the spiny-sharp rocks made climbing slow. Halfway to the top I came out of a fissure and got a view of the waves exploding on the serrated rocks below. Gigantic walls of foamy water shot up the cliffs and misted over me.

Near the top, the rocks funneled closer together and I had to wedge-step my way up until I reached a shelf above. It was a short climb to the top from here.

As I took a step a shadow moved to my left, and I jumped a second before I felt the blade slash across my bicep. I shot my arm out and blocked the next stab coming from above Curly's head. From unsolid footing I sprang against Curly and crashed him into the rock he had hidden behind.

It knocked some of the breath out of him, but he held onto the long kitchen knife, which he probably got from the hotel. I grabbed his knife arm with both hands and bashed it against the sharp rock.

Conley Clark

He dropped the blade, then kneed me in the groin, which bent me over.

Curly went for the knife. I pushed through the pain and tackled him as he came up with the blade. We went down hard on the sharp rock, which, ripped hide from my hip. It was a hell of a time for the thought to pop into my head that if I had become a lawyer I could have avoided all this. But there it was.

Curly and I got to our feet at the edge of the cliff, then he charged and his momentum carried us over the edge. We separated in the air, then plunged into the thundering surf.

When I surfaced I saw Curly's bloody body on the jagged rocks at the base of the cliff, his legs dangling in the water. I turned toward the wall of a ten-foot wave as it crashed over me. The wave drove me under and into the sandy bottom. It felt like my shoulder and head had been bashed with a sledge hammer covered with number four sandpaper. I tried to get my feet under me to push off, but the force of the water tumbled me across the bottom.

A few seconds later the fury of the wave was spent, but the powerful rip grabbed me and took me back out. My air was almost gone. I spun until I felt sand, then planted my feet and pushed off, kicking as hard as I could. After a few seconds I broke the surface. I vacuumed in the biggest and finest breath I'd ever taken.

I glanced toward Curly's body and saw the water erupt around him. A huge bull shark surfaced and snapped down on Curly's legs, then the bloody body and the shark were gone. The last thing I remembered was another wave cresting over me.

I felt the beach under me. Then I felt hairy lips on mine, then the smell of onions and beer being blown into my lungs. I opened my eyes and was eyeball to eyeball with the thick brown face of a soaking wet hombre.

I turned my head and heaved up about a pint of salt water, then heaved some more. When the man saw I had decided not to divorce, he pulled his face back and grinned, a gold tooth gleaming in the sunlight. It was a beautiful face.

Leaning over the hombre's shoulder were Jackie and Danika.

TWENTY-EIGHT

Danika, Jackie, my rescuer Hector and a couple of members of Hector's family were after me to go to the hospital. I let my mind cruise around inside my body while my eyes checked the outside to see if I agreed. The knife slash on my biceps wasn't deep enough to rip muscle and, except for a slight queasiness from too much salt water, the rest of me seemed more or less intact. All I really needed was a few days in a hammock under a beach cabana, but that would have to wait. I wanted to spend some time with Hector, maybe buy him a meal and several Cervezas, but that would have to wait too, so I thanked him with inadequate words and we said our goodbyes.

Danika and Jackie put my arms over their shoulders, and we made our way down the beach, heading toward the cove.

Danika asked, "What happened?"

"One of Castille's men followed you. I followed him. He and I did a cliff dive together, and a shark chose *him*."

Miguel was anchored about thirty yards offshore, at the edge of the cove. I waved him in to shore, then we waded up to our knees and Jackie and Miguel helped Danika up and over the gunwale and into the boat. Jackie formed a stirrup with his hands for me. I stepped into it, and Danika and Miguel grabbed me and hoisted me up and over the gunwale, then pulled Jackie on board. Miguel climbed over me and went to the back of the boat and cranked up, then headed across the bay.

When we were underway, Danika tore off a strip of her blouse and wrapped it around the cut on my arm to slow the bleeding. Jackie looked like he was feeling guilty. He tried to find a way out of it.

"It had to be the cop. He must have told Castille we were at your friend Marty's house. They must have followed us from there."

I propped myself up against the side of the boat. "You're not thinking clearly, Jackie. The cop thought you were at the safehouse.

That was the idea. He and Castille don't know about Marty's, and they'd still be waiting at airports and train stations if you hadn't gone rabbit on us. You walked right into it. How'd that not occur to you?"

Jackie looked frustrated. Danika looked remorseful.

Danika said, "I was frightened."

"I understand that."

"We should have trusted you."

"We're your best chance, Danika."

"Yes. I know that now."

Jackie said, "I still can't figure why you and your partner would do all this for us."

I was worn out and didn't really want to have this conversation. I asked, "Why'd you risk your life to help Danika?"

"That's different. I love her."

"As much as you love Danika, Koot and I hate what the Castilles of the world do to people."

Jackie looked at me for a while, maybe trying to figure me out, then he glanced at Danika and back at me.

"From now on, we'll do whatever you say."

"Castille's men are on their way. I say we get out of here."

At the hotel, Jackie and Danika crammed their clothes into their suitcases while I called Carlos and asked him to take us to La Paz, a city on the Sea of Cortez side of the Baja peninsula, a two hour drive from Cabo. It was too risky to fly out of Cabo; we could run into Eyes and his thugs at the small airport. When I hung up with Carlos, I called and booked the three of us on the late flight from La Paz to Houston, then called Koot and filled him in and told him to pick us up at the airport.

When he can't find Curly, Eyes will call Castille. Castille might put men at the New Orleans airport again to watch for Jackie and Danika coming back into the country. Houston was a safer choice.

Jackie snapped the locks shut on his bag, then stood on the bed and slid a panel in the drop ceiling out of its frame and removed a briefcase. Jackie slid the panel back then sat on the bed and opened the briefcase. It was full of cash. Jackie pulled out three stacks of fifties and held them for me to take.

"I want you and Koot to have this."

"Can't do it, Jackie."

He looked hurt. "I know what Frank and I did to get this money was wrong."

"It's where you go from here that counts."

"We only have about ten thousand, and we're going to use it to get away from that sadistic ..." Jackie had white-knuckled the briefcase. He took a deep breath. "Then we're going to make a new start, and it'll be an honest one."

Danika turned to me. "I am sad that you judge us, Tag. If you had been where I have been..."

"I'm not judging you—either of you. Under the circumstances, the money serves a good purpose. But I still can't take any of it."

"What about Koot and your friend Carlos?"

"Carlos would refuse politely. Koot would be insulted."

Jackie looked at Danika, then put the money back in the briefcase and snapped it shut.

Jackie said, "I think I understand."

"You'd be one of the few. Now we have to get going."

I wanted to wait for Carlos at the street so we could leave quickly when he arrived. Danika grabbed her suitcase and Jackie clutched his luggage and briefcase, then we left the room and walked to the open stairs leading down to the courtyard. When we reached the bottom of the landing, I spotted Eyes and two of his men get out of a rental and enter the courtyard.

I shoved Jackie and Danika into an open room the maid was cleaning and closed the door. I held my finger to my lips for them to keep quiet.

The maid stuck her head out of the bathroom. She looked surprised, but not alarmed.

I said quietly. "Un momento por favor."

She gave us a bemused look, then went back to the bathroom. I glanced at my watch. Eyes and his men had gotten here fast from the airport.

I cracked the curtain enough to watch Eyes and his men cross the courtyard and head for the stairs. The two men with Eyes, one a swaggering pretty boy, the other a pug with a heat rash, checked out the women in bikinis around the pool, but Eyes was looking up to the second floor, looking for Jackie and Danika's room number. He saw it, then looked for Curly's room.

I eased the curtain closed and listened to the footsteps ascend the stairs. When they reached the second story landing, I grabbed Danika's luggage, opened the door and motioned for Danika and Jackie to follow me. We heard the men's steps above us as they walked toward Curly's room, which was at the end of the landing. We moved directly under them. When we reached the end of the building we'd have to risk a dash across open courtyard to the Laundromat, a good fifteen feet away. We'd be visible from the open second floor walkway for two or three seconds, but if we could time it to their knock at Curly's room, maybe they'd all be facing the door.

If we made it to the Laundromat, we could cut through to the street and hide in a shop or beside a building, then watch for Carlos. I pointed to the Laundromat. Jackie and Danika nodded that they understood.

I looked and saw Carlos enter the courtyard. He glanced at the women by the pool, then he saw me. I pointed up and his eyes went to the men on the landing above us. Then I motioned for him to go back out to the van. The expression on his face told me someone above noticed Carlos looking our way.

I quickly herded Jackie and Danika back against the wall. Carlos turned and left the courtyard. I saw the toe end of a pair of shoes at the railing above. Then the pug leaned out over the railing and spotted us.

He squawked, "They're under us."

I barked, "Drop the luggage. Go."

We bolted for the Laundromat, Jackie and Danika ahead of me, Jackie holding the briefcase. I glanced up and saw Eyes and the two men run back down the walkway for the stairs.

When we got through the Laundromat and onto the street, Carlos was starting the van, some forty yards away. I glanced back through the Laundromat and saw Eyes and his men hit the bottom of the landing and sprint toward us.

Carlos squealed tires and raced up to us, then slammed on brakes in front of us. I popped open the side door and the three of us leaped in. Carlos didn't wait for me to close the door. He floored it just as Eyes and his men burst onto the street. The pretty boy raced for the van and managed to grab the handle of the open side door. Just as he pulled himself in I braced myself against the other side of the van and drove my heel into his chest. He fell into the street and rolled. I looked back and saw Eyes and the pug run for their rental car.

I closed the van door and climbed up front with Carlos. In the front passenger seat was a fresh gallon of water. The kid had kept his end of the bargain.

I put the water on the floor and crawled into the seat. Carlos turned off Zaragoza onto a narrow residential street. We were headed in the direction of the Transpeninsular. We hadn't gone two blocks before Carlos had to stop for a pack of bony dogs dawdling in the middle of the street. He sat on the horn, and all but a couple of mongrels moved to the side of the road. Carlos blew again.

I reached to the floor and grabbed the bag of sopaipillas Carlos gave me this morning. I tossed the bag onto the sidewalk, and the pastries spilled out. The two hounds that blocked us were the first to spring on the food. Carlos jammed the accelerator. I looked back and saw Eyes and the pug turn the corner and speed toward us.

At Leona Vacario, Carlos slowed at the red light just long enough to find a small opening in the stream of cross traffic, then he punched it through the intersection. The light was still red when Eyes and the pug got to it, but the driver barely slowed. A car slid sideways into a parked car to avoid hitting the rental.

I turned toward the front and tried to figure out what I was looking at in the next block.

Carlos said, "Sheeet."

We were bearing down fast on two guys cutting wall-to-wall carpet that had been rolled out into the middle of the street. Carlos blasted the horn, and the men lunged to the curb as we wheeled over the carpet.

At the next intersection Carlos made a hard right, then an immediate left and then whipped into a narrow alley behind a row of small casitas. He turned into the backyard of one of the casitas. We watched for the rental. If they found us here, we'd be trapped.

Carlos said, "Back in a jiff."

A jiff. Carlos has been chartering too many fishermen from Omaha.

Soon, he returned with a revolver stuck in the waistband of his pants. He got in and placed the pistol on the dash. "We wait here a little."

After a few minutes I got out of the van and eased down the alley to the street. No sign of the rental.

We got back on the street and headed for the highway. Eyes and the pug would be cruising the streets for us, so we were on edge. I had Carlos pull in behind a pharmacia so I could buy diabetes meds. I had lost mine in the water—again. Fortunately, a prescription wasn't needed in Mexico. I also picked up some Keflex antibiotic. A diabetic with an open wound is ripe for infection, and the ocean is full of bacteria that could stage an unfriendly takeover. I didn't have time to get stitches, so I bought some steri-strips to pull the two sides of the wound together. I got ointment and bandages and a bag of tamales for the trip. I scanned the area for Eyes, then we pulled onto the street.

I took my meds and the Keflex as we got on the Transpeninsular. Danika put some ointment on my scraped hip and cut arm, then laid the steri-strips across the knife cut to pull both sides of the wound together. Then she bandaged my hip.

Night draped us before we had traveled forty miles into the desolate wilderness on the La Paz road. The heat had dropped from suffocating to stifling, still hot enough that the breeze gave little relief. We talked about what had happened.

Danika said, "Carlos, I'm sorry this became dangerous for you."

Carlos turned back to look at her, serious. "You were in need of help. There is no more to say."

So we rode in silence.

Today, death stepped out of the shadows and put a clammy hand on me. This time, like times before, I was able to slap the hand away. Curly wasn't so lucky. I wondered how many more men like Curly, who killed for no other reason than "Boss's orders," I'd have to deal with before *my* luck ran out.

TWENTY-NINE

We tracked and backtracked and worked our way deeper toward the center of the sculpted hedge maze. When we reached the core, Adrienne and I removed our clothes and I lay on my stomach on the soft grass while Adrienne lay across me with her breasts pressed into the contour of my scarred back. I felt at peace.

Then the plane bumped down in Houston and Adrienne and the feeling of peace vanished. But there was still a maze—and we had to find our way out of it.

Koot met us outside the security check area. It was after midnight, and we still had a five hour drive back to New Orleans.

Koot looked at Jackie and Danika, "Is this gonna be a regular thing?"

Jackie said, "It won't happen again, Koot."

Danika said, "We are very sorry. I had...how you say...my panic attacked."

"It'll do that sometimes," Koot said.

"We are very much grateful to you and Tag."

Koot said, "From now on we're a team, okay?"

Danika and Jackie nodded.

We walked to the lot, climbed in the Outback and headed out of Houston.

I sat up front with Koot. He looked at me.

"So you got your plumb line twanged pretty good?"

"Touch and go this time, partner. I actually saw my life flash before me."

"Yeah?"

"That was a disappointment."

"Do better."

"Thanks for the encouragement."

Koot looked at me some more.

I said, "You got something else to say?"

Conley Clark

"Yeah. Next time you leave base camp I'm gonna be with you. Got it?"

"Yes, my Sherpa."

From the airport we made our way to I-10, which would take us all the way into New Orleans. Danika and Jackie soon fell asleep in the backseat. In a low voice I told Koot about Curly providing a meal for a bull shark, about Hector pulling me back from the brink, and about getting away from Eyes and his men.

Koot said, "Grady and the lieutenant want to meet. They're worried Jackie and Danika might run again."

"First I'm going to wake this dealer, Shaman, and see if he has a name for us. You take first watch at Marty's. We'll get with Grady and the lieutenant later this morning."

"This guy Shaman any trouble?"

"He tried to play that hand. Now we have an understanding."

"What if he's forgetful?"

"I'll remind him." I nodded toward Danika and Jackie in the back seat. "Action's coming, partner, but tonight, you're a guardian angel."

Koot blew out his breath and nodded.

I took a swig of cranberry juice I'd gotten at the airport, then said, "We need to find the Sojourn and make sure Castille knows who stole it. We do that and maybe he lets Danika and Jackie walk."

"That's a big 'maybe'."

"Finding the stuff is a big 'maybe'."

I got two hours of sleep and woke as we rolled into New Orleans at dawn. The city was quiet, and a low fog absorbed the pink of first light. We got off I-10 at Tulane Avenue and drove through the cottony vapor toward Marty's house.

At Marty's we let ourselves in with the key he'd given us, which roused Marty. He shuffled into the living room in his aubergine velour robe and shower clogs, adjusting his hair piece as he entered.

Marty said, "Christ, you guys keep shitty hours."

We all looked at each other, then erupted in laughter. With guys trying to kill us, we'd been short on laughter. Now it poured out like water over a spillway. Maybe today would be a good day.

Grady had gotten the address for Willard Coquille, a.k.a. Shaman, by running Coquille's license plate number that Trish took down for me at the party. Grady had given the address to Koot while I was in Cabo. I took a quick shower to wash off the sweat and ocean salt, put on a change of clothes Koot had in the car, then drove over to Shaman's place.

Shaman's apartment was in a two-story building in what used to be a tony neighborhood off St. Charles. The building was a dirty mustard stucco with a symbol that looked like an Egyptian hieroglyph embedded over the arched entryway. At each corner of the facade, a date palm nuzzled against cracking plaster. Both trees were dead. The Egyptian motif in this neighborhood of mostly Victorians and revivals invited attention, like a big-busted woman brandishing her décolletage in front of the missionaries.

I parked on the street and walked to the building entrance. I found the name on the panel, only Coquille used Shaman instead of his real name. Probably wasn't expecting forms from the I.R.S. He wasn't expecting me either at 7:00 a.m.

I rang the buzzer on the panel and stayed on it for a couple of minutes. No answer. Maybe Shaman and Darius had gotten fully loaded last night and were fully unconscious now.

I found the apartment number next door to Coquille's on the panel and buzzed. In a few seconds the voice of an elderly woman answered.

"Yes, who is it?"

"I apologize for disturbing you, ma'am. I'm the exterminator. Mr. Coquille next door to you gave us the key to his apartment before he left town. I'm supposed to spray for a bad roach infestation, only he forgot someone would have to buzz me in."

"If you ask me, it's the people who go in and out of his place at all hours that should be sprayed."

"Yes, ma'am."

"Well, I can't just let you in. You could be just another one of those degenerates."

"I understand. We'll reschedule with Mr. Coquille when he returns in a week or so. Of course, by then many of the roaches will migrate to other apartments."

"Oh, for heaven's sake."

"And they lay eggs."

"The filth."

"Yes, ma'am."

"You spray the place real good. And spray some in his corn flakes while you're at it."

The buzzer sounded, and I went in. I walked the one flight up, found Shaman's apartment and hammered the door.

I heard about six locks snap open at the apartment next door. I grabbed the fire extinguisher off the wall and held it down by my side. It was the old kind of extinguisher with a hose. From a distance, or if her eyesight was weak, it might look like a tank of bug spray.

Finally locks stopped clicking and the woman stuck her head out of the door. She looked at me, then at the fire extinguisher, then back at me.

"You're not an exterminator."

"In my own way, ma'am, I am."

She gave me disgusted, then closed the door and snapped through the sequence of locks. I hated deceiving little old ladies.

I banged on the door some more. Finally the dead bolt slid out and the door cracked open. It was a teenaged girl with a shaved head and a *DNR* tatoo on her forehead. I'd seen DO NOT RESUSITATE tatoos on other parts of people's bodies, usually homicide victims, but this was the first one I'd seen on a noggin. Like an auto zoom the girl's eyes searched for focus. She was wearing only a long black silk shirt which barely covered her pubic hair.

"Yeah?"

"Tell Willard that Boudreau is here."

Flat. "Who's Willard?"

"The guy you're sleeping with."

She gave me a blank look, then stepped away from the door. I pushed it open and saw a shadow behind a wall off the foyer. I pulled my Kahr and stepped back into the hall out of the doorway. "It's not worth it, Darius."

Darius Lewis stepped out from behind the wall into the doorway. We were aiming at each other. He lowered the .22 and let it dangle in his hand.

He said, "Wasn't expecting *you*. Just being cautious."

"When you protect a sleaze bag—caution is a good idea." Lewis had white adhesive tape over the bridge of his nose and cotton stuck in one nostril.

I said, "Sorry about the nose."

"Yeah."

"You were a hellofa football player, Darius. People remember you. You could do a lot better than being meat for this guy."

Darius shrugged, then I heard from behind him, "The fuck you coming around here this hour, Boudreau?" Shaman was standing in the bedroom door in his faux leopard skin briefs. "We just got to bed 'bout an hour ago."

"I'm on a different clock, Sham-man—and the seconds are ticking."

"The fuck, man. We were at Jackson Park at noon, like you said. You wasted my time."

"I apologize, Willard. I had a problem I had to take care of."

"Nobody calls me Willard."

"Have it your way, Sham-man."

Coquille walked to the bar and shook a cigarette from a pack and lit it. Then he picked some tobacco off the tip of his tongue with the cigarette hand.

I said, "I'm kind of in a hurry, Sham-man. You got a name for me?"

"I got nothing you don't start showing some respect."

"You're a drug dealer. You don't get respect."

"I get a lot of respect."

"Respect. You think spouting some pseudo-cosmic-liberate-your-mind babble is getting that for you? You're their supplier, Sham-man. You don't provide the stuff—I'm guessing you don't get the time of day from those kids."

I glanced at Darius and saw him lower his head and work at stifling a grin.

Shaman went on. "They see me with a nice ride and a roll of bills and they want that."

"That's not respect, Sham-man. That's envy with a short memory. Now tell me what you've got."

He took a long drag on his cig. He was probably considering telling Darius to shoot me, but I think he knew that wouldn't happen. He might have been considering standing up to me himself. I knew he wouldn't, but his pride had been bruised and he needed a little time to weigh one wound against the certainty of another. I let him have a few seconds.

Finally he said, "How is it you're still alive, Boudreau?"

"A good diet."

"Uh hunh. I been asking around about the Sojourn, man. Took some chances. Some people don't like it when you ask questions."

"I don't like it when I don't get answers."

"You a hardass bastard."

I waited. He took a drag on his cig, trying to convince himself he was in control and had all the time in the world.

Finally he said, "Found out who's been trying to move the sweet stuff. I told him I had an interested buyer, like you said. It's set up for tonight, 9 o'clock. Is this going to be a buy or a bust?"

I ignored the question. "Name?"

"You gonna keep your word? Let me run my business?"

"It's like I said."

He hesitated, maybe still not trusting I'd leave him alone. Then he said, "A street pimp named Kiki."

THIRTY

Kiki boosting Castille's Sojourn didn't add up. Shopping the drug around New Orleans would be extremely risky, and Kiki wouldn't climb that far out on a narrow limb. I think someone else stole it and was forcing Kiki to front for him.

Then again, maybe Kiki wanted to get away from Nads and was willing to risk it all for a score big enough to start a fantasy life somewhere. Of course, it would have to be somewhere on another planet if Nads found out Kiki had been ambitious to the tune of eighty-five large and didn't cut him in on it.

Kiki might have had the opportunity to take the drugs at one of Castille's parties. Maybe he wandered into Castille's office or another room and found a bag of the party stash left out, grabbed it and stuck it in his car, then returned to the party. If he did it about the same time Danika and Jackie left the party and made their run, the suspicion would fall on them, not Kiki. But that was too much coincidence for me.

The irony in all this was as thick as a consigliere's take of the profits. Kiki works for Nads. Kiki is selling drugs stolen from Nads' rival. I get Kiki to set up a meeting with Nads so I can ask Nads to front me eighty-five thousand dollars to buy the drugs stolen from Castille back from Kiki. It's better than a mini-series.

I went home to see if Kiki had called about the meeting with Nads. When I got in the house, Seven pretended I hadn't been away for a day and generally ignored me. Of course, if Koot hadn't fed them yesterday, she would have been reading me the feline riot act. Santana jumped me with his usual gale force enthusiasm. I put out some fresh food and water, then checked the answering machine.

Adrienne had left a message for me to call. She sounded on edge. Koot told Adrienne yesterday that Jackie and Danika bolted and that I went to Mexico after them.

The next message was from Kiki. The meeting with Nads was set for 2:30 this afternoon at the India Palace. Kiki sounded pretty edgy too, but I was sure he didn't know we were the prospective buyer. I was guessing he was being threatened, and was scared.

If I can get the money from Nads, we'll make the buy tonight, then follow Kiki and the money. Hopefully, the money will lead us to someone else. We find out who, get the money back for Nads, get the drugs and trade with Castille—the Sojourn and the one who stole it—for Danika's and Jackie's freedom. If it turns out Kiki was the one who stole the drugs, so be it. Whether Castille would keep his end of any bargain was the wild card in all this.

No one shadowed me on the way to Adrienne's, but I knew I'd be hearing from Castille soon, and the volume would be turned up from here on out. Adrienne, Blanche and Brent were there when I arrived. Everyone was anxious, so I skipped the greeting I wanted to give them.

"Jackie and Danika are okay."

Adrienne's shoulders relaxed, and the breath she had been holding streamed free. Adrienne came over and hugged me. "God, I can't take much more of this."

The heat from Adrienne's body radiated through me. I felt that, given time, that warmth might heal some old wounds.

Brent said, "You went to Mexico and saved Uncle Jackie and his friend from the bad guys. That's really cool, Tag."

Blanche said, "Way cool."

The danger was not over, something Adrienne and Blanche were aware of, but none of us wanted to think about that now.

I said, "Why don't we pick up some gumbo and go celebrate with your Uncle Jackie and Danika?"

Brent said, "Uncle Jackie likes jumbo shrimp."

"Then let's gumbo and jumbo—to go."

Brent grinned and said, "Tag's the coolest, isn't he, Mom?"

Adrienne gave me a look I liked. "He covers the entire temperature range."

Brent said, "Huh?"

Blanche said, "Never mind. Let's go see our other darling boy."

Brent helped Blanche put some things in a suitcase Adrienne had laid out for Jackie and Danika: Toiletries, some packaged food, a blanket and pillows.

While they packed, Adrienne led me out on the porch.

"Why did they run—after all you and Koot have done to protect them?"

"Castille is trying to kill Jackie, and Danika would probably wish she were dead if Castille got her back. They cracked under the strain."

She pushed her hair straight back and held it on her head and took time to consider that.

"I guess if someone were trying to kill me...maybe I'd do the same." She looked at me. "Can you keep them alive?"

"We're working on something. If that doesn't pan out, we may have to cut off the serpent's head."

"You mean go after Castille?"

"Yeah."

"But he has men around him."

"But I have Koot." I smiled.

Adrienne didn't. She let out a big sigh. "If they survive this— what then—go someplace else and Jackie continues being a criminal?"

"He's got someone he cares about now. That can make you reassess your life. I think Jackie has done that. We get through this —I think their chances for a decent life are good." Adrienne smiled weakly. I said, "In my spare time, I've been wondering about the chances for you and me."

"I've thought about the same thing." She smiled. "In my spare time."

"Should I be giddy?"

"You know how grateful ..."

"Yeah, you've said that."

"Hold on. It's just that with this nightmare we've been in, I haven't had time to sort out the rest of what I've been feeling."

"You'll keep me updated?"

She smiled. "Nightly."

"Nightly would be good."

We went back inside. When Blanche had finished packing, I put the suitcase in the trunk of the Sebring. Brent wanted to sit up front with me, so Adrienne and Blanche sat in the back. I stopped at a seafood place on Carrolton and picked up some shrimp and gumbo, then we headed up to Marty's. When we got to his house, I drove past and did a sweep around the block for lowlife. It was clear.

Koot watched from the window as we climbed the steps to Marty's Victorian. When we entered the house, Jackie, Danika, and Marty were sitting around the living room drinking coffee.

They all stood, then Brent walked cautiously over to Jackie. It had been a while, and Brent looked like he wasn't sure how to act.

Jackie said, "Hey, nephew."

"Hey, Uncle Jackie."

Jackie tousled Brent's hair.

Blanche came over and hugged Jackie. Then she looked him in the eye. "It's time you changed your ways, Jackie Kanawhite."

"I have, Blanche. I swear."

"You never could lie to me, so I'm inclined to believe you."

Blanche turned toward Danika.

"Our darling boy is not really the horse's patoot he's been trying to be. But then I'm sure you already know that."

Danika looked puzzled. "Patoot?"

Brent turned his butt toward her and pointed, then giggled.

"Ohh." Danika smiled and looked at Jackie and then at Blanche. "He has been a very good horse's patoot."

That got some laughs, and Danika looked embarrassed. It was cute.

Blanche said, "If Jackie cares for you, then we care for you."

Danika looked like that was hard to take in. "Thank you."

Jackie put his hand on Danika's arm, then turned toward Adrienne, who had been hanging back. He stepped over to her.

"Hello, A."

"Jackie."

Jackie looked contrite. "Why did you get involved?"

"You're my family, Jackie."

"I didn't think you wanted to lay claim to that anymore."

"Stop with the melodrama. I just didn't want you bringing trouble to Brent and me."

Jackie nodded slightly. "We're caught under a squall line here, A. I'm sorry you got caught under it too. But we're really glad you sent Tag and Koot. They're the reason we're still alive."

"And you're going to stay alive."

Adrienne put her arms around Jackie, and they hugged for a long time. Blanche teared up. I guess for all the regrets and lost time. I let fall a couple of tears too. Some tough guy. I looked over at Koot. He never cried, but his eyes were jolly.

Finally Adrienne broke the embrace.

"Now, let us meet Danika."

Danika joined them in the middle of the living room.

Jackie made the introductions. "The one who always gets the first and last word is Blanche. And this is my nephew, Brent."

"Hello, Brent."

Brent smiled, a little shy.

"And this is my sister, Adrienne." He looked at Adrienne and back at Danika. "This is Danika, the woman I love."

Danika said, "Jackie has told me all about you and Brent and Blanche."

"Yes, well, Brent is innocent."

Adrienne took the suitcase from me. "We brought you some things."

Danika said, "Thank you."

Adrienne touched Danika's arm. "I'm so sorry for what you've been through. If anyone can help you get away from that life and that terrible man, Tag and Koot can."

Danika said, "And Jackie."

Adrienne looked warmly at Jackie. "And my brother Jackie."

Conley Clark

THIRTY-0NE

While everyone ate, I went in Marty's bedroom and called Grady. I told him Koot and I had to take care of something tonight and asked him to take an evening shift at Marty's. He agreed to come over and didn't ask what Koot and I were up to. He knew I wouldn't hold anything back unless I had good reason. This deal would be dirty, and Grady and the lieutenant couldn't have knowledge of it. Grady hated being left in the dark, but he knew how it worked.

After I got off the phone, Koot, Marty and I went out on the porch while Adrienne, Jackie, Danika, Blanche and Brent continued catching up. We sat in the wicker chairs and pumped our lungs against the glutinous humidity.

I said, "A deal is set for tonight."

"Will Nads come through with the money?" Koot asked.

"I'm working on that."

Marty said, "We're talking eleventh hour here, aren't we?"

I said, "I come up with the money, you still willing to make the exchange?"

Kiki didn't know Marty, so he wouldn't connect Marty to Koot or me.

Marty said, "Do I need to worry?"

"We'll be close."

"I want you spooning me."

Koot said, "Front and back."

I said, "You won't have to worry about the bag man. He's not dangerous."

Koot turned to me. "You know him?"

"Kiki."

Koot looked surprised. "Kiki—with delusions of grandeur?"

"Probably didn't have a choice."

"That sounds more like it. So we let Marty do the deal with Kiki —then secure Marty—then follow Kiki to the mystery man."

Marty said, "Then what?"

I said, "From there we make it up as we go."

Marty rolled his eyes. "The professionals."

After a couple of hours I took Adrienne, Blanche and Brent home. On the way I said to Adrienne, "It'll be safer if you and Brent stay with Blanche for a few days."

Adrienne nodded, then she said, "Brent is supposed to spend the night with Clayton."

"That's fine. Tell him you'll be at Blanche's, but not why."

"Where will you be?"

"Trying to catch a thief."

I had a little over an hour before I was to meet Nads, so I drove to the *Vieux Carré* early to grab something to eat. With all the hubbub and the planning, I had forgotten to eat at Marty's. I parked at the townhome on Saint Philip and walked down to the Kosher Creole Kitchen on Decatur.

I ordered red snapper etoufee over rice, a side of boiled okra and onions and an unsweetened iced tea. The food was steaming, and the spices in the etoufee balanced perfectly with the flavor of the snapper. I tried to take my mind off the problems ahead long enough to savor the meal, but the problems and the flavors wrangled. At about 2:20 I paid the bill and walked to the India Palace for the meeting with Nads.

When I arrived at the restaurant, Giancarlo met me at the door.

"Boudreau."

I handed him my Kahr. He motioned for one of his soldiers to pat me down.

I said, "As many years as I tried to bust you guys and you still don't trust me."

"Boudreau, all you got is jokes."

"I've got all my fingers."

"That could change."

Early in his career as a soldier Giancarlo had his pinky cleaved on his right hand for screwing the wife of a capo. These guys talk about "family" like it's a thing of honor, but I didn't know many heads of families that cut off its members fingers for an in-and-out.

I played a dangerous game tweaking him about his finger, but the frustration of years of not being able to nail these guys...I couldn't help myself.

The soldier finished patting me down, then he stepped back and nodded to Giancarlo. Giancarlo stepped aside for me to approach. Nads sat at a booth in the back of the restaurant under a painting of the Hindu god Kali, the destroyer. No doubt, Nads' favorite booth.

Except for Liano, his soldiers and one Indian server standing in the corner, the restaurant was empty. As a precaution, Nads usually ate after regular serving hours when the diners had left. If people lingered after regular hours, Liano sent his soldiers in while he sat in the car. The soldiers stood over the diners until they got the message and cleared out. Restaurant owners weren't known to address the diners' complaints.

Nads was bent over a spread of samosas, tandoori chicken, spinach paneer, lemon pickle and some pooris. Nads was sort of a Mafia oddball in his preference for Indian food over Sicilian. He glanced up as he stuffed a samosa in his mouth.

Still chewing. "Whatta you want?"

"I need some money."

"Now, after all these years, you want money from me. I guess it's never too late to wise up."

"I want money—and I'm going to ask you for something else."

"One thing at a time. So how much you want?"

"Eighty-five large."

Nads stopped chewing and cocked his head and looked at me.

"You serious?"

"As a bad prostate."

"Then maybe they ought to call *you* Nads."

"You get it all back. I keep nothing."

"Sit down, Boudreau."

I slid in the booth.

Nads picked up a chicken leg and gnawed on it. "What's the eighty-five for?"

"Two people's lives."

Nads said, "I give you the money, two of my men go with you."

"Can't do it."

"Then negotiating's over. I'll give you five thousand to run errands for me. That's probably five more than you got put away for retirement."

I opened the left side of my sport coat to show Nads some papers in the inside pocket. Then I slowly reached in my pocket and retrieved them, then placed the papers on the table.

"What's this?"

"It's the deed to my house and a signed and notarized affidavit turning it over to you. I need eighty-five. I don't get your money back in a few days, you get the house. It's worth one sixty on the market now. With the hundred I got in equity, you sell it and pocket about fifteen profit."

Nads pushed his plate away and swung his legs to the side of the booth.

"When do you need the money?"

"Now would be nice."

Nads nodded and Giancarlo came.

"Hundreds okay?"

"Ben Franklin'll be fine."

He instructed Giancarlo, then Giancarlo turned and left. Liano brushed crumbs from his lap.

"It's no secret, Nads, you hate your competition."

"Castille. That Cajun piece of shit."

"We share the same sentiments."

"It's time I deal with him."

"Right. But the problem for you, as I see it, is that you're under indictment for, what, the fifth or sixth time? I lose track. You can't afford to start a war with Castille. Even your high-priced friends downtown won't be able to help if that dam breaks." I let him mull that over for a few seconds. "But Koot and I are outside your little rivalry."

"I'm listening."

"If we can find out the where and when of Castille's next designer drug shipment, we can bring the police to the party. Something else—Kanawhite is still alive. I'm convinced it wasn't you that had Caveccio taken out, but I think you would have Kanawhite killed for skipping on your business arrangement."

"Where is he now?"

"Castille is still trying to kill him. He helped one of Castille's call girls, a woman named Danika, escape the life. They're in hiding. Kanawhite wants out of the business, Nads. He and the woman want a run at a decent life."

Nads laughed. "A decent life? The guy fell for a hooker."

"Hooking wasn't a choice. Anyway, Kanawhite's part of the deal. I get Castille, you let Kanawhite out."

Nads ignored the proposal. "So if they're in hiding, how come you need to deal for them?"

"It gets complicated."

"Uh huh. You were going to give Castille my money to get him off their backs, right?"

"Always a step ahead, Nads." I didn't want to explain about buying the drugs and giving them back to Castille.

"Always will be. How you plan to get the eighty-five back to me if you use it to bargain with?"

"That's my problem. One way or another you get your money back—maybe with profit. Plus, we'll get Castille. You can't lose."

"You're willing to gamble your house, the only thing you got worth anything, to save a coupla nobodies I bet you barely know." Nads laughed. "I never understood how a guy as tough as you could be such a chump."

"Is that worse than a hump? I can never remember."

Giancarlo came back in the restaurant carrying a Sak's Fifth Avenue shopping bag. He brought it over to the booth. I glanced in. The money line was two thirds to the top and the bag was bulging. I've seen that much cash only a couple of times before, both times when we busted dealers. Seeing it reminded me of the family money I'd never see.

I said, "You let Kanawhite out of the business, I work on getting Castille."

"How 'bout this—you get Castille, I'll think about letting Kanawhite out."

I had nothing left for leverage. I slid out of the booth and took the bag from Giancarlo. "I'll be in touch."

"I know you will. And don't worry about anything. It don't work out for you, I know a homeless shelter I can get you into."

Nads laughed. Giancarlo stared at me. Nads wanted Castille. Giancarlo wanted me, but he'd settle for seeing me lose my house.

THIRTY-TWO

We had a cell phone number set up under a fictitious name so there would be no trace back to Marty. I had given the number to Shaman to pass along to Kiki when the deal was set up. Marty was supposed to receive a call at 8:00 p.m. with instructions for the buy. Koot, Marty and I met at Koot's studio at 7:45. At exactly 8:00 the phone rang, and Marty answered it.

Marty listened, then responded, "Yes, eighty-five thousand in cash. Yes, in a brown briefcase. Corner of Chartres and Canal."

We had told Marty not to agree to the swap unless it was in a public place. Canal at Chartres was good. Canal was at the edge of the French Quarter. It was Friday night, and the area would be packed with diners and the party crowd. It was safer to have people around, but also meant it would be harder to track Marty in the swell.

Marty paused again to listen to his instructions. He paled. "I understand."

Marty hung up and walked to the water cooler, filled a paper cup and drank.

I said, "He threaten to kill you if you weren't alone?"

Marty nodded feebly.

"Kiki's not a murderer, but the mystery man is an unknown. No one would think badly of you, Marty, if you weren't up to this."

Marty took his handkerchief out and mopped his forehead.

"Is there any liquor?"

Koot said, "Afraid not."

Marty had a hard time catching his breath.

I said, "You wanna bag it?"

"Yeah. But then people would expect me to do that."

"This is serious, Marty. A lot of people would be afraid."

"You guys aren't."

"Don't believe everything you think."

174   Conley Clark

"Yeah, but you jump in anyway."

I shrugged. "Just remember, Marty—whatever you decide to do —you'll still be the same back-slapping, ass-kissing, breast-fixated political ferret we've come to know and like."

Marty snorted and nearly choked on his laugh. Koot grinned.

Marty cleared his throat and straightened his coat and tried to be serious, but hadn't quite gotten there. He placed his hand on his hair piece and said, "How's the hair?"

Koot said, "You look dapper, Martin."

"Then let's get this campaign underway."

Koot and I looked at each other, then I said, "Let's get you suited up."

We had Marty take his shirt off, then Koot strapped the Kevlar vest on him. We had picked a green shirt from Marty's clothes. The dark color and thick nap of the material, plus the sport coat would conceal the lines of the vest underneath.

Koot said, "Marty, when you get there, he may have you move again. Follow instructions, but under no circumstances will you get in a car with anybody. Understand?"

"Got it."

At 8:10 we left in the Outback, and Koot drove down Canal toward the Central Business District and the Quarter. We listened to the news. Hurricane Katrina had bullied its way onto shore in Miami, claimed six lives, then turned south and downgraded to a tropical storm. While hovering out in the Gulf, it got its second wind and upgraded again to a cat 1, moved back on shore and rumbled across the Everglades.

The levee system, built to withstand a category 3 hurricane, has caused some unintended side-effects. When the Army Corps of Engineers began leveeing the Mississippi in the 19th century, it cut off the region's main source of river silt, the basic material for building deltas. This, along with the weight of massive building and the destabilizing seeping of water, oil and gas from beneath the ground, has caused the bowl which New Orleans sits in to steadily sink. If Katrina punches through the levees in even a few places, New Orleans could find itself under water again, like it did in '65, when Betsy flooded the city.

When we got downtown Koot took a right off Canal onto Baronne and then cut down to Carondelet, where we found a parking space a few blocks from the meeting place.

We got out, and I took the briefcase with the eighty-five thousand in it out of the back and handed it to Marty, then we walked toward Canal.

When we reached Canal I said, "Koot will track you from this side of the street. I'll cross to the other side with you, then fall back behind you."

Marty said, "Not too far back."

"You'll be covered."

Koot said, "This is a good thing you're doing, Marty."

Marty took a deep breath, then said, "I keep telling myself that. Let's do it before I get tired of hearing it."

Marty and I crossed Canal and turned toward the river. The meeting place was a couple of blocks away. Koot paralleled Marty from the other side of Canal. I distanced myself enough so Kiki, or whoever else might be watching, wouldn't see me; but I stayed close enough that some street punk with a gun and a thing for briefcases couldn't come out of the shadows and get away with the score of his sad little life.

Marty being short made it hard for me to spot up on his head in the walking and staggering crowd of people. I lost him a couple of times, but glanced across the street and saw that Koot seemed to have him in his sights.

When we neared the corner of Chartres, I stepped into the recessed entrance of a liquor store. Marty continued to the corner, then stopped and stood against the wall of a hotel.

I watched him from the liquor store entranceway. Within a minute Marty pulled his phone out and answered it. A few seconds later he hung up and walked back up Canal. He was being moved around before the exchange took place.

I stepped farther back into the entranceway so Marty wouldn't see me when he walked by. If he saw me, reflex might make him look too long, which could cue Kiki or the mystery man to my presence. After Marty passed, I eased to the edge of the door and watched for Kiki or someone who looked like a tail, but didn't see anyone that aroused suspicion. I fell in behind Marty again.

When he got to the corner, Marty crossed back over Canal. Koot melted into a doorway on the other side of the street and watched Marty approach.

When Marty reached the curb he continued walking up St. Charles. I stopped at the corner before crossing Canal and scanned the sidewalk behind me and across the street.

Conley Clark

At the side of the Courtyard Marriott, Marty stopped and answered his phone. A few seconds later a streetcar turned off Canal onto St. Charles and temporarily blocked my view. Then the streetcar stopped and Marty got on. It hadn't occurred to us to tell Marty not to board the trolley. We'd just been taken out.

I raced across Canal against the light and was nearly tatooed by a Hyundai on one of the south bound lanes. When I got to St. Charles I ran full out. Koot was already in front and heading for the Outback, which was about three and a half blocks away. He widened the gap on me going up Gravier. By the time I reached Carondelet, Koot had reached the wagon,while I was still a block away. With the pounding I had taken lately, I had lost some steps—not that I could catch the gazelle, even in peak condition.

Koot jumped in the Outback and peeled away from the curb. I stopped to catch my breath and waited for him. He jammed on the brakes, and I hopped in. Koot floored it, heading for St. Charles.

I wondered if Kiki or the alpha male controlling him was just taking precautions, or if Shaman told Kiki that I was the one who set up the deal. I didn't think Shaman could stomach the idea of me coming after him for giving me away, but you never know. Maybe I had poured too much salt on his cut pride. My manners were atrocious when it came to drug dealers.

Koot pushed it as much as he could in Friday night traffic. A few blocks beyond Lee Circle we caught up with the street car and followed along side as the streetcar headed uptown, but we couldn't see if Marty or Kiki were on board.

Marty might have been instructed to get off and walk again, or the deal might have already been made and Kiki got off before we caught up. We had no choice but to stay with the streetcar and hope we weren't chasing phantoms.

Two stops later, at Jackson Avenue, Kiki got off, clutching the briefcase. Koot whipped in behind a parked car on the street. Kiki scanned the area, but didn't see us. He crossed the street, then got in his old white Caddie fin job and headed south on Jackson toward the river.

Koot let him cross the streetcar tracks and the downtown bound lanes of St. Charles, then pulled out and cut over the neutral ground and the tracks and followed. I took out my cell phone and dialed Marty. I could hear him fumbling with the phone after he punched the answer button.

Finally he got control of it. "Yeah?"

"Marty, you okay?"

"Never better. Damn that was exciting."

"What have you got?"

"I've got a sports bag full of pills. Hope it's not vitamins."

"Get off the streetcar and catch a cab home. We're on Kiki."

"I did it, Tag."

"You did it, Marty."

At the river, Kiki turned onto Tchoupitoulas. Soon he turned into the entrance of an abandoned warehouse and docking area on the bank of the river.

Koot pulled past the entrance, killed the lights and parked on a side street. We got out, crossed the railroad tracks and moved toward the warehouse. Large, slow-drifting clouds blocked the moon, which gave us cover for an approach. We moved along some old boxcars until we were about thirty yards from the warehouse. I didn't see any lights through the transom windows or through the cracks in the bay doors. We drew our weapons.

I said, "Let's find out what's behind door number one."

We moved quickly across the open space to the partially closed bay door, then we squatted and peered in. The warehouse was dark. Koot slipped in, and I followed.

From the back of the warehouse, I heard muted voices. Koot and I split up and worked our way down the walls, staying low. There was little cover except for a few pallets of old barrels stacked two-high around the perimeter and in the middle of the space. I could just make out the dirty neon green lettering on the drums. It was TRICHLOROETHYLENE, an industrial solvent.

The voices became more intense. I heard a scuffle, then a cry. I thought I saw the silhouette of someone fall to the concrete floor. Another silhouette moved slowly away from the downed figure and toward the back of the warehouse.

I moved quickly across the warehouse to the person on the floor. The moon broke from behind the clouds and cast a faint light through the windows near the top of the warehouse - enough light to see that it was Kiki. His throat was cut. The alpha male never intended to let Kiki live.

Air leaked from the slit in his throat and bubbled the blood at his carotid. His eyes were Sanpaku, and had almost disappeared up into his head. He was near the end.

I took Kiki's hand and held it. He squeezed my hand, as if he were afraid I'd let go.

"Kiki, I'm here."

Dying is the one thing we all do alone, and I had no idea if one human being could really comfort another at the moment of death. I wanted to believe so.

Kiki moved his other hand slowly off his chest and pointed two fingers toward his eyes. I thought at first he was trying to tell me he couldn't see, then it dawned on me. Two fingers pointing at the eyes was the sign on the street that a cop was near by. Kiki was telling me it was a cop that had killed him. Maybe Castille's cop.

Kiki's hand fell to his chest, and the bubbles at his throat stopped. I felt his wrist. He was dead.

Clouds moved past the moon, and the warehouse was dark again. Near the back of the warehouse I heard Koot yell, "Stop!" Blue flame burst from the corner of the building and bullets ripped into metal.

Koot returned fire. I caught a glimpse of a shadowy figure and fired as he ducked behind something large. A strong chemical odor drifted my way, and in a few seconds I felt dizzy. The barrels of solvent had been hit.

I ran across the warehouse toward where I had seen Koot's muzzle blast. I hoped nothing was on the floor that would trip me and give the cop a downed target. The killer caught my movement in the dark and fired rapidly. I heard a shot chip the concrete at my feet and heard another one hiss by my head.

I could barely see the barrels when I dove behind them. The chemical fumes were overpowering here. Koot was bent over and solvent was pouring at our feet.

"We have to get out of here," I said.

Koot mumbled, "Feel sick."

Three shots burst and hit the barrels again, then I saw the shadowy figure bolt from his cover. I fired two rounds as he went through the back door and couldn't tell if I'd hit him.

I lifted Koot and helped him through the back door, then sat him down outside. My eyes were burning, and I was still dizzy. I could just make out a blurry outline of the killer's car as it took off. It sounded like a muscle car.

I aimed and squeezed off four rounds. One popped the right tail light. The car fishtailed around the corner of the warehouse and was gone.

THIRTY-THREE

The Hazardous Materials Unit had finished cleaning up the solvent, and the uniforms had cordoned off the warehouse entrance when Mowery drove up in the unmarked Lumina with his bubble light flashing. Unless there is a mob scene, detectives don't use the light for a homicide. Must have been anxious to see us. But then why did it take him so long to get here?

Mowery got out and spoke to the female HazMat officer. I stood at the back of the ambulance while the EMTs inserted the gurney with Koot on it into the vehicle. Koot had thrown up and his eyes were swollen, but I was told he'd be all right in a few hours. One of the EMTs had given us both Phenergan for nausea and wanted me to go over to Charity Hospital, but I wanted to get the Q & A with Mowery over with first. Before one of the EMTs closed the door I leaned in and put my hand on Koot's shoulder.

"How are your eyes?"

His eyes watered in a steady stream. "It's like I've been cutting radioactive onions."

I said, "It'll be okay."

"Better than Kiki."

"Yeah."

"The renegade cop double-crossed the department and his boss Castille," Koot said.

"And set up Danika and Jackie for the fall."

"Yeah."

"Looks like Mowery's the 'up' detective tonight. I'll see you at the ER when he's done with me."

I stepped back, and the EMT closed the door and climbed in the front. The driver turned on his flasher, and the ambulance pulled away.

When Mowery finished speaking with the HazMat officer, he came over. He nodded toward the ambulance that had just reached the street.

"That Loomis?"

"Yeah."

"He take a bullet?"

"Chemical fumes."

Mowery nodded once. "I'll catch up with him later."

"Koot will be just fine, Mowery. Thanks for asking."

"Let's go inside, Boudreau."

We entered the warehouse. A bank of halogen lights with cable ran to the HazMat truck and lit one side of the warehouse. Big fans were aimed toward the back and front bay doors. Some of the fumes still lingered, but it was bearable. We walked to the far side of the building where Kiki's body lay. The Forensics Light Unit was combing the area. One unit officer was lifting prints from Kiki's body.

Mowery asked, "We gonna find any of your prints on the body?"

"His hand."

"Why?"

"I held his hand while he died."

"That's touching, Boudreau. It really is."

"I doubt you'll lift any of the killer's prints."

"He had gloves?"

"Unless he's stupid. I don't think he's stupid."

"You sound like you never came across a stupid killer before. What makes you think this guy wasn't a dimwit?"

"Just a hunch."

"Uh huh. You know something you're not telling me?"

"Not a thing."

"So Kiki was alive when you got to him?"

"Yeah."

"He say anything?"

"His throat was slashed, Mowery."

"Yeah. That kind of thing happens when you're around."

Tonight I wasn't feeling the anger these cheap shots usually brought on. I had reserved it all for myself. I couldn't shake the feeling that if we had gotten here a few seconds sooner, Kiki might still be alive.

Mowery spread his hands. "What, no comment?"

"Get on with it, Mowery."

"Why were you and Loomis here?"

"Kiki called and said he was in trouble and asked us to meet him here. We got here too late." For now, the lie ought to hold. "We exchanged fire with the killer before he drove away."

That part was true, but I left out the part about putting one in the tail light. Since the Boudreau fan club and the DA would salivate over finding out we did a drug deal with Mafia money, I left that part out too. We'd have to continue to keep it from Grady and the lieutenant as well.

Mowery said, "Why would Kiki call *you* if he were in trouble?"

"Mowery, did you know every Sunday Kiki took barbecue ribs to his mother down in Plaquemines Parish?"

"I'm asking the questions."

"Or that he never beat his women, or that he put some of the runaways wanting to give the street life a try on a bus back home?"

"Like I give a shit."

"Most didn't."

Mowery gave me hard eyes. "I think the reason he called you is because the two of you had a lot in common. You're both lowlifes."

"The man just died, Mowery."

"You expect me to show some respect? All right. The pimp was one of our best snitches. How's that?"

I stared at Mowery. He stared back. That pleasantry exchanged, Mowery asked, "What kind of trouble was Kiki in?"

"He didn't say."

"I think you're lying."

"That's a given. You haven't asked much about the killer, Mowery. You trying to figure a way to pin this one on me too?"

Mowery's neck veins bulged. He stepped in close. "You keep your mouth shut, Boudreau, except to answer questions."

I glanced toward the bay door and saw Grady enter the warehouse and trudge across the floor. I had called and left a message with Rosie because Grady would want to know about Kiki's murder, and because he needed to know it was the cop. The rest Koot and I would keep to ourselves for now.

Grady stepped past us and bent down to look at the corpse, then he stood.

Still looking at Kiki, he said, "A creampuff like Kiki in that world. It was bound to come to this." He looked a few seconds longer, then stepped over to us. "Whatta we know about the killer?"

I said, "Mowery was just about to ask me that."

Those bulging veins again. Mowery asked, "What'd the killer look like, Boudreau?"

"Too dark to get a look."

Mowery asked, "Did you get a make or a license number?"

"The chemicals blurred my vision."

"You don't know much, do you?"

I yawned.

Grady asked, "You get any metal into him?"

"I might have clipped him. Hard to say."

Grady asked Mowery. "Forensics get anything for ballistics?"

Mowery, defensive, like he hadn't been on top of it, "They dug some slugs out in here. We'll run them for a match."

Grady asked, "Where's Loomis?"

I said, "The ER. The fumes got to him. They said he'd be okay in a few hours."

"Good. You gonna get him?"

"Yeah."

Grady turned to Mowery. "You done with Boudreau?"

Mowery, like he owned me. "For now."

Grady and I left Mowery with the forensics guys and went outside and over to his car. We leaned against the Crown Vic.

"What happened here, Hot Rod?"

"Kiki let me know before he died that it was a cop." I pointed to my eyes with two fingers.

Grady understood. "Sonofabitch."

"Yeah. I'm guessing Castille's boy. Of course, I forget to mention that to Mowery." Grady nodded. "It was interesting it took Mowery so long to arrive on the scene."

"I'll keep an eye on him. If he's our boy, he'll play his hand soon enough," said Grady. "Where does Kiki fit in here?"

"I can't tell you yet, Grady. Koot and I are on the other side of the fence right now."

He said, "Whatever you and Koot are doing, we can find another way to do this. We don't need any dead heroes."

"It's already in play."

Grady drew in a breath then forced it all out. He reached in his side coat pocket and got a macaroon, then popped it in his mouth and chewed.

"You guys drive me nuts."

"That's what the department shrink is for."

Grady chuckled mirthlessly.

I said, "Jackie and Danika are gonna need you to stay close while Koot and I work this out."

"I'll keep an eye on them." He chewed a few times and swallowed.

I said, "Besides Mowery, any thoughts who it might be?"

Grady shrugged. "A cop's pay. Temptation yammers in everybody's head."

"In your case it doesn't matter. You're a lousy listener anyway."

"That's what Rosie's always telling me."

THIRTY-FOUR

On the way to the ER I called Marty. He said he took a cab home and hid the drugs in the basement, then started working on a bottle of Tuaca. I told him about Kiki's murder. Marty told me Kiki had seemed very nervous during the exchange. Kiki probably suspected he wasn't going to make it.

Saturday night was blood and cocktail night at the Charity ER. Friends and families boozed together, then carved each other up and funneled into the ER to be put back together.

When I got there, the bleeders were in a queue, standing room only. I saw a nurse I knew stuffing gauze bandage into a gaping stomach wound. The victim didn't flinch. Probably fully anesthetized before he came in.

I'd met Sunny, the nurse, here years ago after Koot and I answered a domestic call and brought in a balding stick figure who had been worked over with a Dirt Devil by his wife. Sunny and I went out for three months, which was about two months longer than any of the others, before she too decided I came with too much baggage. We remained friendly when our paths crossed, which was mostly here at the ER when I was still on the force.

Sunny had taken care of Koot when he'd come in tonight. She told me he had been given oxygen, then hydrated with an IV and his eyes were treated for the burning.

I went to the waiting room and after about an hour, Sunny woke me and told me Koot was being released. Koot and I left the hospital, and I drove toward his house.

I asked, "How're you feeling?"

"Like the bulb needs changing."

"Let's fold in the flaps for the night. See how you feel tomorrow."

"Sometimes you can be a reasonable man, Boudreau."

I turned onto Broad. Two uniforms in a patrol car had stopped a couple of guys in a Trans Am and were making the driver blow into a breathalyzer.

Koot said, "You think Kiki's killer got a look at us tonight?"

"He was just a shadow to us. I'm guessing we were the same to him."

Koot shifted his head around, like he was still trying to find his bearings. "We got the drugs, but it might not be enough."

"Yeah. Unless we can prove Castille's boy did the boost, Castille's gonna stay focused on Jackie and Danika."

"Might not hurt to tell Castille about his man anyway. See what shakes out."

"Too risky. If Castille believes the cop, then Castille will tell him we're on to him. If our boy doesn't suspect we know a detective is on the take, he might get careless."

Koot said, "He trips up, maybe Grady and the lieutenant nail him."

"Right now—I've got my own problem. When Nads finds out I don't have his money, he's going to take my house. Can the kids and I move in with you?"

"Nads is not gonna take your house."

"You going to sweet talk him?"

"Need be."

"I made the deal, Koot, eyes open. Nads gets the house."

Koot looked out the window and didn't say anything. I turned onto Orleans, and we rode in silence. A guy in stretch tights was jogging along on the sidewalk, reflector tape all over him and his shoes.

Finally Koot said, "You ever wonder how it might've turned out if Kiki had made different choices with his life?"

"I like to think we all get another go-around. Maybe next time he will."

I dropped Koot off at his place and headed home. Tomorrow I'd get the Outback to Koot and pick up the Sebring at the studio. When I finally got in bed, it was after 1:00 a.m. My head was still gauzy with the effects of the chemicals, and I needed sleep like a vampire needs a neck.

I had no idea how long I'd been asleep when the banging at the door started. It took a while to get myself to a sitting position. I looked at the clock. 2:45. Not even a decent nap.

I pulled on a pair of sweat pants and took the Kahr from the night stand, then dragged myself to the door. Santana had come into the living room. I held the gun behind me and opened the door. Giancarlo looked past me at Santana. Santana growled.

I said, "He doesn't like to be woken in the middle of the night like I do."

"The dog, Boudreau."

I grabbed Santana by the collar and pulled him into the kitchen, then closed the door. Without an invitation, Giancarlo entered the house and looked around.

"Anyone else in the house?"

"Besides the three flight attendants—just me."

Giancarlo did a quick walk-through of the house, then came back into the living room.

"The gun, Boudreau."

I handed Giancarlo my gun. "What's this about?"

Without answering, he stepped to the door, nodded, then stood aside. Nads walked in, followed by a guy I'd never seen before and two of Nads' soldiers. The new guy's eyes darted around like minnows, and he was pale and sweating. He was holding his right hand, his index finger wrapped with a bloody rag.

Nads nodded, and one of his crew took the guy by the arm and dragged him to a chair, then pressed him down into it.

Nads said to me while looking at the guy, "This numbnuts likes the peep shows. Only he didn't know I owned the place. He's been kind enough to answer some questions."

"Who is he?"

"One of Castille's grunts. Not one of his brightest, that's for sure." Nads went and stood over the guy in the chair. "Tell Boudreau what you told me."

The guy straightened in the chair and kept glancing over at Giancarlo. Giancarlo stood near the door, expressionless. Giancarlo was known to carry a cigar cutter for "interviews." Judging by the blood on the bandage, Giancarlo probably took off a joint of the guy's finger. Since Giancarlo's own pinky had been taken off with a cigar cutter, he was partial to the method.

This is the kind of thing you have to be prepared to stomach when you make deals with psychopaths as I had. My stomach let me know I hadn't been prepared.

The guy said, "Castille's operation is in an old salt mine...at Jefferson Island...about two and a half hours from the city. There's a...there's a large shipment of Sojourn...that's the drug he makes...going out in a coupla nights."

The guy's head bobbed like trash in the ocean toward Nads, then me, then Giancarlo, then back to Nads. You could smell the fear.

Nads said, "This is a tell-all, hemorrhoid."

"Sorry. Castille is always there...when a shipment goes out. Likes to oversee it personally. Doesn't trust anybody."

Nads said, "There's a surprise."

Nads took a map out of his suit coat and handed it to me. To the guy. "This map better be right," Nads jerked his head toward Giancarlo, "or your scrotum comes off next."

The guy's eyes saucered. "I swear on my mother's..."

"Don't drag your mother into this, numbnuts."

The guy kept twisting his head back and forth. He said, "It's a good map. You follow that map. It's a good map."

I asked the guy, "You know a homicide detective on Castille's payroll?"

"Don't know nothing about that."

Nads said, "Anal pucker here is gonna be our guest long enough for some scores to be settled. Then he's decided to find work in Alaska. That right?"

"Absolutely. Start clean."

Nads looked at me. "You think you can work with what I just gave you, Boudreau?"

"I'm on it."

Nads smirked. "So, Boudreau, who's the better detective—you or me?"

No point in going into the difference between detection and torture with a guy that uses violence like you'd use a Visa card. I had to admit though, it was the information we needed, and I wouldn't lose sleep over a piece of a thug's finger if we could bring Castille down.

"You got the goods, Nads."

Nads grinned, and just as quickly went stony.

"You got my eighty-five thousand?"

This was hard. I had lived in this house for ten years and had more than half the mortgage paid off. I liked the house and the neighborhood. I liked the deck and the shade oak in the backyard. Now I was going to hand it over to Cosa Nostra.

I said, "The deal went bad. The guy got away with the money."

"So, I'm guessing the deal was for the drugs that the asshole stole from Castille?"

No surprise Nads knew about the theft. His snitches went out like computer viruses.

"That's right."

"You get the drugs?"

"Yeah."

"So sell the drugs and pay me with the cash."

"Can't do it."

"Why not?"

"Same reason you don't sell them."

Nads didn't like the answer, but he couldn't argue the point.

He said, "So you were going to use the drugs to barter with Castille for the hump and the hooker?"

"Uh huh."

"You give Castille his product back, he turns around and sells it to kids."

"If I have to let the drugs get out on the street to protect Jackie and Danika..." I shrugged. "Right and wrong is sometimes shifting sand."

"How 'bout shifting *hands*. The deed to your house—from your hands to mine. I sell the house, I just made a little profit."

"That's right."

"And you're on the street for being a chump Samaritan."

"Right again. There's something else. Kiki was killed tonight by the guy that took the money."

"Kiki was in on this and you didn't tell me?"

"He was being used. We needed Kiki to lead us to the guy with the drugs."

"So when this asshole got the money—my money—he cut Kiki out of the picture."

"He slit his throat."

"Somebody works for me gets killed or wants out, and you've got something to do with it, Boudreau."

Kiki was no more than a vending machine to Nads—something to generate cash flow. Nads would have to find somebody to replace Kiki, which was the only reason he was upset.

"I guess it's pointless to remind you I'm not the one that killed Kiki."

"Very astute. If you didn't have a job to do that I want done, namely, get Castille, it wouldn't matter you don't have a house. You wouldn't be needing it. We clear?"

Nads threat made my blood rise hot. I stared at Liano. He stared back. We stood there staring—my hot blood against his cold. I struggled to get the rage under control.

Finally I said, "Castille will be taken off the board, Liano. But I won't be doing it for you."

Liano eyed me a few seconds longer, then turned jolly again. The human emotional spigot.

"You got spine, Boudreau. You and Loomis always did. You take that coonass Castille down and you can have your house back. Then you pay me the eighty-five in installments—plus the vig, of course. Kanawhite and the hooker can set up house. Everybody's happy."

"Like in a fairy tale."

"Exactly; like in a fucking fairy tale."

THIRTY-FIVE

After Nads and his crew left, I got about three hours sleep then called Koot.

I said, "You got the spiders out of your head?"

"Yeah, but they left some webs."

"We've caught a break. Nads came to the house. He snared one of Castille's crew. Giancarlo had a one-on-one with the guy with a cigar cutter and suddenly we have the location of Castille's operation. It's in an old salt mine down in Vermilion Parish."

Koot said, "That's seriously good news."

"The guy said that a shipment of Sojourn was going out tomorrow night and that Castille would be there."

"The lieutenant and Grady can pull uniforms from another district for the bust and keep Second District Homicide in the dark so the puke with the badge can't warn Castille," said Koot.

"First we make sure the guy gave us the right location, and get the layout of the place. You feeling up to a night prowl?"

"Whatta you think?"

"I think that halitosis is better than no breath at all."

"Un huh. Swing by the studio around 6:00."

"Marvelous."

I hung up and fed the kids, then drew blood and tested my glucose. Steady at one-twenty. I made myself a cup of Irish Breakfast tea to triage my haggard brain. Sometime soon I was going to have to get a decent night's sleep. I took the tea, my phone and the newspaper out to the deck. The paper was full of the usual, crime and punishment, celebrities acting out. I saw where Hurricane Katrina had downgraded during the night to a tropical storm with 70 mph winds. Enough to break some limbs and toss things around, but not enough to fear.

The phone rang. I took a swallow of tea, then answered it.

Adrienne said, "Good morning."

"Morning."

"Are you busy?"

"I'm in between busy right now."

"Brent is with Clayton, so I thought I might cook you breakfast."

"Absolutely."

"Yummy." Yummy came out a purr. "It's good to start the day with something hot."

"Hmm. Is that before or after breakfast?"

"Your choice."

"Give me about thirty seconds to get there."

"I'm glad not everything you do is that fast."

"I'll shave in the car."

I hung up and realized I wasn't as tired as I thought I was.

I didn't let driving in heavy traffic distract me from the image I had of Adrienne answering the door in something short and sheer. When I rang the door bell, I noticed my pulse was out of the gate ahead of me. I got the same reaction when someone held a gun on me, but it didn't give me an erection.

The door swung open and Blanche stepped out on the porch.

I blinked. "Blanche."

"Disappointed?"

"Of course not." I knew she knew I *was* disappointed, and she knew I knew it. "It's always good to see you, Blanche."

"Well, that's very gratifying, but I'm afraid I don't have time to visit. I'm going to pick up some things for our darling boy and that dear girl Danika, then I'm having beignets and coffee with a retired orthodontist."

"I hope the man has a lot of self-confidence."

"He'll need it, won't he?"

"When you get back, I'll take you and Adrienne to see Jackie and Danika."

"First things first. Your hormones are falling all over themselves, so go on in."

"Blanche, why are you always yanking my chain?"

"Because you're so adorable."

"I'd hate *not* to be adorable to you."

"Taggert Boudreau, there is nothing you or Koot Loomis could do for the rest of your lives to get on my bad side."

Blanche hugged me then smiled at me with her eyes, then she said, "She's in the shower. Why don't you surprise her."

With that, Blanche descended the steps laughing. Then she blew a kiss to the old timer tending his roses next door and got in her Corvette convertible. She started the 'Vette and raced the engine to announce her entrance into traffic, then launched into the fray.

I went in the house and walked down the hall to the bathroom, where the door was open and the shower was running. I leaned against the door frame. The contours of Adrienne's body refracted through the frosted glass of the shower door and the steam. It was like viewing an impressionist painting brought to life—a particularly gorgeous painting.

"I'm with the Missionaries for Mirth. Can I give you my testimony?"

"I'm all ears."

"Not quite."

Adrienne asked, "Will you scrub my back?"

"Absolutely."

I quickly undressed and stepped in the shower. Adrienne put her arms around my neck and pressed her breasts into my chest. She said, "And the rest of me is pretty dirty too."

"How about I start with these and work my way down?"

"Yummy."

After about an hour of hallelujah love-making, we dressed and went into the kitchen. Adrienne made Spanish omelets, which she served with buttered grits, toasted bagels, mango chutney and hot Guatemalan coffee. A cross-cultural feast.

After I had savored a few bites I said, "I have some good news."

She gave me sexy. "You've already delivered it."

"Yeah, well, that was just the morning edition."

"I think I'll become a regular subscriber."

I took a sip of hot coffee, then leaned across the table a little closer to Adrienne.

"We know where to find Castille and his operation."

Sexy went serious. She considered what I'd said for a few seconds, then asked, "Will you go after him?"

"Yes."

"Not just the two of you?"

"We'll bring the police in."

"Tag, I'm afraid."

"Jackie and Danika will be safe."

Adrienne looked at me. "Not just for Jackie and Danika."

"Hey, the cops can take care of themselves."

Adrienne continued to look at me. "Sometimes you hide behind humor. It's as if you don't want anyone coming too close."

I shifted in my chair. She had called me out. I hadn't been serious about anyone for a long time, so I hadn't had to look at some things about myself.

I said, "I'm sorry, Adrienne." She continued to look at me.

"When I was a drunk and deformed with guilt, I ran off every woman I was with. I guess I've been afraid I'd do the same with you."

"I'm still here."

"I was more concerned about after the danger is over for Jackie and Danika."

"How is it that you'll risk getting killed, but you're afraid to risk opening up to me."

"If I get killed, the pain's over."

A slight wry smile. "Maybe you could work on that."

"I will."

"And Tag..."

I think I squinted. "Uh oh."

"...Don't stop making me laugh."

I grinned. "Don't stop calling me out."

"You can count on it."

Conley Clark

THIRTY-SIX

I went to the studio to wait for Koot to finish his evening class. In the office was a fruit basket wrapped in yellow cellophane. I read the attached card. It said: "Koot, because of you I no longer feel at the mercy of the world. You are so much more than an instructor to me. Thank you for being you. Gail." Well, well. Another one of Koot's admirers.

Gail. I was thinking she was the one married with three kids. Disappointed at home, and when Koot had a talk with her, she'd be disappointed all over again. Koot was anti-adultery on principle.

When the class was over, the woman with the nice legs who'd wanted to spar with me stuck her head in the office and said, "When are we going to go at it?"

"Right after the heart transplant."

"Chicken."

I shrugged. "You're on to me."

She popped her towel within a couple of inches of my leg, then swaggered out of the studio. Loved the swagger.

I wanted to make sure Katrina was still no more than rambunctious, so I turned the TV on to catch the weather. The hurricane had left Florida and was tracking toward the Mississippi and Louisiana coasts, while gaining brawn. If it stayed on course, it would make shore in a couple of days.

When the last student was gone, Koot grabbed the two-way radios and locked up, then we left in the Outback. The four-wheel drive might be needed in the low country.

We grabbed some oyster po'boys at a little takeout place near the studio, then got on the Ponchartrain Expressway and headed west. Koot pushed it up to seventy-five and set the cruise control. It was interstate all the way to Lafayette. We crossed the Mississippi River out of Baton Rouge at 8:30. We'd be there a little before 10:00 p.m.

At Lafayette we turned onto Highway 90 and headed south until we reached the state that led to the salt mine. At about the four-mile mark, Koot slowed and we looked for the sign for the mine. There were few houses on this road and no street lights. Outside the twin beams of the wagon lights, visibility fell off fast.

After a couple hundred yards, we caught a glimpse of a sign. Koot stopped, backed up and stopped again, then angled the headlights at the sign, which sat back from the road. It was all warped wood, and the lettering had sun-bleached to a ghost image. We could just make out the words: *Canton Salt.*

Beside the sign was the entrance road, which was gated and chained. Koot backed onto the road again, then continued slowly past the entrance until we saw two tractor ruts leading into a sugar cane field on the opposite side of the highway. Koot killed the lights and turned onto the ruts.

Large purple stalks of cane arched over the Outback as we advanced into the field. The ribbon-shaped leaves hung from the stalks like little banners for a good harvest. Above us, the stars and the moon were crystalline.

When the Outback was out of sight from the paved road, Koot stopped and shut off the engine. He grabbed his wire cutters from the glove compartment and stuck them in a hip pack. I gave Koot one of the two-way radios and put the other in its case on my belt. We bent cane stalks back opening our doors, then we got out and moved up the rutted path toward the paved road.

We stayed in the cloak of the cane field until a pickup truck passed, then we jogged across the road to the chain-link fence that fronted Castille's property. The fence was an eight-footer topped with coiled razor wire.

Koot pulled the wire cutters out of his pack and handed them to me. Then he squatted. I stood on his shoulders and balanced myself, then Koot stood slowly and I was hoisted up to the barbed wire. I cut the wire and bent it back on each side of the cut, leaving about three feet of passage over.

The lights from a car appeared down the road, heading our way.

Koot said, "You're going over."

Koot got his hands under my feet and pushed. I scrambled up and over the fence and landed on my feet, then fell back on the ground, jamming the shoulder holstered Kahr into my arm pit. Koot flattened in the reedy grass until the car passed, then popped to his feet and went up the fence like the upshot of a bungee jump. He leaped down from the top and landed on his feet, ready for action.

Conley Clark

I said, "You need to rest—eat an energy bar or something?"

He was already out in front. "Get it in gear, Boudreau."

"Show off."

The moonlight penetrating the forest allowed us to see well enough to move quickly. We settled into a steady jog through the slash pines. The smell of sap was strong, and was both sweet and pungent. We had jogged maybe three hundred yards when we came to the far edge of the thicket, where we stopped.

Koot said, "Bad guy at 10 o'clock."

Seventy yards to our left, a guy was sitting in the lit open door of the old mining guard shack on the entrance road. About sixty yards directly in front of us was a large reinforced steel A-frame that jutted out of the ground maybe fifteen feet high. A purplish vapor light on top of the frame illuminated the entrance to the mine and the area around it.

A large pizza-sized pulley hung from the apex of the frame with a thick rope running through it. One end of the rope was attached to an electric rotating drum off to the side of the mining shaft and the other end was attached to an open elevator cage, suspended from the A-frame and above the mining shaft. The drum would rotate and lower or raise the cage in and out of the mine. Basic, but it got the job done. Standing near the elevator shaft were two guys with automatic weapons, smoking cigarettes.

To the right of the mine shaft, maybe seventy yards, I could see the moon reflecting off what looked like a fairly large lake. In the middle of the lake, I could see the lights on the silhouette of an oil drilling barge and derrick. These drilling barges were anchored in inland bodies of water all over South Louisiana.

Just behind the area of the elevator shaft was a small stand of trees. I said, "We need to get to that grove, and from there to the elevator."

"Right."

"To the lake, then we'll cut around behind."

We backed into the cover of the pines again and made our way toward the lake to put more distance between us and the guy at the shack, and to move out of the sight line of the two guys near the elevator. We were lucky the tree cover ran all the way to the lake. At the lake we were far enough away from the guard shack that we wouldn't be seen, but were still in the sight line of the two at the elevator.

We'd have to be in the open for a few seconds until we reached the trees behind the elevator. We waited. When one of the gunmen took something out of his pocket and showed it to the other guy, I said, "Let's go."

We sprinted out of the woods toward the thicket. If the guys with the semiautomatics spotted us in the moonlight, we'd either have to stand and fight in the open or swim. I wasn't in the mood for either. Then we were in the trees.

We moved quickly through the grove to an old rusted front-loader near the mine shaft. We were only a few steps from the gunmen. A breeze was blowing our way, carrying the sound of their conversation. Something about losing money on the dog fights.

Pit bull fights are still popular in some parts of Louisiana. Fight rings often threw cash at some veterinarian to cut the dogs' vocal chords, so there'd be no barking to give away the location. These guys at the mine wouldn't have a problem with that.

From this position, we got a better look at the elevator cage, which was a solid steel frame covered on three sides and on top and bottom with sheets of aluminum. The elevator door was see-through steel mesh.

When the thugs finished smoking, they flipped the butts toward the front loader as they walked toward the elevator.

I whispered, "I'm going to catch a ride. You're my eyes up top."

"Turn your pager to vibrate."

I reached to my belt and pressed the button on the pager.

"Got it."

"I page you, it means someone up top is waiting for the elevator. I'll stay close to the shaft so we have a shot at getting a signal on the radio."

I made sure the two-way radio and pager were snug on my hip.

The two gunmen reached the elevator.

"Watch yourself, Tag."

The thugs lifted the steel mesh door and entered the cage, then closed the door. One of them threw the switch and the elevator descended. Just as the top of the cage dropped below ground level, I sprinted for the elevator shaft. On the run I leaped for the thick rope and grabbed it. The force of impact made the cage beneath me shudder. I was counting on jerks and shudders being normal in an old rig like this. The thugs didn't start blasting holes through the roof, so I must have figured right.

I was about fifteen feet above the cage. The rope was coated with light oil, probably to preserve it, which made it more of a slow slide than a climb down to the cage. I stepped lightly on the framed aluminum roof, then went to my stomach and slid to the edge of the cage so I could peer over. Nothing but darkness. The cage dropped deeper and deeper into the earth before I saw the light of the first level below.

As the cage passed slowly by the first level, I looked into an immense room lit by banks of lights attached to generators. The room was maybe a hundred feet across and forty feet high.

Salt forms underground in massive domes, some domes a few miles wide and seven or eight miles deep. To get the salt out, these colossal formations are blasted by explosives and scooped out by gigantic bulldozers, leaving behind these cathedral-sized rooms that honeycomb the dome at different levels for several hundred feet down.

Stacked up and lined along the dirty salt walls of the room were maybe a couple hundred crates with POWDERED MILK stenciled on the sides in blue letters. The Sojourn tabs would be buried in containers of powdered milk, then the containers would be placed in these crates.

The cage dropped into blackness again. We were probably a few hundred feet down and the temperature was getting warmer. At the next level was another huge salt room. This one was sectioned off with flimsy partitions. Through an opening between two of the partitions, I saw a woman sitting on a cot, reading a magazine. This would be the living quarters for the women forced to make Castille's drugs.

A guy with a holstered pistol on his hip was sitting against a salt wall, pawing a woman sitting in his lap. The woman's face was as blank as an uncarved headstone. Castille probably let the men who pulled duty down here take the women at will, as compensation for having to live in the dirty, stifling underground. The women got no compensation—other than being allowed to live another day.

Just before the cage dropped from view, the woman behind the partition glanced toward the elevator and saw me. Then darkness again. If she told the guard she'd seen me, more men with guns would be waiting for me at the next level. I drew my weapon for the reception.

As we descended, a familiar smell wafted up through the shaft. After another hundred feet or so, we reached the third level and the elevator stopped. I scooted back from the edge and waited. No welcoming committee. The woman hadn't given me up.

After the two guys with the semiautomatics got out and joined another guy in the corner of the gigantic room, I moved closer to the front edge of the cage so I could have a better look. In the middle of the smoke-laced cavern was the factory, and the smell of drug soup cooking was strong.

When I'd worked Narcotics, we'd raided several clandestine labs, but none of the operations came close to the size of this one. And with slave labor, Castille could run the lab around the clock.

About a dozen women in coveralls worked around four conference-sized plywood tables. Most of the women looked to be in their late thirties and early forties, no longer young enough to prostitute for Castille. A few were younger. Maybe the younger ones couldn't or wouldn't fake pleasure enough to suit the customers, so they were brought down here to a salt perdition.

At each table, ingredients were poured into several round Pyrex cooking flasks. The flasks sat in what looked like large electric crock pots, and the tables were full of these cookers. A web of power cords and hoses was woven beneath the tables.

At a smaller table, women filled freezer bags with the finished product of pills and placed the bags in round containers, then they poured powdered milk in around the bags and sealed the containers.

Drums and gallon bottles of chemicals sat in a corner. Hydrochloric acid, Red Devil lye, ether, starter fluids, paint thinner, acetone, stove fuel, ammonia, Freon—these were just some of the chemicals used in making designer drugs. Breathing this stuff cooking had to be ten times worse than chain-smoking. A fan circulated the steamy fumes, but did little to break up the concentration of stench.

I settled in to wait for someone to take the elevator back to the top. I had counted two men on the first level, one on the second level and three on the third. I was sure there were more. I hoped most of them would be up top loading the shipment when we came in force tomorrow night.

I must have waited about thirty-five minutes before the elevator jerked into motion and started the slow ascent. No one had gotten on which meant someone would be getting on somewhere above me. My pager vibrated on my hip. I waited until the cage was well above the third level so I couldn't be heard from below, then I tried to radio Koot, but couldn't get a signal. I was too far below ground.

When the cage reached the second level, the guy with the pistol was looking over one of the partitions, getting his free peep. The woman who had seen me earlier came from behind another partition and glanced at the guy, then she looked my way. She'd be wondering why I was here. As I passed, I gave her the okay sign.

Conley Clark

She nodded once, and I hoped she understood someone would be back for her and the rest of the women.

When I was well clear of the second level, I tried the radio again and got a signal. I punched the button. Koot would mute the audible so he wouldn't be given away.

Koot spoke low. "Tag. One gunmen and one woman up top." I'd be clearly seen by them when the cage reached the surface. "If the gunman sees you, I'm taking him."

When I reached the first level, I used the ambient light from the room to look over the back side of the elevator. There might be just enough room between the cage and the steel frame of the shaft for me to hang on the back side, out of sight when I reached the top. If I was wrong, I'd be ground round. When we rose past the first level, I punched the radio again.

I said, "Koot, If I don't make it, it'll be up to you and Grady to get Castille."

"You're babbling, Boudreau."

"I'm just saying—the women down here are depending on you."

"What's going on?"

I could see the light at the top of the elevator shaft.

I said, "I love you, Koot."

I punched off and moved to the back edge of the elevator. When it was about thirty feet from the top I slid over the back side and pressed my body hard against the cage while I clung to the top edge. The steel frame of the elevator shaft scoured my butt as I ascended and pressed my pelvic bone into the cage so hard I thought it would snap. My chest was pinned, and I couldn't breathe.

Finally, the cage broke the surface of the ground and stopped. I felt someone step inside. I tried to quickly pull myself up, but was wedged in too tight to get leverage. I managed to inch myself up far enough to grab a beam on the head-frame above, then slowly pulled myself up. I crawled onto the roof of the cage just as the switch was thrown.

The cage descended. I quickly got to my feet and leaped up for the landing. I caught the edge of the steel flooring, but my hands were oily and sweaty and I was losing my grip. Just as I was about to drop, two hands grabbed my wrists—then I was on solid ground.

Koot and I ran for the cover of the trees. When we were in the trees, we stopped. My butt was raw and I wasn't sure I'd be making love to Adrienne anytime soon, but I was in one piece.

I said, "You ever get tired of dragging me out of the fire?"

"When it gets in the way of my social life."

"You don't have a social life."

Koot shrugged. Then he looked like he'd rather be somewhere else.

He said, "So... I guess I've gotta say I love you too."

"Nah. You've had enough challenges for one night."

"Good. Let's go home, and I'll scramble some eggs."

THIRTY-SEVEN

In the morning I called the station and got Grady and the lieutenant on the speaker phone in the lieutenant's office. I told them about Castille's operation and about the shipment tonight. They got as excited as I was about the prospect of bagging Castille.

After we talked it over, the lieutenant decided to pull some uniformed officers from another district for the bust. They'd be told about the need for secrecy without being told why. The lieutenant had told the Second District commander about the rogue detective, so the commander supported what we were doing.

Koot and I were going to meet with Grady, Lieutenant Tolleson and the uniforms later to go over the layout of the mine and the approach plan. After I hung up, I thought it was Grady calling me back when the phone rang.

"Tag, they've got Brent." Adrienne had choked out the words.

"Adrienne, what happened?"

"He was skateboarding in front of the house. They took him."

"You saw them?"

"No, they called after they...after they...oh, God."

"All right, listen to me."

"It never occurred to me..."

"Adrienne, it's not your fault."

She screamed, "He's just a boy!"

"Brent needs us to keep it together, so we can help him. You can do that." I heard her take a couple of deep breaths, trying to rein in the fear. "Tell me what they said."

She took another deep breath and let it out. "They said they'll call you on your cell phone."

"Call me?"

"Yes."

"Okay. Did they say when they'd call?"

"Soon. They just said soon. They said if we brought in the police they would...they would..."

"We won't do that, Adrienne. Have you told anyone besides me?"

"Blanche. I'm at her house now."

"Are you going to tell Weems?"

"I think he should know."

"Can he be trusted not to call the police?"

She thought about it for a second, then said, "I won't call Clayton."

"All right. I'm on my way."

I hung up and put on a pair of cargo pants, a shirt and split leather boots. I strapped on the shoulder holster with the Kahr and took eight extra ammo clips from the closet. I put on my baseball jacket and grabbed a small bottle of Rescue Remedy and slipped it in my jacket. Then I got in the Sebring and pushed it hard toward Blanche's place.

I dialed Koot's cell. Only a handful of people had his cell number, and it was the only phone he'd answer during one of his classes. I heard a click and then heard Koot's voice telling a student, "The aggressor leads the dance," then he corrected someone's snap kick, then he answered the phone.

"Loomis."

"Castille has Brent."

"Where are you?"

"On my way to Blanche's."

"I'll meet you there."

"Call our man at motor vehicles and get an address to go with the license plates."

"I'm on it."

Before we lost them, we'd copied the license number of Heckle and Jeckle's Cobra. If we got an address, maybe we'd get lucky and they'd be holding Brent there. It was a place to start.

Blanche lived in a Tudor cottage on the lake side of Audubon Park on Prytania. I parked in the driveway, then went to the door and rang the chimes: *Bolero*. Blanche answered the door.

She spoke in a low, shaky voice. "I've never seen her like this, Tag."

"Has she taken anything?"

"No."

I took the Rescue Remedy out of my pocket and handed it to Blanche.

"For crisis. Double dose dropped under the tongue."

"She doesn't like taking drugs."

"It's not a drug."

Blanche took the bottle. "She's in the living room."

Adrienne was sitting on the couch, a portable phone in her lap. Her eyes were red and swollen. When she saw me she got up and met me in the middle of the room. She threw her arms around me and put her head on my shoulder.

"Tag, I want you to do whatever you have to do to get Brent back."

"We will."

She took her head off my shoulder and looked at me without a blink. "*Whatever* you have to do."

"Adrienne, you have to know something. We have the drugs that were stolen from Castille, but that won't be enough to get Brent back. Castille thinks Jackie and Danika stole from him, and he's going to want them as part of the bargain for Brent."

Barely audible. "No."

"Our only option is to agree to a meeting, then try to find Brent with the time we have."

She closed her eyes and nodded, then dropped into the chair behind her.

Blanche pulled the eyedropper from the bottle of Rescue Remedy and stepped over to Adrienne.

I said, "This will help."

She looked at the eyedropper.

Blanche said, "Under the tongue, and don't give me any static."

Adrienne opened her mouth and curled her tongue back. Blanche dropped in about six drops.

Blanche said, "Does this stuff make you dopey?"

"No. It just takes the edge off."

Blanche filled the dropper again, then tilted her head back and squeezed several drops into her own mouth.

When Koot arrived, Adrienne said, "Tag told me you lost your boy to these kind of men."

Koot said, "They don't win today."

Adrienne nodded. "Thank you."

Koot kept his feelings in tight compartments, but Adrienne had connected Koot to the memory of his son, and I knew that had twisted him inside. He struggled to swallow, then he struggled to speak. Finally, he just looked at Adrienne and nodded.

We waited in silence. We didn't have to wait long. I answered the phone on the first ring.

"I'm here, Castille."

"So you thought you could defeat me, cher?"

"The choke chain is on me, Castille, and you're holding the end."

"Did you kill my man in Mexico?"

"He made the play first."

"I'm also willing to kill to get what I want."

"Is the boy all right?"

"Do you have the Sojourn?"

In the background, Adrienne was pleading to speak to Brent.

"Yes, I have the drugs."

"I thought so. I give you the boy, you give me my drugs, and Kanawhite and Danika."

"You're asking Adrienne to trade her brother for her son. You know she can't do that."

"Would she rather I kill the boy and find my whore and Kanawhite later?"

I felt my stomach clench. I tried to keep my voice from betraying me. "Kanawhite and Danika didn't steal your drugs, Castille."

"And you know who did?"

"It was your cop."

Castille was silent for a few seconds, then he said, "Who would that be?"

"You have more than one on your payroll?"

"So, you're just guessing. A pathetic attempt to stall for time, cher. I'll tell you what, Boudreau. Kanawhite can stay where you have him hidden. You bring the Sojourn and Danika to Greenwood Cemetery, Metarie Road entrance, 4:00. Otherwise, we kill the boy and then we'll find the two of them anyway."

My head throbbed. Adrienne's eyes were painful pleas.

"The boy is scared, Castille. Let him speak to his mother."

"I give up something—you give up something." Then he hung up.

I wanted to keep talking, pretend Castille was still on the line listening to reason. Instead, I looked at Adrienne and shook my head. Adrienne's shoulders sagged. Blanche put her arms around her. I wanted to do the same, but we had less than two hours to find Brent. After 4:00, I was sure Brent would be dead.

Even if Castille got what he wanted, he might still kill Brent just because we made him look bad in Cabo. I had a feeling he'd try to take Koot and me out too.

"Adrienne, we're going after Brent."

The look she gave me knotted my stomach tighter. Blanche and I exchanged looks. She'd take care of Adrienne.

Koot stepped over. He had the look. He'd already turned painful memory to fire-etched readiness.

"This time he comes home, Tag."

THIRTY-EIGHT

We had an address to go with the license number of the Cobra; it was on Romulus, next to the horse track. We left Blanche's place in my car and drove up Carrolton to Esplanade, then worked my way into the neighborhood just north of the track. The regular racing season was over, but a special race week had the horses running and we could hear the track announcer's voice wash over the neighborhood, going through the lineup before post time: Patriot, Critical Mass, Lapaloosa Girl, Hang Time and some others.

Romulus was a short street that dead ended at the fairgrounds. I pulled past it and parked on Belfort. I chambered a round in the Kahr and Koot snapped a clip into his Glock and stuck his backup Smith and Wesson Chief's Special in an ankle holster. We concealed our weapons, got out and walked up Belfort, then turned down Romulus and headed toward the address. Judging by the way the numbers ran, 1210 would be a house or two from the end of the street. When we were half way down the block, an ice cream van turned onto Romulus, its kiddie Muzak tinkling through the neighborhood. If kids came to the street, it would be bad if Castille's men spotted us and leveled fire.

Koot stepped into the street and held his hand up for the driver to stop. We stepped to the driver's open window. The elderly Asian man had a jar of peanut butter between his legs with a spoon stuck in it. A paint-splattered portable CD player sat on his dash. Country and Western music. The kiddie tunes mixed with C & W was a strange brew, something Picasso might have listened to while churning out fractured people.

Koot said, "Sir, we have a police situation here. Please turn your van around and exit the area."

The man said, "Show me your badge."

Another pesky citizen asserting his rights.

I said, "Sir, we're not the police, but there may be trouble a few houses down from here. If children come out to the street, they could be in danger."

"Why not say that in the first place? I will turn around."

"Thank you."

A couple of kids came out of their houses and ran to the van. The Asian gent said, "Children, no ice cream today. Go back inside and have a nice glass of water. Very good for you."

The kids looked puzzled, then pissed, then they went back inside. The elderly man turned the van around in a driveway, then nodded solemnly as he drove by us. A reasonable person. We didn't come across those too often.

We continued down the block until we were a couple of doors away from the house, a bungalow with four chunky, dry rotted columns in the middle and at the ends of the porch. The eaves of the gabled roof were rotting, and the small lawn was badly rutted where cars had parked. Two dead holly bushes framed the crumbling concrete steps. My real estate friend would call it a fixer-upper wannabe.

Heckle and Jeckle's Cobra wasn't around, but an early model Malibu was parked on the street in front of the house. Koot and I drew our weapons and moved quickly to the side of the house, staying low. A TV blared in the front of the house, the noise running neck and neck with the noise from the track.

We made our way to the back of the house and moved to the door. I tried the doorknob. Unlocked. Koot dropped down low. I turned the knob slowly, then opened the door quickly. No unfriendly greeting. I slipped in with Koot at my back, and we moved down the hall. We cleared the kitchen, the bathroom and the two bedrooms, then we moved the rest of the way to the living room and peered in.

A woman was sprawled on the couch with her legs on the coffee table, watching the Shopping Channel, the volume on the TV at full blast. She was nude. On the coffee table was a half empty quart of scotch and a half full glass.

We moved quickly to the couch. The woman saw us and opened her mouth. With the TV and race noise, it was hard to tell, but I think she screamed. Koot moved behind the sofa, ready to grab the woman in case she had a surprise hidden between the cushions.

A bag of coke lay on the couch beside her. Three chorus lines of the powder ran on the glass of a framed picture lying on the coffee table. The photo was of the woman and Heckle. Heckle's tongue was running up the woman's face. Classy.

Koot ran his hand between the couch cushions. No gun.

I tried to shout over the noise. "Stand up."

She let her legs fall to the floor, but when she tried to stand she teetered and fell back on the couch. I walked over to the TV and turned it off. That left the sharp voice of the track announcer as the horses came out of the gate. The woman tried to stand again, but only managed to sit up at the edge of the couch.

"Ya scarrred the shit ou' of me. You thh cops?" The slurred speech, the floating eyes. All too familiar.

I said, "The cops come later."

I took off my jacket and held it out for her to cover up. Instead of taking it, she smiled and sat up straighter, pointing her nipples at me.

Koot said, "Stand up."

She smiled some more and this time got to her feet. Probably thought we wanted the full view. Except for the bruises, she had an attractive body.

I yelled, "Where is the boy?"

Her eyes were all over the place. "Thh boy. I tol' thm not to hurrt him."

Koot was getting tense. He shouted, "Where do they have him?"

"Thhe woo kill me if I..." She looked like she was about to pass out. Koot grabbed her and shook her shoulders to keep her conscious.

I said loudly, "They're going to kill the boy if we don't get to him soon. You understand?"

She slumped. Koot lifted her and shook her again.

"They sa' thhe woo not kill hmm."

I touched a bruise on her arm and one on her face.

"Your boyfriend did this to you. You think he won't kill the boy if his boss tells him to?"

Koot's face reddened. He shook her harder. That wiped the smile off.

She said, "Hey!" She was angry, and her eyes picked up some focus. "Aw right, aw right. They took hmm to Mahdi Gras warehass. In Algiers."

We knew the warehouse. It was used to store old parade floats. At one time there were public tours.

I said loudly, "You'd better not tell them we were here. They'll know you gave us the warehouse location."

Koot let the woman go, and she flopped on the couch. He bent over and blew the coke lines off the photo, then grabbed the bag and ripped it open and slung it across the room. A white powder storm filled the air. A boy taken and now a woman beaten put Koot over the edge. He bent close to the woman.

"You wanna be a victim the rest of your life?"

That pissed her off again. She spewed, "Na a victimm. I do wha' I want."

Koot straightened and pulled his card from his pocket and dropped it on the coffee table. He yelled, "You want out of this shit life, you call me. There are people who can help."

We left the house in a cloud of coke dust as Lapaloosa Girl beat Critical Mass to the wire by a nose.

I drove through traffic and onto the expressway, then crossed the river on the Greater New Orleans Bridge. From the bridge we could see the Mardi Gras warehouse on the bank of the river. It was nearly 3:00. They'd be taking Brent out of the warehouse in about a half hour and head to the meeting place.

After we crossed the river we curved around onto Franklin and turned back up toward Algiers Point and the warehouse.

The corrugated metal building was the size of a large airplane hanger and took up all the space between the quiet river street and the levee behind. The building probably stayed locked until after Mardi Gras, when they moved the floats into storage. I wondered if the owner knew Castille was using the building. Maybe they had some illegal business together, or maybe Castille had something on the owner.

I drove by slowly and saw the Cobra parked at the side of the building, near the back. It was the only car in the lot. At the next block, I came back around and parked on the opposite side of the building, near the front corner where there were no windows.

We got out and walked to the front entrance. Beside the two large closed bay doors was a people door. It was locked, so we went to the side of the warehouse where the Cobra was parked. We moved quickly down the side of the building until we came to another people door. Koot tried it. That one was locked too.

About eighteen feet above us was a bank of windows, the kind that pivot open from the middle of the window frame. Two of the windows were open, but were too high for one of us to boost the other up to them. Stacked beside the building were some ten-foot lengths of four-by-fours.

Koot said, "This'll do."

We pulled one of the four by fours from the pile and leaned it gently against the building so it wouldn't bang the corrugated metal walls.

Koot said, "This time I go."

"Hey, be all you can be."

I stooped so Koot could climb up on my shoulders. When he was steady on my shoulders I stood up, then held the timber to steady it. Koot reached up to the end of the timber against the building and muscled himself up. The end of the timber was the size of a piece of toast, yet Koot got part of one foot on it, then, using the side of the building to steady himself, he slowly stood up. Then he got part of his other foot on the end.

The window frame was another three feet above Koot's head. Koot got his balance, then slowly bent his knees, then leaped and caught the window frame.

He pulled himself up to the window and looked in, then pulled himself through the narrow space under the glass pane and into the warehouse.

I brought the timber down and placed it back in the pile, then drew my weapon and moved to the door. In a few seconds, Koot unlatched the door and I slipped in quickly and eased the door shut behind me.

The huge building was jammed with floats from past Mardi Gras parades. Papier maché heads of famous personalities, mythological figures and cartoon characters were mounted on the floats or hung on the walls around the warehouse, each head the size of a Zamboni. Marilyn Monroe, Michael Jordan, Goofy, Bogart, Neptune, Oprah.

Through the floats, we could see an office in the corner of the building. Glass windows all the way around gave anyone in the office a view of the warehouse. Heckle and Jeckle were inside watching TV. They'd have Brent nearby.

Koot and I used the cover of the floats and made our way closer to the office, but didn't see Brent inside with Castille's guys. Just outside the office was another door. I pointed to it, and Koot nodded. We got on our stomachs and crawled under the office windows toward the door. When we were near the door we heard a moan that sounded like it came from behind us. I knew it was Brent.

We turned around and crawled back under the windows toward the sound. Then one of Castille's men yelled, and we rolled to our backs and took aim at the office door. Then he yelled again and I realized he was clamoring at the TV.

Conley Clark

We quickly crawled past the office and back to the cover of the floats. We heard the moan again. It was coming from the float next to us. We moved to the side of the float that couldn't be seen from the office, then peered over. Huddled under Mick Jagger's gigantic lips was Brent, his hands and feet clasp-tied and his mouth covered with duct tape.

I looked in the office. Heckle and Jeckle were still fixated on the tube, so I crawled over the side and onto the bed of the float. Brent was in an awkward position on his side. I rolled him toward me. His eyes were fearful until he recognized me.

I whispered "The cavalry's here, bud."

I got my nails under the end of the tape. "This is going to snatch your mustache off. No noise, okay?"

Brent nodded. I yanked and Brent winced silently. I took out my Swiss Army knife and cut the plastic ties from his hands and feet. Brent scratched hard above his top lip.

I said, "You had enough of this place?"

He nodded. "Is my mom all right?"

"She's fine. Let's go over the side, okay, nice and low."

Brent crawled over the side, and Koot lowered him to the ground and I followed. Koot led Brent to the exit, while I covered the rear. When we were about ten feet from the door, it opened and a guy stepped through with a boxed pizza in his hand. He dropped the pizza and went for his gun, but before the pie hit the ground Koot shot the guy twice in the chest and he collapsed in the doorway.

I tossed the keys to Koot. "Get him to the car."

Koot said, "Let's go, Brent." They jumped over the body as they escaped the building.

Then, BAM! BAM! BAM! One guy ran from the office firing, one fired from inside the office door. I fired three times, and the office window exploded. Heckle went down in a shower of glass. I knew two slugs caught him. He wouldn't be beating women or kidnapping kids anymore.

Jeckle made it to one of the floats. He fired twice, and I could hear the slugs passing through Darth Vader's head just above me. I ran for a float closer to the door. Two more rounds hit the metal wall behind me. I ducked behind Elmer Fudd's chin and squeezed off four rounds to keep Jeckle pinned, then dashed through the door. Koot had backed the Sebring to the entrance. He flung the door open, I leaped in and Koot scorched the Michelins out of the lot.

THIRTY-NINE

When I was sure we hadn't been followed, I told Brent he could get up from the floor in the back. He rose cautiously and peered out the back window. When he was convinced that the shooting was over, he climbed in the back seat.

"You okay, Brent?"

He looked dazed. "Are those men dead?"

"Two of them are."

Violence in real life is not like in the movies. There's no emotional distance. It's all sweat and fear and adrenaline. At least that's the way it is for most of us. With Koot it's mostly just adrenaline. Brent had seen someone killed, and he had been afraid for his own life. I was concerned about how he would handle the experience. He seemed confused.

"My mom says people should never resort to violence."

"I think she's changed her mind on that, Brent. What do you think about what happened?"

He creased his brow. In a few seconds he said, "I'm not glad those men are dead—but I'm not sorry either."

Brent would go through some ups and downs with this, but I had a feeling he'd be okay.

We went straight to Blanche's house. We needed to get Adrienne, Blanche and Brent to a safer place until this was over. Marty was going to have a full house.

The look on Adrienne's face when we walked in took away some of the edge of being shot at. She and Blanche engulfed Brent. I gave them their time while Koot watched the front of the house.

When Adrienne and Blanche let Brent up for air, Brent said, "Those men tried to kill us, Mom. Koot and Tag shot two of them." He waited. I think he wanted his mother to help him get perspective.

Adrienne said, "The world is full of violent people, Brent. I didn't want to look at that." Adrienne looked at me, then back at Brent. "Tag and Koot did what they had to do to bring you back to me. And I'm glad."

Brent looked at me, then back at his mom. "So am I."

I said, "Adrienne, Castille's men may be on their way here."

Adrienne and Blanche stiffened. The look on Brent's face showed a new understanding of a part of life that most people never have to face.

He said, "Mom, Aunt Blanche—we have to go."

I said, "You can stay at Marty's until it's safe to come home."

They threw some things together, then we left. We got to Marty's at about 4:00, the time we were supposed to have made the exchange with Castille. Another disappointment for Castille. We planned to disappoint him one more time.

I had called the lieutenant on the way to Blanche's house and told him what happened. I had to listen to his harangue about Koot and me being uncontrollable. Then Grady got on the phone and told us he'd meet us at Marty's.

Marty had just come home from a luncheon fundraiser when we arrived. Danika and Jackie were playing rummy at the dining room table.

I said, "Marty, you have room for three more?"

"You protect 'em, I'll pack 'em in."

Brent told Jackie, Danika and Marty about the kidnapping and about the rescue, and was swarmed again. He looked like he was enjoying the attention.

After the telling was done, Danika said, "This cannot continue. You are all in danger because of me. Maybe I should go."

Adrienne said, "We won't let you do that."

"Castille will never let us go, Tag."

I said. "Have faith in us a little longer."

"I wish I had your courage."

"Courage is when you keep going, despite fear and hopelessness. You've been doing that for years."

Danika closed her eyes and took a deep breath, then opened her eyes again and nodded. She would stay put.

I heard Adrienne thank Marty for his help, then tell him she needed to talk to him outside. Marty got the look—like he thought it might be something he didn't want to hear—then he followed Adrienne through the back door.

I was guessing Adrienne wanted to make sure Marty had no expectations of being with her in return for his help. Maybe she'd tell him how she felt about me. Then maybe she'd tell *me*.

At first Marty might have helped as a way to get next to Adrienne, but I also knew Marty wanted to do the right thing, something he rarely got to do in the political hippodrome he mucked around in. I think taking the risk with the drug buy made Marty realize he was braver than he gave himself credit for. By doing the right thing I think Marty discovered, or rediscovered, that was reward enough. I was pretty sure of it when they came back in the house. Marty was fine, even jovial.

Grady arrived, and while the doting on Brent and Danika continued, Grady, Marty, Koot and I went in the kitchen and sat at the table.

Grady said, "So Castille wanted to trade for the boy."

Marty quickly added, "For Jackie and Danika."

Marty knew Grady and the lieutenant couldn't know about the drug deal, so he had quickly tried to deflect suspicion about it where there was none.

Grady said, "I thought it was for Saints' season tickets."

Grady was annoyed. I knew it was mostly at Koot and me for going Brent's rescue alone.

Grady said to Koot and me, "You left two bodies at the Mardi Gras warehouse?"

Koot said, "Bodies that won't be there by the time you send Homicide."

Grady said, "We have to stay focused on tonight. As far as the lieutenant is concerned, 'No bodies—no homicide.'"

I said, "Good."

Grady still looked annoyed. "You two getting the boy back is good—very good—but this cowboy crap has to stop."

Koot said, "We were up against the clock, Grady."

I said, "They threatened to kill Brent if the police were spotted."

Grady understood, but like the lieutenant, he had to get it out of his system. He mumbled, "Friggin' outta control, the both of you."

Marty said, "How about some coffee?"

I said, "No time."

"What now, somebody's cat stuck in a tree?"

I gave Marty the broad strokes about tonight's bust.

Grady said, "NOPD has been trying to find where Castille makes his stuff for over a year, then these two find the place in a few days." He looked at Marty and nodded toward Koot and me, then smiled for the first time. "I guess they're still pretty good detectives."

I'd tell him some other time about Nads and Giancarlo and the joint of an informant's finger.

FORTY

Koot and I sped to the Second District station. When we walked in, the lieutenant was telling all the Homicide detectives gathered for the Thursday afternoon staff meeting that it had been canceled. Trammel and Fortenberry looked curious about the announcement. Stubbs looked bored. Doucette and Mowery looked constipated, as usual.

When he was done, Lieutenant Tolleson looked toward Grady, then looked our way. "Herns, you, Loomis and Boudreau come in my office."

Doucette said, "Lieutenant, what's goin' on? How come we don't know where Kanawhite and the woman have been taken. How come Boudreau and Loomis show up and we get shut out?"

"You don't like the way I'm running things, file a complaint, Doucette."

Doucette gave the lieutenant a hard look, then swiveled it around to me. Mowery leaned back in his chair and crossed his arms. The lieutenant and Grady turned and walked into his office, and Koot and I followed. I looked at Mowery and Doucette as we walked by.

I said, "You guys should get a new look. Maybe get a facial or change your part to the other side."

Mowery said, "You and me, Boudreau."

Maybe I helped provide meaning to their lives.

I was about to enter the lieutenant's office when I glanced toward Fortenberry and noticed blood coming through his shirt at his left shoulder. I stepped over to his desk.

"That's a pretty nasty wound, Hal." I nodded toward his shoulder.

He looked down at the walnut-sized blood stain, then lifted the shirt material away from the wound. He seemed to study the blood for a few seconds before he spoke.

"I was putting a tin roof on a storage shed this weekend. The edge caught me."

"Did you see a doc?"

"Nah."

"Koot's had some experience. Why don't you let him have a look?"

"Thanks, but it's not that bad."

"Okay."

I walked into Lieutenant Tolleson's office and closed the door behind me.

"What does Fortenberry drive?"

Grady said, "An old Chevy pickup and a green Trans Am."

"Koot, show the lieutenant the mine layout. I'll be back in a few minutes."

The lieutenant said, "Where the hell you going, Boudreau?"

"To check out a muscle car."

I left the office and went downstairs and out of the station. The cops parked their personal cars up and down Magazine near the station and around the corner on Napoleon. I walked up to Napoleon. About half way down the block, I spotted the Pontiac Trans Am.

When I reached the car, I walked to the rear. The casing on the right tail light didn't match the left one. It was clean and looked new. I glanced around for cops, then took out my Swiss Army knife, pried out the screw driver and squatted at the right tail light. I took out the two screws and popped the casing off. The reflector behind the bulbs had been punctured through to the frame. I dug into the imploded metal with the screw driver and a spent slug fell out.

I screwed the casing back on and went back up to Lieutenant Tolleson's office and closed the door. I dropped the slug on the lieutenant's desk.

"I dug this out of the right tail light of Fortenberry's Trans Am." Everybody looked at the slug. "It's mine."

Grady said, "Sonofabitch."

Koot lowered his head and sighed.

Lieutenant Tolleson stared at me for a few seconds, then stared through the glass at Fortenberry. He said, "So Fortenberry rips Castille off, then keeps pretending to be the devoted employee."

Grady said, "And the devoted cop."

Lieutenant Tolleson said, "Bring him in."

Grady stuck his head out and told Fortenberry the lieutenant wanted to see him. When Fortenberry entered and saw four sober faces focused on him, he looked nervous.

The lieutenant said, "Detec..." He gritted his teeth. "Fortenberry, let me have your weapon and badge."

Grady stood behind Fortenberry, blocking the view of the rest of the detectives and poised for Fortenberry to make a stupid move.

Fortenberry said, "What's this about, Lieutenant?"

Lieutenant Tolleson said, "The gun and badge, Fortenberry."

Hal glanced from face to face, then removed his Glock from his holster and set it on the desk. The lieutenant handed the Glock and the spent bullet to Grady.

"This is a matter for Public Integrity. You'll go there with Detective Herns and a uniformed officer. Herns will present them with preliminary evidence. They'll have questions."

Fortenberry said, "Lieutenant..."

"Save it, Fortenberry. We're about to go after your boss."

Grady opened the door and escorted Fortenberry out of the office. Grady didn't have a hand on Fortenberry, but you could tell the other detectives knew something was up. I closed the office door.

The lieutenant said, "We can feel sorry about this later."

I said, "Now that you've got your guy, you going to let your detectives in on the bust?"

"Yeah."

"You going to tell them about Fortenberry?"

"It can wait. They don't need this shit on their minds going into a dangerous situation. And if that wasn't enough, this hurricane heading our way is big—a mother—and Mayor Nagin just called for a voluntary evac. We don't have much time."

The lieutenant stood and we followed him out of the office. He gathered the detectives again. "Detectives, we have an opportunity here. Boudreau and Loomis found Dumont Castille's drug operation."

Mowery and Doucette looked at each other. They had been part of the ongoing effort to find Castille's factory and wouldn't like that we'd found it first.

"Castille will be there tonight for a shipment. We're going in."

Trammel asked, "Lieutenant, isn't this Narcotics' bust?"

"No, we're bringing in a murderer. If we find drugs on the scene, so much the better."

The lieutenant didn't want to shut Narcotics out, but he didn't have time to wrangle over a plan with them and who gets to lead going in.

Mowery asked, "What about Herns and Fortenberry?"

"They're taking care of some other business."

The detectives glanced around at each other. You could tell they all had questions.

The lieutenant said, "Castille's operation is in Vermilion Parish. I've cleared it with the sheriff's department down there. I'm bringing in some uniformed officers so we can go in strong. I'll brief you on our approach before we go. Now make your calls to your families, grab a bite to eat, then be back here in forty-five minutes for the briefing. We'll be leaving in a couple of hours."

Doucette said, "Boudreau and Loomis aren't tagging along on police business are they, lieutenant?"

"No, they're not tagging along. They're going to *lead* us there."

I took a couple of seconds to enjoy the look on Doucette's face.

Mowery said, "Then they're gonna stay out of the way?"

The lieutenant said, "Mowery, Doucette, in a few hours you're gonna be entering a damned piranha tank. You'd better get your minds on piranhas."

Without waiting for another complaint from Rabid and Rabider, the lieutenant motioned for Koot and me to follow him into the office. We went over the layout of the salt mine while the detectives were either on the phones, out for food or getting shotguns and semiautomatics requisitioned. Some of the uniformed officers the lieutenant had requested from another station had come upstairs to wait for the briefing.

We had been going over the plan for a few minutes when the lieutenant took a call. He mostly listened, then in a minute he hung up. He looked shaken.

"I made a mistake, fellas—a bad one. Public Integrity found out Fortenberry sold his Trans Am over a week ago."

Koot said, "To who?"

"Stubbs. We got the wrong cop."

We looked at each other.

I said, "Stubbs would have called Castille by now."

Koot said, "Castille knows we're coming."

The lieutenant shook his head. "I should have checked on the car."

I said, "It got by all of us."

The lieutenant said, "Castille thinks we're coming later. He'll take time to load his shipment. We go *now*."

The lieutenant stepped out into the main room. Trammel and three uniforms were sitting around talking.

"Trammel, get on the radio and get Mowery, Doucette and Stubbs back here on the double."

Trammel reached out. Mowery and Doucette had gone across the street for burgers. They were back in a couple of minutes. Stubbs showed up five minutes later. When Stubbs walked in, Lieutenant Tolleson went over and stood in front of him. I eased up behind the lieutenant.

Lieutenant Tolleson said, "Stubbs, let me have your weapon."

That got everyone's attention. It was pointless now to try and keep the detectives in the dark about having a parasite in the Second District.

Stubbs said, "What's the deal, lieutenant?"

"Right now it's about giving me your weapon."

Stubbs' eyes bounced back and forth between us and the detectives, then he glanced toward the two ways out of the room. Koot moved silently to the midpoint between the two stairways.

Doucette, Mowery and Trammel were cops with cops' instincts. Trammel placed her hand on her weapon. Mowery unsnapped his holster strap. Stubbs picked up on it, but you could see he was still thinking about making a move. Finally, he opened his coat and showed the gun at his side.

He said, "Easy. Why is everyone so amped?"

The lieutenant stepped over to pull Stubbs' gun from his holster. When he reached for it, Stubbs grabbed him around the neck, pulling him in to his body with his left hand. He grabbed his weapon with the other hand, then put it to the lieutenant's head.

Trammel, Mowery and Koot drew down at the same time. Stubbs' voice pinched up an octave. "Get away from the stairs, Loomis." Koot didn't move.

The lieutenant said, "Forget about walking out of here, Stubbs."

Stubbs backed the lieutenant up so no one could get behind him. He breathing was shallow, eratic. He went red.

"Boudreau, you and Loomis had to stick your goddamned faces in this. Why would you help a whore and her party boy?"

I held my hand up. "This doesn't have to end badly, Stubbs."

Still hot. "I asked you a question."

"It's what cops do."

"You're *not* fuckin' cops."

"Reasons are the same."

"Right. Serve and protect. It's all bullshit. Most homicides should be misdemeanors. Scum killing scum for a dime bag—for a pair of ju ju flake tennis shoes—or over some extracurricular hump."

"We let justice be decided in the streets—it's a short fall to the bottom, Stubbs."

There were footsteps on the stairs. Grady and Fortenberry topped the stairs and stopped.

Stubbs said, "Yeah, well, I'm not taking the fall." Stubbs tightened the grip around Lieutenant Tolleson's neck. "I killed one. What's one more?"

Mowery said, "The difference between living or dying right here."

Stubbs' eyes glazed as he looked around at the faces in the room. After several seconds he let the lieutenant go and put his gun to his own head and gritted his teeth.

I said, "Don't do it, Ernie."

Stubbs stood there with the gun at his head, trembling.

The lieutenant held out his hand and said, "It's over, Stubbs."

Stubbs stood with the gun at his head, then he asked himself a question—the age-old question.

"Who am I?"

Then he handed the gun to the lieutenant and it was over.

FORTY-ONE

After two uniforms took Stubbs away, Grady and Hal showed up at the station. Lieutenant Tolleson and I apologized to Hal for the mistaken accusation. The apology was rushed, which none of us wanted, but we had lost time we didn't have dealing with Stubbs. I was relieved when Hal let us off the hook.

The lieutenant addressed the detectives and uniforms.

"We're about to walk into a bad situation, and you didn't need this hanging over you, but it's done and we've got to put it aside for now. Stubbs warned Castille, but Castille thinks we're coming later tonight. So we go now. Herns will brief you."

Grady said, "The drug operation is in an old salt mine. There's only one elevator to move the crated drugs and lab equipment out of the mine. We don't think they'll have enough time to get it all out before we get there. That's good. There are women in the mine. Our main concern is getting them out safely."

Lieutenant Tolleson said, "Boudreau and Loomis have been to the mine. Boudreau will give you the layout." The lieutenant looked directly at Doucette and Mowery. "Anybody has a problem with that, you can sit this one out." No one said anything. The lieutenant nodded to me.

I picked up the magic marker and drew a basic layout on the white marker board. "The chain will have to be cut at the main entrance. About a hundred and twenty yards down the entrance road is a guard shack. We go in fast without lights and take out the guard." I pointed to the elevator location. "The elevator into the mine is here. First level down is the crated drugs. The women's quarters are on the second level. Third level is where they cook the stuff. Women will be on the second and third levels."

Lieutenant Tolleson said, "First we secure the surface, then Herns, Mowery, Doucette, Fortenberry and two uniforms will get the women out of the mine."

The lieutenant waited for questions, then he said, "We've been waiting a long time for this."

Hal cut his eyes my way and said, "Let's go catch the *real* bad guys."

Koot and I rode with Grady and Lieutenant Tolleson. Doucette, Mowery, Fortenberry, and Trammel were behind us, followed by eight uniformed officers in two patrol cars. When we got near the mine gate, Grady killed the lights. The three cars behind us went dark, and we eased up to the entryway and stopped. A uniform jumped out with a pair of cable cutters and cut the chain on the entrance gate and quickly pushed the two halves of the gate open.

As Grady eased the Crown Vic to the gate, the other cars lined up on his bumper. The uniform hopped back in the patrol car and, we took off fast. When we were about seventy yards out, the guard saw or heard us and stepped out of the guard shack, opening fire with a semiautomatic. The lieutenant, Koot and I stuck our heads out our windows and returned fire. The Crown Vic's windshield took a bullet and splintered. One of us shot the guard, who went down.

Grady shouted, "Anyone hit?"

No one. We roared up to the guard shack in a shower of flak coming from Castille's men at the mine entrance. Grady and the other three drivers slid to a stop, one behind the other. We all bailed out and got behind the vehicles. which were soon riddled with ordnance. One of the uniforms caught a bullet in the arm, and another officer tied on a tourniquet to stop the bleeding.

Castille's crew blasted from behind a tractor trailer, their faces lit by muzzle fire. The truck would be loaded with the shipment of Sojourn.

I slapped Koot on the shoulder and nodded toward the guard. We stayed low and moved back to where the guard was lying by the shack, keeping the cars between us and the gunfire. The guy had caught one in the chest and one in the side. He was bleeding pretty badly. Koot picked up the semiautomatic lying beside the guy and tossed it out of reach.

I yelled over the thunder of gunfire. "Are the women still in the mine?"

The guy looked scared. He grabbed my shirt and pulled me to him. "I can't die. I've got plans."

I leaned to the guy's ear. "The sooner this ends, the sooner we can get you help."

Conley Clark

He didn't answer at first. Koot ripped off part of the guy's shirt and stuffed it in the guy's gaping chest wound, then placed the guy's right hand on the patch to hold it in place. Shots hit the guard shack just above our heads. Wood chips peppered our hair.

The guy glanced down at his shirt, which was dark with blood, then tried to speak. I leaned down close so I could hear.

He said, "Women...in the mine."

"Where is Castille?"

"Barge... on the lake."

The oil drilling barge we had seen last night.

"How many of his men on the barge?"

"Three."

"What's he doing?"

The guy choked on blood trying to speak. Finally he got it out, barely audible. "Don't know."

More bullets slammed the guard shack. The window fractured and dropped. The shack looked like a voter card with all the chads punched.

I said to Castille's man, "Hang on."

Koot and I moved back to the cars, where the firefight had intensified—probably the rest of Castille's crew had come up from below ground. We moved to Lieutenant Tolleson's and Grady's position.

I shouted over the gunfire. "Castille is on a drilling barge in the lake. Only three men. Koot and I can take them."

"Take a couple of men," the lieutenant shouted.

"You've got your hands full here."

Lieutenant Tolleson looked down the line. Another uniform had caught a slug in the foot that came in under the car. She was still fighting, but she wouldn't be able to move in toward the mine when the time came. That made them two officers short, and they needed to go in strong to get to the women below. The lieutenant thought about it for a second, then nodded.

I pointed toward the woods about forty yards behind us. "Cover us to the trees."

The lieutenant nodded.

Grady shouted, "You two watch your hot dogs."

Koot said, "Always."

Grady nodded.

The lieutenant yelled for his men to cover us. When the fusillade started, we broke for the woods. We got half way to the tree line before Castille's men turned fire on us. Shots speared the ground around us, then we were in the trees. We moved well back into the pines so the trees would take most of the blind fire Castille's men sprayed at us. After several seconds they stopped firing at us and redirected at the detectives and officers.

It took us a couple of minutes to circle around the gunmen's position and reach the lake. In the moonlight we saw a boat house and dock down shore. We sprinted, and I was breathing hard when we got there. While I was catching my breath, the gazelle was already in a skiff starting the engine. I climbed in, and we headed for the barge rig, about two hundred yards out in the lake.

When we got near the rig, Koot idled down so we could approach quietly. We snapped new clips into our weapons.

Koot asked, "What's Castille up to?"

The drilling rig was active, which meant there'd be a drilling crew. Not a likely place for Castille to hide money or drugs.

"We're about to find out."

FORTY-TWO

We slipped in beside the barge and tied off. Farther down the barge, a drilling crew boat was tied to the docking platform, the boat Castille and his men had come in.

No one in sight, so we grabbed a railing and pulled ourselves up to the first deck. From there we headed to the pipe deck. Before I joined NOPD, I had worked on a drilling rig in the Gulf for ten months. Knowing the layout might prove useful.

We moved down the walkway, then climbed the stairs to the pipe deck. When we neared the landing, I stuck my head up far enough to see one of Castille's crew holding a semiautomatic on a couple of roustabouts. The roustabouts were attaching thirty-foot sections of six-inch drill pipe to the crane cable, then the crane hoisted the pipe up to the rig floor where a couple of roughnecks pulled the pipe into the enclosed drilling area.

Through the wide V door opening of the rig floor I saw Eyes holding his weapon on the roughnecks while they connected pipe to the drill string. Only, the blowout prevention stack stood about eight feet off to the side from where they were drilling. Nothing was making sense.

I nodded toward a pipe rack that held a couple of dozen sections of drill pipe. We dashed behind it.

Koot said, "I got him."

I grabbed a large pipe wrench that lay close by. "I'll get his attention."

Koot darted for a large pressurized tank. From there he made his way to the cover of a hydroclone lying on deck. He was now twenty feet from Castille's man.

Koot nodded, and I heaved the heavy wrench. With the drilling noise up on the rig floor, I wasn't worried about Eyes hearing the wrench hit. When it struck the deck, the gunman turned toward the noise.

When Koot made his move, the roustabouts looked his way, which caught the gunman's attention. He wheeled around. Koot leap-kicked him in the face before he could get a shot off. Lights out.

I moved to the roustabouts while Koot picked up the weapon beside Castille's man and slung it into the lake. I told the men to go down to the crew boat and wait. I kept an eye on Eyes while the men descended the stairs to the lower deck.

Koot and I were about to move toward the deck above when the floor under our feet began to vibrate; suddenly the whole barge rig was shaking. Metal girders all over the barge twisted and moaned. The pipe wrench danced on the metal deck like water droplets on a griddle.

Then it dawned on me. Castille had forced the driller to skid the barge over with the hydraulics to make room for a new well bore. Then Castille had the crew attach a new drill bit and pipe to a mud motor and gyro, then the new drill was aimed at the salt dome. He had forced the driller to puncture the salt mine below and now the lake was emptying into it—and the women were still down there.

Castille figured he wouldn't have time to move the drugs and all of the equipment out of the mine before we arrived. By emptying the lake into the mine, he could seal the evidence and drown the women so there'd be no witnesses.

Castille or one of his men knew something about drilling—enough to come up with the idea to make it look like a drilling accident—like a miscalculation by the oil company. And Castille was willing to drown the rig crew to complete the scenario. Only we got here early.

I could see the lake water already circulating around the barge, drawn toward the hole under us. Salt dissolves quickly, which meant the hole would widen rapidly. There wasn't much time to get the women out.

Eyes and Castille showed at the rig floor opening, heading for the crew boat. When they spotted us, they quickly moved back behind the doorway and opened fire. We returned fire as we ran for the cover of the pipe rack. From there, Koot fired on their position while I got on the radio to Grady.

"Grady, what's happening?"

"What's left of Castille's crew gave up. We still have to get the women on the second level, but Tag—water is pouring in through the damned walls."

"Get them out now, Grady."

"What's going on?"

"Castille forced the barge crew to drill into the mine. The lake is coming in, and it won't take long to flood the mine."

"Shit." Grady hung up.

Koot and I kept raking Castille's and Eyes' position, but the barge was shaking so violently now we might as well have been firing blindfolded. Eyes broke for the stairs. We tracked his descent, but our shots sprayed wildly. Eyes tripped and toppled at the bottom, then got up and used the partial cover of some P tanks as he headed for the stairs leading to the crew boat.

Koot moved to head Eyes off. Movement for the both of them was a one-step-forward-two-steps-sideways progression. We were all struggling to stay on our feet.

I glanced out at the lake. The slow circling water had now formed into a gigantic whirlpool, and was picking up speed. We needed to get the crew off the barge before the whole rig went under.

I fired at Castille on the rig floor while Koot circled around the pipe deck. As Eyes neared the stairs, Koot stepped from behind the crane and came down hard with his fist on Eyes' gun arm and the gun skidded across the deck. A jackhammer of blows would usually follow, but Koot lost his balance on the convulsing deck. Eyes grabbed onto a cable above him and swung his body forward and kicked Koot in the chest, sending him backward over some cement casings.

Eyes went for his gun, which was bouncing all over the deck. I stepped into the open and tried to move closer to Eyes to increase my odds of hitting him, but staggered like a drunk. Fortunately, Castille, from above, was shooting at me like one. But even drunks can get lucky.

When Eyes reached his gun, I stopped and fired. The second shot caught him in the meat of his bicep, and he spun and went down. I had aimed at his chest.

When I surged toward him, Eyes came up with the pipe wrench and swung. He caught me in the hip; my body jerked, and the Kahr flew under the pipe rack.

Castille was still firing at me from the rig floor and didn't seem to care that Eyes was in the firing line. Scumbag fealty. Koot rolled to the cover of some cement casings and fired at Castille.

Eyes lunged at me, and we went down. When we hit the deck, Eyes was on top of me and got off two solid punches to my jaw.

When he drew his arm back the third time I thrust the palm of my hand hard up under his chin and his head snapped back.

I heard a loud creak just before the post on the pipe rack collapsed and the pipes crashed to the floor and rushed toward us. I got my foot under Eyes' stomach and shoved, then rolled to my feet and dove clear of the careening steel. I looked back and saw Eyes get swept off his feet and buried under the heavy pipe.

I made my way around behind the P tanks to Koot. He had taken a slug in the leg from Castille. The noise of the barge breaking up grew louder.

I shouted, "Can you make it to the crew boat?" It was a short crawl to the stairs.

"Yeah. What are you gonna do?"

"Get the rest of the crew out."

"You'll need cover."

"I need you to keep the guys at the crew boat from taking off. Hold the boat for five minutes. No one shows—get the men to shore."

The whirlpool was circling faster now. It was like someone had pulled the plug on a gigantic bathtub.

I shouted, "Give me the Glock." Koot gave me his gun and the extra clips from his belt. He still had his .38 in his ankle holster. I said, "I'll cover you to the stairs."

Koot got himself pointed toward the stairs, then looked at me. I shouted, "What?"

"You can't save everybody, Boudreau."

"How many times have I said that to *you*?"

"You die, I'm gonna be pissed."

"It's good to get that out of your system. Now move."

I snapped a new clip in and strafed Castille's position.

When Koot had made it down the stairs, I lurched for the side stairwell leading up to the rig floor. As I climbed the steps I clung to the railing to keep from being hurled off. The violent shaking made my teeth feel like a palsied dentist was drilling my mouth.

When I reached the top of the steps, I slipped through the door and crouched behind the drawworks engine. I could see part of Castille's shirt behind the BOP stack. He hadn't seen me break for the rig floor and was still looking for me down on the pipe deck.

I motioned for the six crew members huddled near the drill shack to come. They used the wall to steady themselves as they staggered to me, then they crouched behind the engine.

Conley Clark

I leaned close and spoke just loud enough for them to hear me. "They're waiting for you at the crew boat."

Castille's view was partially hidden by the stack, so I motioned for them to go. When they reached the head of the stairs Castille saw them. I emptied a clip at the BOP stack, which kept Castille pinned long enough for the crew to clear the landing and descend.

I popped another clip in. Castille broke for the main door down to the pipe deck, but I cut him off with more fire and he lunged for the drill shack for cover. As I turned to follow the crew down the stairs there was a horrendous, ripping noise as the giant barge pitched sideways. I tumbled out from behind the drawworks engine and grabbed the hoist cable to keep from sliding down the deck. Castille shot at me, and suddenly the rig floor exploded into a wall of fire. The concussion of the blast sent me back against the wall. The shot had sparked gas escaping the well bore. Castille was trapped.

I crawled on the tilted deck to the side door, then made my way down the listing stairway. When I reached the pipe deck, I saw the crew boat out in the lake heading for shore. The whirlpool was monstrous now and threatened to draw the boat back, but the crew boat's powerful engine strained against the force of the water and, foot by foot, the boat advanced. I knew they would make it to shore.

I half crawled, half slid across the pipe deck, which was canted at a radical angle, until I reached the next set of stairs. I was about to descend the stairs when I saw a shadow move behind me. I rolled to my back. Eyes, face bloodied, stood over me with a cement casing held high over his head. Just as I brought the Glock up and Eyes brought the casing down, the barge pitched again and Eyes and the casing were hurled over the railing and slammed into the deck below. He wouldn't be getting up again.

When I reached the bottom of the stairs, I saw that the lower level was now under water. I couldn't swim against the swirling water to get to the skiff. Then Koot appeared in the skiff and pulled up to the barge. I fell into the boat, and Koot revved the small outboard full out.

We inched forward against the force of the water, which now sounded like the front edge of a monstrous wind. I looked toward the far side of the lake and watched small and large boats being sucked away from their moorings and pulled into the current of the giant eddy. An empty pleasure craft, maybe an eighteen-footer, sped toward us from our right and shot across our bow and narrowly missed us. We watched it being pulled toward the vortex of the whirlpool until it flipped up on its end, then vanished into the swirling void.

I looked back and saw Castille high up on the tilted derrick, trying to escape the flames. The barge pitched one last time, upended and whale moaned as it slid into the roiling waters. As the barge went under, Castille scrambled in desperation up the last few feet to the top of the derrick—then disappeared into his watery tomb.

After about a hundred fifty yards, our progress began to slow, then it stopped. The force of the water was drawing us back toward the same fate.

I shouted, "Turn into the stream—then slingshot."

Koot turned the boat until we were moving with the circling current. The vortex had dropped lower, and we found ourselves on an increasingly sloped wall of water, like a high-banked race track. We had circled about halfway around the lake, the water rushing faster and the boat rushing with it.

Koot throttled full, angled the bow slightly against the current. The force behind the trajectory shot us across the face of the whirlpool. When we were within ten feet of the rapidly receding waterline, which was now about thirty yards from the old shoreline, the power of the water captured us again.

We looked at each other then leaped from the boat as far as we could toward the water's edge. I plunged under and felt my legs dig into the mud, but the riptide energy of the water bent me like green bamboo. I felt my anchoring slip. Then the water was gone and I was lying face down in the mud. I looked up and saw the edge of the water racing toward the vortex.

Koot lifted his head out of the mud and attempt to wipe his face. Later, I'd remember it as comical.

Koot said, "Cuttin' it pretty close."

Uselessly, I wiped my face.

"Yeah. We've gotta stop doing that."

FORTY-THREE

Grady, Fortenberry and a couple of uniformed officers threw us a rope and pulled us, one at a time, out of the mud. We checked to see if all the barge crew members onshore were okay, then we went back to the mine.

It's rare you get to see justice play out so clearly. Castille and Eyes were sealed in the same watery crypt they tried to condemn the women to. Including Castille, Eyes, Curly, Heckle and Jeckle and the guy at the guard shack who didn't make it, thirteen of that crew were dead. The remaining eight at the mine saw the odds tilt against them and gave up.

The EMTs arrived at the scene followed by the parish sheriff and two of his deputies. The EMTs triaged the wounds of the two uniformed officers and Koot, then ambulances took the three of them to an ER in Lafayette. A couple of EMTs stayed behind and checked on the women, who were being questioned by Marie Trammel.

Marie was trying to guide the women away from the dead bodies of Castille's crew, but a few of the women stepped over and spit on the corpses. The women were free of Castille and his men, but only time would tell if they'd free themselves of the hatred and bitterness.

I was spent, so I went over and sat on the fender of Grady's Crown Vic while Lieutenant Tolleson and Grady spoke with the parish sheriff. The car was scrap. Pieces of safety glass dangled from the door frame where windows used to be, and the body on the combat side of the car was peg board. The other three cars looked pretty much the same.

After a while, a white sedan pulled up and a tall suit with a crew cut got out, scanned the scene, then tramped over to the lieutenant. I recognized the guy from NOPD Narcotics. You'd think he'd be happy we had taken out a major crime ring, but I'd seen happier faces in a lineup. After the lieutenant explained that there had been no time to bring Narcotics in on the bust, the guy didn't look any happier. The usual territorial machismo.

Three NOPD patrol cars and a paddy wagon showed up leading the Medical Examiner and the forensics team. After the detectives and uniformed officers loaded the survivors of Castille's crew in the wagon, Fortenberry, Mowery and Doucette wandered over.

Doucette said, "A lot of cops worked hard and long to find this operation. How'd you and Loomis manage to find it?"

"A lucky break."

"Un huh. You always have to be the hero, don't you, Boudreau? You think this changes how the cops in the department feel about you?"

I was too tired to bite.

Fortenberry said, "Boudreau and Loomis stuck their necks out same as us, Doucette."

Mowery said, "You're out of line, Doucette."

That was out of the blue. If I'd had the energy, I would have raised an eyebrow.

Doucette said, "The both of ya fuhgotten about Charlie Guiterrez..."

Fortenberry said, "I haven't forgotten anything, Doucette. I just never believed it went down the way you wanted us to believe it did."

Doucette turned to Mowery. "You believe this shit?" Mowery didn't say anything. "What's with you?"

"We've got a crime scene here."

After a few thick seconds Doucette said, "Coupla friggin' dupes." Then he turned and walked away stiffly.

Mowery turned to me. "I went to see your ex yesterday. She still believes you didn't set up Guiterrez to be murdered."

"What made you think she'd change her mind?"

"I didn't think she'd change her mind. I just wanted to hear her say it again."

We looked at each other for a few seconds. Mowery nodded, I nodded, then he turned and walked over to where Grady and the lieutenant were dealing with the guy from Narcotics.

In his own way, Mowery let me know he may have been wrong about me. He had invested a lot in hating me, a lot in Doucette's testimony, so it must have been hard for him to acknowledge doubts. I wasn't sure why he would have doubts after all this time. Maybe it was because Koot and I put ourselves between Castille and a couple of people who needed help. Maybe it was my winning smile. Anyway, It felt good, Mowery and Hal standing up for me.

Hal said, "Nothing like being shot at to make you want a drink."

"How about I buy you a cup of coffee instead when we get back to the city. We can talk through it."

"Thanks, Tag. I'll poll my nerves again when we're done here. If I still feel like a drink, I'll take you up on the offer."

"You got it."

Hal nodded.

"Hal, sorry again for making you as the bad cop."

"Forget it." Fortenberry gazed over toward the women who were being questioned. Finally he said, "These women have dealt with worse than being shot at. Don't think I'll need that drink."

"I'm glad."

Hal nodded, then walked over to the women.

The woman who had seen me in the mine came over. Her skin was bone white from living underground, tinted only by branching blue veins and the moonlight.

She said, "Every night for two years I dreamed you'd come for us."

"Now you can dream new dreams."

She put her arms around me and held on for a long time. I was salt and sweat and mud, but she didn't seem to mind. Then she let go and looked at me.

"Thank you."

I nodded and smiled.

She smiled, then an EMT came over and guided her to an ambulance.

Later, Grady and I picked Koot up at the hospital in Lafayette. The two officers had already been treated and taken back to New Orleans. Koot had bathed and was in green scrubs and on crutches. He was lucky. The bullet had passed through his calf muscle clean, just missing bone and the Peroneal artery. After a few weeks on crutches and some frustration with not being able to teach, Koot would be back to his driven self again.

It was after midnight when we pulled onto I-10 out of Lafayette. The Crown Vic was the only one of the four cars we came in that still ran. The windows had been shot out, but the front windshield was more or less intact, so we didn't have to eat bugs. A couple of body bags thrown over the seats kept us from getting glass in our butts.

After a while, Grady looked at Koot, who had his leg stretched out in the back seat, then he looked over at me. He spoke up over the noise of the wind.

"A lot of people got their lives back tonight."

Koot leaned forward and slapped Grady twice on the shoulder. "No more hiding in the shadows for Jackie and Danika."

I thought of the lost years for the women, and of a few lost years of my own. Danika and the rest of the women would never get back those years, but the body bags beneath us were empty, the air was damp and sweet, and seemed, to me, full of promise.

When we arrived at the Second District station, before Grady went upstairs to file the report he told us that a wit had come forward placing Eyes and another one of Castille's men at Caveccio's place the night of the murder. With their deaths, the taxpayers catch a break. No trial.

Koot and I left for Marty's in the Sebring. We were going to wake everyone, but they wouldn't mind. The porch light glared on and Marty answered the door in his pajamas. He was pointing an old .22 bolt action rifle at our stomachs. Adrienne and the others were peering out into the living room from the hall. Marty glanced back and forth between Koot on crutches and me looking like a mud man from Borneo, then he lowered the rifle.

He said, "For Chrissake, I'm afraid to ask who won."

When the others recognized us, they trailed each other into the living room, everyone in robes or pajamas except Adrienne, who wore a lavender nightshirt. When the plug was pulled on the lake, I wondered if I'd ever see her again.

We stepped inside and closed the door. I said, "It's over."

Koot said, "Castille's dead, and what's left of his crew won't be bothering you again."

Adrienne drew in a sharp breath.

Danika looked unconvinced. "Are you sure Castille is dead?"

"Dead and already underground," I said.

Adrienne came over and looked at Koot. "What happened?"

Koot said, "Nothing a little fishing won't cure."

Adrienne looked at me. "You okay under there?"

"Mud baths do wonders for the complexion."

Jackie said, "What about the crooked cop?"

"We got him. He'll be tried for murder and a number of conspiracy charges."

Everybody stared at us some more, working on acceptance.

Conley Clark

Finally Blanche said, "I wish I believed in hell, then I'd be satisfied they'd all find a home."

Adrienne hugged Koot as he propped himself against the door, then she hugged me. Then there was a breakout of hugging.

The celebration moved to the kitchen, where we all sat around the dining table and talked. I told Danika and Jackie that the lieutenant had some questions and wanted me to bring them by the station in the morning. Koot and I answered everyone's questions about what happened at the mine. Hearing the details seemed to cement the reality for them that this chapter of fear was closed.

We talked about the hurricane, which was about thirty hours away. Koot and I told Adrienne and Blanche we'd come by to help shutter their homes. Everyone had made their evacuation plans.

After a while, Koot and I left to get a few hours sleep. I dropped Koot off, and on the way home, I thought of how I was looking forward to spending time with Adrienne and Brent without being hip-deep in the acid-stress of the last several days. And I thought of how I was looking forward to spending a lot of time with Adrienne alone.

FORTY-FOUR

Lieutenant Tolleson made a case for Jackie with the DA about Jackie's dealings with Nads. The DA considered what Jackie had done to help Danika and agreed not to indict. Koot and I told Jackie we'd see to it that Nads kept his agreement to let Jackie out of the racket. Jackie and Danika thanked us about a dozen times, then left to make arrangements to leave for Spain.

That afternoon Kiki's friend Mae, Kiki's mother, two hookers, a man I didn't know, Koot and I gathered at the river's edge to scatter Kiki's ashes. Mae hadn't taken seriously Kiki's request to have his ashes made into a diamond for her.

I never expected Kiki to reach old age. I also never expected an addict who lived in that world to keep his essential humanity—but somehow Kiki did. To most people Kiki would always be the street pimp and drug addict who got what he deserved. Maybe he did. Maybe we all get what we deserve.

Koot and I swung by Mama's, one of Nads' "legit" restaurants, and told the manager we had news Liano was waiting for and that we'd be in the park at Jackson Square.

We sat on a bench and waited. The air was still, and the sky clear. It was eerie in light of what was coming.

"Tag, I don't think New Orleans is ready for this one."

"Yeah. The draining of wetlands has put less marsh between us and Katrina to absorb the surge."

"And the levees are out of their league against a cat 5."

"Plus the bowl has gotten deeper."

Since the Army Corps of Engineers started building the levee system in the 19th century, it has created unintended consequences. The levees cut off the area's main source of river silt, the basic material for building deltas. This, along with the weight of massive city development and the destabilizing seepage of water, oil and gas from underground, has caused the basin that New Orleans sits in to sink steadily. If Katrina punches through the levees, even in just a few places, the city could find itself underwater again, like it did in '65 with Betsy, only this time—deeper.

A Caddie Seville pulled up to the park entrance on Decatur. Giancarlo and another one of Nads' crew got out and strolled into the park. Giancarlo sat down by me on the bench, and the other guy, a stump with a lacquered coiff, stood by Koot. Koot stared at Giancarlo. It was his way of saying "This had better go well."

Giancarlo glanced at Koot and then turned toward me and sighed. "Are we going to be able to do this without drawing attention?"

I looked at Koot. He nodded slightly, assuring me he had his say.

"Absolutely," I said.

The Sicilians patted us down, trying to be as discreet as possible in a park full of people. We had left our guns in the trunk of the car. When they were finished, Giancarlo nodded toward a Town Car that had pulled up. Nads, the sumo and a couple other guys got out of the Lincoln and walked over with Liano. Giancarlo and the stump joined the rest of the soldiers in a ring around Nads and scanned the park for enemy sightings.

I moved to the center of the bench and Nads sat on the end.

I said, "Castille and his lieutenant and eleven others are dead."

Nads said, "I heard Castille was flushed down the biggest toilet in the world." He looked at his men and laughed. Cue the return hilarity. "I also heard one of New Orleans' finest turned out to be bent. What a shame. A real black eye for the department."

"Sorry he wasn't on *your* payroll?"

Nads flicked his hand out. "Got all the help at the department I can use."

Unfortunately, that might have been true.

Koot said, "Castille and his crew are off the board. You gonna cut Jackie Kanawhite loose?"

"You got my money back from Stubbs?"

"One thing at a time," I said.

Nads crossed his legs, then straightened the crease in his pants. "Yeah, Boudreau, he's out. I didn't make much from those humps anyway."

I glanced at Koot. So far, so good.

Nads said, "Now what about my money?"

"Stubbs copped to working for Castille, but told Public Integrity nothing about a drug deal or the money. Looks like he stashed it."

Stubbs figured Koot and I wouldn't come forward about the drug deal and money and expose Marty or ourselves to prosecution. I guess he had answered the question of "*Who am I?*"

Nads said, "I got a dead pimp. What'd the bent dick tell 'em about that?"

"He told them he killed Kiki because Kiki found out he was on Castille's payroll and was going to turn him in."

"Then I guess I'll have to sell your house—correction—my house, and make a tidy profit."

Koot shifted on the bench. He said, "You don't wanna do that, Nads."

"That a threat, Loomis?"

Koot looked at Nads for a few seconds, then said, "No threat. We just need some time to pay you."

Nads said, "When they branded your head it must have cooked your brains, Loomis. I can sell the house and get my money *now*. Or at least after this friggin hurricane blows by."

I said, "Yeah, you could. You get my house, and Stubbs gets away with your money."

"No one takes from me, Boudreau. You know that."

I shrugged. We did know that and we knew how this thing would play out. So did Nads. All this banter was just ping pong. Nads could make more money by selling my house, but this was a matter of pride. Nads would say a matter of honor. He would send Giancarlo to see Stubbs in prison. Giancarlo would give Stubbs a choice—give back the money or die in prison by lethal injection—with a shank.

"You're holding the deed, Nads."

"I'm always holding the deed, Boudreau." Nads brushed imaginary dirt from his tie. "You two were going to take Castille off the board whether we had an agreement or not, but the fact that you did is money in my pocket. Less competition."

"Glad we could help," I said.

Nads stood and straightened his suit. "Helping me sticks in both your throats like a jagged chicken bone. I just want you to know—I like that. I like that a lot." Nads grinned. "We'll talk soon."

Nads and his men moved away in a Sicilian knot.

FORTY-FIVE

I got a call from Grady asking me to listen to a message left on Stubbs' answering machine a few days ago. I did, then I drove over to Stubbs' duplex. The front door was open, and I entered and moved toward the noise coming from the back yard. When I stepped out the back door I saw Danika, covered in soot, exit an old furnace room. She held a briefcase, and I didn't have to look in it to know the briefcase was full of money.

I said, "You and Stubbs stole the drugs from Castille."

Danika froze. "Tag, you frightened me." She looked like she was quick-sorting several story options in her mind. Then I guess she decided it wasn't worth it. She seemed resigned.

She said, "How did you..." Then she got it. "The message I left on Ernie's machine."

I nodded. "So, while Stubbs was supposed to be keeping an eye on you for Castille, you two hooked up and cooked up a plan."

"Yes."

"And you were just using Jackie."

"I was just using Ernie too."

"Stubbs took the drugs, sold them, then betrayed you."

Danika shrugged. "He used me better."

"Why involve Jackie in all this?"

"Ernie knew that Jackie loved me and would help me get away from Castille. Since I had been on Jackie's boat many times, Ernie thought staging an accident was the perfect way for me to escape. Jackie was eager when I suggested the idea. Later, Ernie and I were supposed to meet overseas. I was going to get my share of the money and leave Ernie."

"But Stubbs never planned to meet you."

Danika smiled, sardonic. "So little trust in the world."

"And Stubbs knew suspicion would fall on you and Jackie for the drugs, not him."

"It's clear now Ernie planned it that way."

"Jackie knew nothing about the drugs or Stubbs?"

Danika tried to wipe soot from her face with the back of her hand. "No."

"And it was Stubbs' idea for you to hold up near New Orleans for a few days."

"I guess Ernie wanted me dead, so he told Castille where to find us. But it was a huge risk for him. If Castille had taken us alive, so he could get his drugs, I would have told Castille that Ernie helped me steal the Sojourn."

I said, "Stubbs told the investigators that Castille didn't care about the drugs, he just wanted you both dead. With slave labor and cheap ingredients, it was easy for Castille to make more drugs."

"I guess Ernie thought of everything. He said he was going to find someone to sell the drugs for him, so Castille would not find out it was Ernie."

"He found someone, then he murdered him. His name was Kiki."

Danika closed her eyes. When she opened them, her voice was weak.

"I didn't think anyone would get killed. Jackie's friends, then this man. And taking the boy. I am sorry."

Despite the deceit, her sorrow seemed genuine. She did what she thought she had to do to break free of Castille, but things went bad.

"Why didn't you tell us about Stubbs when you suspected he wanted you dead?"

"I didn't want to believe it. I still hoped for the money. I needed it to start my life again."

I hadn't figured Danika the type for denial, but I knew from experience that desperation could send you there.

Danika looked hollow as she moved to the porch steps and sat.

"I pretended to love Ernie. I pretended to love Jackie. But after what Jackie did for me, after what you all did for me, I am ashamed."

"Not too ashamed to take the money."

"Why shouldn't I take it?"

"It's not nearly enough, considering what you've been through."

"Thank you."

"But I can't let you have it. It was a loan, and the loan's due."

She looked surprised. "I don't understand."

"I borrowed the money for the drug buy. Stubbs got away with the cash, and we didn't know it was him until later."

"You were going to give Castille back his drugs, so he might let us go?"

"No one else can know about this. Understand?"

Danika looked at me for several seconds, then she got up and stepped over to me. A tear mixed with soot coursed black down her face. She said, "Adrienne is a very fortunate woman." Then she handed me the briefcase.

I gave her my handkerchief. "I guess you'll be leaving the country."

"Yes..." She wiped wet soot off her face. "With Jackie."

Last night I was too tired to lift an eyebrow in surprise. Today was different.

"It is true that I don't love Jackie. But he risked so much for me, and paid so dearly...I will go on pretending. I have no love in me, Tag. But maybe in time I can find it again, then maybe I can give it to Jackie." She wiped away black tears. "Of course, this all depends on you."

I could tell Jackie he'd been used, but there's a chance he wouldn't want to know. I didn't doubt that Danika was sorry for what she'd done, and that she'd try to make Jackie happy. For a while, maybe that would be enough.

I said, "Don't you two have a plane to catch?"

FORTY-SIX

I had been beaten and shot at, attacked by a moccasin and nearly shredded by a Komodo dragon. I came within an inch of being crushed in a mining shaft, went into diabetic collapse, had my eyes burned by chemicals, was attacked with a knife, swallowed more ocean than I could handle, and was nearly sucked down a watery black hole—but I was going to be spending time with Adrienne Kanawhite, so I was feeling good.

Blanche and Koot were nailing ¾ inch plywood to windows at the front of Adrienne's house when I arrived. Blanche came over and sat on the chaise lounge. She patted the cushion beside her, and I sat. She said, "As soon as Koot gets off his crutches I'm signing up for his Kenpo class. I realize now my charm would be wasted on some men."

"Only the extreme hard cases."

Blanche looked at me for a few seconds, then said, "I want to say something."

"Then it'll be said."

She grinned. "You think you know me pretty well."

"There's very little I can predict about you, Blanche, except that you say what's on your mind."

"Good. I would hate to be too predictable."

Blanche got serious. She placed her hand on mine and said, "Adrienne just needs some time."

"To get over all this—of course."

"More than that." Blanche was about to say something else when Brent walked out the front door and over to the sofa.

I said, "How's it goin', partner?"

Brent said, "I don't like seeing a therapist. If I need to talk to someone, I'd rather talk to you."

"We can talk anytime you want. But don't give your mother a hard time on this, okay?"

Brent gave me resignation, then he brightened. "When am I going to see the *Cirque de Dufas*?"

"Santana and Seven give shows daily. We'll catch one after Katrina is gone."

"Cool. Have you ever been in a hurricane?"

"Not like this one."

"How will it be different?"

"It's going to change a lot of lives."

"How?"

"We'll soon see, little man."

After we secured Adrienne's home, then Blanche's, Adrienne took me to lunch at a Thai place around the corner. It was one of the few businesses still open. The smell of coconut milk and basil drifting from the kitchen made me realize how hungry I was.

I said, "New Orleans is going to get pushed pretty hard when this hurricane makes landfall tomorrow. What are your plans?"

"Blanche has a sister in Baton Rouge. We're leaving in a few hours. Where will you and Koot go?"

"Probably just point the car north."

The server brought water and menus.

Adrienne said, "Jackie and Danika are on their way to Madrid."

I didn't like keeping things from Adrienne, but she'd never hear from me about Danika, though I thought she'd probably understand.

"Danika may never want to come back to New Orleans," said Adrienne.

"She'll need some time away from here, but if Jackie wants to come home, they could end up here again."

Adrienne pushed her hair behind her ear. "I'm glad Jackie is finally happy."

"I'm pretty happy myself."

Adrienne looked at me for a long time. Finally she said, "Do you know how deeply I feel about you?"

"You never got around to telling me."

"That's because I wasn't sure I wanted to get involved any more than we already were."

"And now?"

"Tag, you take on danger as readily as most people run away from it. That's who you and Koot are. Thank God that's who you are. But Brent idolizes you. If you didn't come home one day..."

I didn't like where this was going. "So this is about Brent?"

"I almost lost my brother and my son. Your clients bring betrayal, deceit, theft, violence and lay it at your door. Any of that can lead to the kind of trouble we just went through."

"What are you telling me?"

Adrienne closed her eyes for a few seconds, then opened them.

"Blanche thinks I'm a fool, and Brent will hate me when I tell him. But I can't see you anymore."

At the house...Blanche tried to warn me this was coming. It felt like someone had run a grinder over my chest.

I said, "Time to go."

Adrienne placed her hand on mine.

"I love you, Tag."

Suddenly the smell of food went fetid.

"Yeah. Ain't love grand?"

FORTY-SEVEN

Strands of ashen-white clouds lolled over the horizon, and a warm breeze nudged in from the east. Without a forecast, you'd never know that in less than fourteen hours a 145 mph beast will rage through New Orleans. After we boarded up Grady's house, Grady helped me nail sheets of plywood to my windows and doors while Koot sat on the porch and watched. Koot, the good scout he is, had prepared for this years ago by installing industrial-strength storm shutters on his place. Grady held plywood in place while I drove wide head nails into the window frame. The sun had kindled to white and the heat reached into my shoulder, leg and jaw and baked in some relief from a lingering soreness.

Grady said, "Tag, when were you going to tell me what Danika's phone message meant?"

"When you retire."

There was a lot the police would never know. Koot, Marty and I had taken the drugs to a deserted cay, drenched them with gas and lit it. Nads got his money back, and Giancarlo paid Stubbs a visit in prison anyway, telling him to keep his mouth shut about the Sojo deal, so the money couldn't be traced back to Nads. Stubbs knew Nads could easily have him killed, so I wasn't worried about Stubbs taking revenge on us at the trial.

The indirect benefit of Giancarlo's visit was that we didn't go to jail, and I got the deed back to my house. It felt good to be a homeowner again. I just hoped the house would still be here when we got back to town.

Grady shook his head back and forth. "Cops keeping secrets from cops."

I hated keeping things from Grady about as much as I liked him calling us cops.

Grady said, "I guess most of the women will return to their country after the trial?"

I said, "Some will. Some told us they were too ashamed to go back. A few said they couldn't return because their people thought they brought disgrace to the family."

Koot said, "Nice families."

I said, "Marty is going to line up help for the women who want to stay in New Orleans—counseling, finding jobs, a place to live. Right now, the women are being taken to Baton Rouge until Katrina is spent."

Grady said, "Marty was a big part in all this."

"Yeah." Grady knew about Marty giving shelter, but no one would ever know, except Koot and me, the risk Marty took doing the drug deal.

Grady said, "How's the boy?"

I said, "He seems to have accepted seeing a therapist when he gets back. I think he'll be okay."

Koot said, "Except for being pretty pissed at his mom."

Grady said, "I'm sorry, Sport Model, it didn't work out with you and Adrienne."

Koot said, "She's pretty miserable, according to Blanche."

I said, "If I were a better man, I wouldn't be so glad."

Grady said, "It's gonna be all right, Tag."

I shrugged. "Yeah. A hundred thousand skin cells replaced every minute. Maybe tomorrow I'll wake up a new man."

After Grady left to stay with family in Houston, and Koot went home to pack, I sat on the patio, drank black tea, and felt nothing. Santana paced the perimeter around me, as restless as I was leaden. When the phone rang, I got up to answer it without thinking, the habit of someone accustomed to answering distress calls.

Adrienne said, "Am I disturbing you?"

"Hmmm."

"Yes, well, forget I said that. Is it all right that I called?"

"Yes."

There were a few seconds of thickset silence, then Adrienne said, "I'm afraid."

"I know."

"And Brent is so angry with me."

"You want me to have a talk with him? Explain fear to a boy who was kidnapped and saw a man killed?"

"I didn't call so you could get back at me."

"Sorry it came out that way."

"You're angry with me too?"

"I understand your reasons."

"But you're still angry."

"Yeah, I guess I am."

I realized I hadn't taken a breath since we began this conversation. I drew one.

Adrienne said, "You can't promise that someday, someone with a vendetta against you won't come for Brent and me, trying to get to you."

"No, I can't promise that. No one could. But I'd do everything I could to keep that from happening."

I heard Adrienne take a long breath, then a long exhale.

"I need more time with this."

"We all have needs."

"What do you need?"

"To know that you and Brent are safe right now."

"We're here in Baton Rouge. If you're trying to make me love you, I already do."

"Yet you're there, and I'm here."

Silence, then Adrienne said, "For now."

Adrienne asked if she could stay in touch, then we hung up.

I poured another cup of Irish tea, then went out to the patio again. A few people were still in the neighborhood battening down. I wondered how well New Orleans would stand up to the pounding it was about to take, and I wondered how soon it would rise from the aftermath. And I mulled over my conversation with Adrienne. I drank tea and thought of the man who stated in his will to leave him in bed for three days after he died—in case he came around. At the moment, I was feeling the man's optimism.